THE
GRAVEDIGGER'S
BALL

ALSO BY SOLOMON JONES

Bridge

Ride or Die

C.R.E.A.M.

Payback

The Last Confession

THE GRAVEDIGGER'S BALL

A COLETTI NOVEL

SOLOMON JONES

Minotaur Books ✺ New York

THE GRAVEDIGGER'S BALL. Copyright © 2011 by Solomon Jones. All rights reserved. Printed in the United States of America. For information, address St. Martin's Press, 175 Fifth Avenue, New York, N.Y. 10010.

www.minotaurbooks.com

ISBN 978-0-312-58081-0

First Edition: October 2011

10 9 8 7 6 5 4 3 2 1

To my soldiers in the Words On The Street program.
Keep writing. I believe in you.

ACKNOWLEDGMENTS

First, I must thank God for granting me the talent to write. I am forever indebted to my wife, LaVeta; my children, Eve, Adrianne, and Solomon; and my parents, Carolyn and Solomon, for inspiring me to be my best. To Laurel Hill—the historic Philadelphia cemetery that served as an inspiration for this story—thank you for your support and partnership. To the U.S. National Park Service and the rangers at the historic Edgar Allan Poe House, thank you for your valuable assistance. To the historic preservation community, thank you for your passion and perseverance. Special thanks to the young writers from my Words On The Street literacy program, and to Verizon, Art Sanctuary, the *Philadelphia Daily News,* Barnes & Noble, Clear Channel Radio, and Minotaur Books for helping to make that program a reality. Thanks to Congressman Chaka Fattah, the Black Male Development Symposium, Pennsylvania State Representative Tony Payton, Drs. Ernest and Iris Moody, Janice Gable Bashman, and Joan Shadwick for sponsoring students in the program. Thanks to South Philadelphia High School, Fitzsimons High School, and Mastery Charter School/Shoemaker Campus for being the first schools to participate. To my agent, Jill Marr of the Sandra Dijkstra Agency, thank you for believing. And to you, my readers, thank you for your undying support. You are the reason that I write.

THE
GRAVEDIGGER'S
BALL

CHAPTER 1

It was 9 A.M. on a Wednesday, and a late autumn breeze swept in off the Schuylkill River as Detective Mike Coletti strode through the Fairgrounds Cemetery.

As he passed between centuries-old crypts, Coletti thought of his young partner, Charlie Mann, whose crack marksmanship had saved Coletti from the serial killer who was now buried there.

In some ways, Coletti wished that Mann had allowed him to die in the showdown with the killer. That way, Coletti wouldn't be wrestling with a loss no one could understand, or walking toward a grave he didn't want to see.

But Coletti knew, deep down, that the grief he felt was just another in a long line of enemies that he'd spent his life fighting—enemies that in many ways were extensions of himself.

In his youth, Coletti had struggled against his desire to cross the line between cops and criminals on South Philly's mob-controlled streets. In the department, he'd struggled against authority, and in doing so, he'd crippled his career. In private, he'd struggled against the demons of pride, rebellion, and apathy.

Today, Coletti would confront his demons, and he would do it where they lived—in his heart. He would either win the battle that raged within him or he would die fighting, but Coletti couldn't allow his demons to consume him. Not anymore.

He cut an unusual figure as he crossed the sprawling cemetery. His dark Mediterranean features were topped by salt-and-pepper hair. His pants and rumpled trench coat were accented by coffee stains. But it was his facial expression—grim and determined, angry even—that set him apart from the mourners that usually visited the cemetery.

When he finally caught sight of the grave he'd come to visit, he saw something odd out of the corner of his eye. It was a brightly colored vinyl banner strung on the cemetery's wrought iron gate. It looked out of place among the acres of headstones.

"Gravedigger's Ball," it read. "November 14th. A black-tie fund-raiser at Tookesbury Mansion. Go to Fairgrounds cemetery.com for ticket information."

Coletti had heard of the annual fund-raiser that helped to maintain the historic graveyard where burials were now a rarity, but he'd never paid attention, and in truth, he didn't care about it now.

He looked once more at the banner and kept walking.

Then he felt someone's eyes at his back. He turned around and saw two women standing near a grave. The younger one was staring at him as the cemetery's swirling wind blew her blond hair across her face.

Coletti turned away from her, scowling as he thought of the things that had happened the last time a woman had looked at him that way. He thought of the confession in the art gallery, the bodies in the churches, the clues in the prophecy, the Angel of Death.

He thought of the way he'd looked past all those things to stare back at that woman. He thought of the resultant carnage.

Coletti couldn't afford to be distracted anymore. He'd come to the graveyard for a purpose, and he was going to accomplish it.

As he drew nearer to the grave, the dead leaves in the cemetery crunched beneath his feet. He smiled at the way they crackled and split. The sound reminded him of his heart.

Of course, no one knew the true depths of Coletti's heartbreak, and if he could help it, no living person ever would. Where Coletti came from, you didn't pour out your heart. Not if you were pushing sixty. Men from Coletti's generation kept their feelings to themselves, or they whispered them in confessional booths to priests. They didn't tell their wives. They didn't tell their children. They didn't tell anyone. They simply lived with it.

That wouldn't work for Coletti this time. He'd seen too much misery while investigating the string of killings that had almost cost him his life. But in all he'd witnessed, he didn't see the thing that mattered most. He didn't see her lies.

Coletti could live with many things, but he couldn't live with that, so he walked through the cemetery and stopped at the grave of the woman whose deception had almost killed him.

He stood there and took a deep breath as he looked at the small, flat stone that marked Mary Smithson's grave. Then he bent down and placed a white rose upon it as he whispered the words that he'd thus far kept to himself.

"You spit on my heart," he said bitterly. "But at least I know I *have* a heart now. That's more than I could say before I met you."

Coletti glanced over his shoulder self-consciously. He wasn't used to speaking to the dead, but he was here now, and he was determined to get it all out, no matter how awkward it felt.

"I guess the worst part is that I trusted you," he said, looking down at the tiny grave marker. "I let my guard down, and you hit me so fast and so hard I didn't even know it until it was too late."

He shook a Marlboro loose from a near-empty pack and lit it as his heart filled with grief, then with pain, then with regret. Taking a long drag, he released the acrid smoke into the air and stood there, savoring his first and only cigarette of the day.

For a long time, he stared at the grave, his mind filled with a mixture of love and hate so volatile he felt as if it would explode. "You lied to me, Mary. But I lied to myself too, didn't I? I lied when I told myself a young, smart woman like you would want a lonely old cop like me. I lied while you kept on killing, and the craziest part of it all, the part that eats me up every time I think about it . . ." He paused as the anger and grief welled up inside him. "The part that kills me is that I loved you anyway."

Coletti took another drag of the cigarette. Then he plucked it away and stood at the grave as the autumn breeze whispered through his unkempt hair.

"But that's all in the past, isn't it?" He looked down at the ground with a sorrow he'd been holding on to for months. "If I didn't learn anything else from all this, I learned that it doesn't pay to hold on to the past."

But the past was all he had, so he stood at her grave and closed his eyes and tried to picture her. Not as the crazed killer who'd perished in the abandoned warehouse, but as the woman he'd loved almost from the moment they met. He wanted to remember her smiling and full of life, with a sparkle in her eye and a laugh that was almost musical.

Maybe if he remembered her that way he could stop being so angry at her. Maybe he could even forgive himself.

When finally he opened his eyes, he saw something curious. About thirty feet to his left, the young woman he'd seen earlier was walking toward him, taking each step with a sense of purpose that was vaguely familiar. She didn't sashay with the self-awareness of a woman who knew she was being watched. Rather, she moved in fits and starts, with the confused look of someone who was searching for something.

As she moved toward him, Coletti saw that her lips, bow-shaped and thin, were set in a perplexed line, and her brow was furrowed in a look of determination. None of this was particularly interesting to Coletti. When he saw her eyes, however, his curiosity quickly morphed into something between anxiety and fear.

This woman, with eyes that were at once intense and alluring, was a younger version of Mary. She had the same pale skin and wide face, the same sensuality and windswept hair, the same sense of purpose that had driven Mary to the grave. Yet something in this woman's face was different.

As she drew closer, Coletti saw what it was. She was worried about something, and worry was an expression he'd never seen on Mary's face.

Unable to speak, think, or move, the old detective just stared. Before he knew it, she was beside him, and though he wanted to stop himself from looking at her, he couldn't. She didn't seem to care.

Standing there next to him, she silently looked down at the grave for a full minute before she even acknowledged his presence.

"You're Detective Coletti," she said, looking up at him with the same blue eyes that had instantly drawn him to Mary Smithson. "I read a lot about you right after Mary died."

"I, uh . . ." He stumbled for the words before finally blurting out, "You look a lot like her."

The woman smiled sadly. "She was my sister—genetically, at least."

"You must've been closer to her than the rest of the family. I talked to her father after she died, and none of them had any interest in coming here to stand for her burial."

"I'm not surprised," the woman said, glancing at the grave once more. "They're an insular bunch. They don't like to be questioned, and they don't take too kindly to outsiders."

"You sound like you speak from experience."

"I do." She extended her hand. "My name is Lenore Wilkinson. Mary and I shared a father, but not much else."

Coletti reached out and shook her hand. Her skin was soft and smooth, but her grip was surprisingly strong. "Mary mentioned you," Coletti said.

"Mostly angry accusations, I bet. Let's see. . . . My mother was a whore who stole Mary's father and embarrassed her mom in front of the fifty-nine people who lived in that sprawling metropolis called Dunmore."

"You sound a little angry yourself," Coletti said.

"Maybe a little. Wouldn't you be angry if people hated you just for being born?"

"I guess you've got a point."

Lenore looked down at the grave marker. "That's what makes this whole thing such a struggle for me. On the one hand, I hate Mary and her family for the things they said about my mother and me, and on the other hand I'm curious about Mary. I don't understand how she could kill all those people, especially since she was supposed to be the smart one."

"She *was* the smart one," Coletti said in a faraway voice. "So smart she almost killed me."

Lenore looked at him, looked *through* him, really. "And you loved her in spite of that," she said with a certainty that was unnerving.

As he contemplated an answer to the truth she somehow knew, the air between them thickened and the moment seemed to expand. They both felt it. When Coletti turned around to see why the atmosphere had suddenly changed, the stillness was shattered.

The sound of a gunshot exploded through the graveyard. Coletti grabbed Lenore as he dove to the ground and snatched his weapon from the shoulder holster beneath his trench coat.

About fifty yards in front of them and to their left, a dark figure crossed Coletti's line of vision and walked between the gravestones. "Stay here," Coletti said to Lenore.

Coletti got up and ran toward the spot where he'd seen the dark figure, but when he got there, the area was filled only with an eerie stillness. He looked frantically around him as he made his way through the maze of headstones and crypts, spires and mausoleums that peppered the sprawling graveyard.

As he did so, the sounds of nearby traffic seemed to fade. Joggers slowed on Kelly Drive—the tree-lined, scenic road that wound along the Schuylkill's banks. The sky was silent, the river still. Coletti could hear the sound of his own breathing and the crunch of leaves beneath his feet. He was sure the gunman could hear them, too, so he stopped moving and tried to get his bearings.

Everywhere he looked, it seemed, there was an angle, a corner, a hiding place where a man could lie in wait. As soon as Coletti started moving again, he rounded one such corner, and on the other side of a mausoleum, he saw the dark figure again, just a few feet away.

His face was pasty and white. His mustache was thick and crooked, and his high, wide forehead was topped by stringy black hair that was parted and combed to the left. He was wearing a long black topcoat with the wide lapels of centuries gone by and a bow tie that hung limp against a high-collared shirt.

"Don't move!" Coletti shouted.

The man looked at him with coal-black eyes and disappeared behind an ornate headstone.

"Hey!" Coletti yelled, running to catch him. But when Coletti rounded the headstone, the man was gone.

Holding his gun out in front of him, the detective looked left, then right, then left again, scanning the cemetery for the man whose cold, dead eyes made him look as if he'd climbed out from one of the graves.

When he didn't see him, Coletti walked forward slowly, watching and waiting for the figure to emerge from the shadows. Slowly, agonizingly, the seconds ticked by, and Coletti began to wonder if the man he'd seen was himself a shadow.

Doubling back and retracing his steps to the spot where he'd first seen the man, Coletti rounded the corner of the mausoleum and nearly stumbled into a deep hole. He caught himself just as he looked down into what appeared to be a freshly dug grave. At the bottom was a green piece of tarp with a body on top.

The dead woman was gray-haired and thin, lying flat on her back with eyes stretched wide and a string of pearls hanging loosely around her neck. Coletti couldn't see any blood. Just a smear of what appeared to be dirt around her mouth.

For a moment, Coletti stood there, unsure of what he was seeing. He hadn't seen the hole in the ground when he passed by the first time, but there it was now, with a dead woman staring up from the bottom.

Coletti's breath came faster. He held his gun tightly and took ten steps, hoping to see the man in black again. He stopped on the other side of the mausoleum, listening to nothing, and the longer he stood there, the more stubborn the silence seemed. Then suddenly he heard the crackle of footsteps on leaves. He swung around and aimed in the direction of the sound.

"Wait!" Lenore screamed, shielding her face with her hands as she looked down the barrel of Coletti's gun.

The detective sighed and lowered his weapon. "I thought I told you to stay put."

"I was afraid," Lenore said in a quaking voice.

"Looks like you should've been," he said, taking her hand and leading her over to the grave.

"Oh my God," she whispered when she looked down and saw the body.

"That's the woman you were with, isn't it?"

Lenore nodded slowly and swallowed hard. "Her name is Clarissa Bailey. She was showing me around the graveyard."

Coletti spotted something at the edge of the grave. "What's this?" he said, bending down for a closer look.

Lenore looked over his shoulder as he used a stick to turn over the small piece of parchmentlike paper.

Coletti squinted as he read the words that were typed on the sheet. *"Deep into that darkness peering, long I stood there, wondering, fearing, doubting, dreaming dreams no mortals ever dared to dream before."*

He looked at Lenore. "Do you have any idea what that might mean?"

Lenore shook her head and looked away from the body. She appeared to be growing ill. Coletti looked away, too. He could feel himself growing suspicious.

Just then, something rustled the branches of a nearby tree. Coletti turned and aimed his gun in the direction of the sound, but lowered it when he realized that it was merely a bird.

As they watched the black, crowlike creature fly into the distance, Coletti wondered how Mary's sister was connected to the victim. Then he wondered if the only witness to the murder had just flown away.

By nine thirty, swirling dome lights from a dozen police cars filled the cemetery. Boats from the department's Marine Unit trolled the river, a helicopter hovered overhead, and police flooded Fairmount Park, the acres-wide swath of woodlands that flanked the graveyard and extended along both sides of the river.

Officer Frank Smith was among them, and he was determined to find the suspect, because doing so might finally get him out of the park.

He'd been banished to park duty two years before, reassigned from the ninth district after a high-profile drug conviction was overturned because he badly mishandled evidence.

Despite that blemish on his record, he was a cop's cop. Known to his fellow officers as Smitty, he was hewn from a long line of men who'd stood on the front lines of the city's war on crime. He was proud of that distinction and anxious to carry on the legacy of his forebears.

Smitty had done so in the ninth, having foiled bank robberies and muggings on more than one occasion. But here, in the park, he was left to patrol a sector that included five acres of woods, three baseball diamonds, two eighteenth-century mansions, and a broken-down amphitheater.

He spent most of his time rousting couples who stayed in the park after the ten o' clock curfew or writing tickets for people who raced their cars along the park's winding roads.

In Smitty's mind, two years of park duty was ample punishment for his sins. Now, he wanted to get back to doing real police work, and if finding a pasty-faced man wearing old-fashioned clothes was his ticket back, the cop was determined to do that.

He'd spent the past twenty minutes riding through the park with his head on a swivel, looking through the trees for signs of anything unusual. He'd checked the locked doors on the mansion that housed Smith Playground and the historic home on the other side of Reservoir Drive. He'd checked the hiding spaces along the sides of the roads and the open spaces in the fields.

Smitty took one more swing through his sector, riding past a statue of General Ulysses S. Grant and beneath a bridge that connected Kelly Drive to the park. When he turned right on Mt. Pleasant Drive, a sliver of road that ran near the reservoir, he passed Smith Playground and saw something in the woods to his right. It appeared, at first, to be a large animal of some kind—a deer, perhaps. When he looked again, he was sure that what he'd seen was a man.

He parked his car and looked into the forested area known as Sedgley Woods. In warm weather, it was a mix of fallen trees, worn paths, and metallic baskets that served as a disc golf course. On rainy fall days like this one, the woods were largely abandoned, which made the man's presence there all the more unusual.

Smitty got out and walked past what would have been the third hole on the disc golf course. As he moved farther into the woods, he saw the man again. Breaking into a trot, he grabbed his radio to call for backup, but when he pressed the transmit button, nothing happened. He tried again with the same result, and when it was clear that his handheld radio was out, he didn't go back to his car. He drew his gun. He wasn't going to let whomever he'd seen get away.

The skies grew darker, and Smitty followed the man as he veered off the dirt path and into a thicket of fallen trees, moss-covered rocks, twisted vines, and uneven earth. Along the way, the cop stumbled over fallen branches and sunk into piles of leaves. With each step he took, he caught another glimpse of something that appeared to be the suspect. He churned his legs harder in an attempt to catch up to him, but as the woods surrounded Smitty, both his legs and his eyes began to betray him.

He tripped and fell over a discarded beer bottle. He fell again on a slippery rock. And when he got up, trotting past a tree with the names of long-dead lovers carved into its bark, a pasty white face flashed in front of him and disappeared. A second later, the face was visible to his left. Then it showed up on his right, staring at him with those coal-black eyes.

Each time Smitty looked in the direction of the face, he saw only the suspect's black coat. The black of the coat gave way to the high-collared shirt, then the floppy bow tie, and again, the face. The images appeared and disappeared in a deluge of black and white, assaulting the cop's eyes like fists.

Smitty looked in front of him and thought he saw the suspect again, nearly fifty yards away in a deeper section of the woods. He ran to catch up, trudging through a patch of dead vines so thick that they looked like tangled yarn. He fell once more, dropping his hat in the process. Then, with sweat trickling down his face, Smitty struggled to his feet and beat back the vines as he moved deeper into the woods.

He was breathing hard as he jogged through the wilderness, hoping all the while that he'd catch another glimpse of the suspect. The farther he ran, however, the more useless the chase seemed to be. The trees were more numerous than they'd been just seconds ago, and their branches seemed to weave together to blot out all signs of daylight.

"Hey!" Smitty yelled, but the woods simply swallowed his voice. "Hey!" he yelled, louder this time, and still, to no avail. "Hey!" he screamed, his voice now tinged with panic.

The answer he received was darkness, punctuated by the sound of a stick breaking in front of him. He raised his gun and aimed in that direction. Then a tree branch was brought down on his arm with such force that it knocked him off his feet and made him drop the gun.

Smitty yelled in agony and grasped his forearm, knowing that it was broken. When he looked up to see where the branch had come from, the man he'd been looking for was standing over him, preparing to swing again. Rolling to his right, the cop eluded the heavy branch and scrambled to his feet before the man could swing a third time.

Smitty dove for the gun, but the man kicked it away before he could reach it. If he was going to win this battle, he'd have to do it the old-fashioned way.

Smitty slowly rose to his feet and circled left in a fighting crouch. "Come on," he said through clenched teeth.

The man simply looked at him, his coal-black eyes, crooked mustache, and unsmiling mouth fixed rigidly in his ghostly white face.

Smitty charged with his nightstick in his left hand and managed to land a glancing blow before the man sidestepped him. He tried to swing again, but the man blocked the nightstick with his much heavier tree branch and grabbed the cop's broken forearm with his other hand.

Smitty screamed and fell to the ground clutching his arm. The man tried to stomp on him, but Smitty swept his adversary's legs from under him. Fists flew as they rolled among sticks and fallen leaves, each struggling to overcome the other.

Scrambling to his knees, Smitty caught the man with a hard left hook that temporarily swung the battle in his favor. The man rolled onto his back. Smitty tried to jump on top of him. The man put both feet into Smitty's stomach and pushed with all his might, sending the cop sprawling.

Both of them rushed to get to their feet, and, for the first time, the cop got a good look at the man he was fighting. His eyes were black and bottomless. His mustache was brittle and his flesh was devoid of color. His face showed no signs of life. Even the drop of blood that trickled down his forehead appeared to be black instead of red. He looked dead and alive all at once.

Smitty took a step backward as the man in black approached. He took another when the man moved closer. The cop looked behind him and saw a mound of dirt. Then he looked once more at the man in front of him. As Smitty's face twisted in fear, the man's lips parted, revealing a black-toothed smile. Smitty yelled and tried to charge him, but the man swung mightily and the cop stumbled backward toward the mound of dirt. Smitty tried to stop himself, but before he could regain his footing, the ground beneath him gave way.

He fell into a freshly dug hole that had been covered by leaves and sticks. He tried to crawl up the side of the narrow opening, but his broken arm betrayed him and he quickly slid down the dirt wall.

Again and again he tried to crawl out of the hole. When he couldn't try anymore, he looked up and saw the man in black watching him. He was holding a shovel, and when he dropped the first pile of dirt into the hole, Smitty screamed out for help, but the makeshift tomb muffled his voice.

As the man in black methodically filled the hole, Smitty continued his desperate calls for help. In twenty minutes, the hole was filled. Smitty was silent. The man was gone.

The only thing that remained was a single black bird, perched high above the scene. When the bird finally flew away, one thing was abundantly clear. The Gravedigger's Ball had begun.

CHAPTER 2

By ten o' clock, the cemetery was abuzz as officers looked among the dead for evidence to assist the living. Thus far, they'd failed to find anything to prove that a gun had even been fired—not a bullet casing, not a bullet hole, not even a trace of gunpowder.

They'd also been unable to contact Mrs. Bailey's husband. Coletti wasn't one to wait for answers, however, so he asked a uniformed officer to stay with Lenore while he questioned the manager of the cemetery.

The slightly built man in the black suit and bowler hat had been standing off to the side, watching intently as investigators went about their work. Coletti knew from the manager's anxious demeanor and troubled facial expression that he was deeply invested in the cemetery.

The detective was willing to bet that nothing happened at Fairgrounds without the manager's knowledge. That was why Coletti, when questioning him, repeatedly made him go over their procedures for digging graves.

"Please tell me again how a grave could be left open like this," Coletti said for the third time.

The manager sighed in frustration. "As I told you before, there would normally be heavy metal poles holding the Astroturf in place over an open grave, and the area would be blocked off so no one could access it."

"So what happened here?"

"Apparently someone moved the poles!" the manager snapped.

Coletti looked at him with a raised eyebrow. Then the manager took a deep breath and spoke more calmly.

"Look," he said in a conciliatory tone, "I'm as bothered about this as anyone, but you have to know I had no idea there was an untended open grave on the grounds. We tend to take that type of thing very seriously."

Coletti could see, from the troubled expression on his face, that the manager was genuinely concerned about what had happened. But that didn't mean he was off the hook.

"What about her?" Coletti said, nodding toward Lenore. "Are you sure you've never seen her here before?"

"I'm certain," the manager said, sneaking a look at her while nervously adjusting his glasses. "Mrs. Wilkinson visited for the first time today. Clarissa was so excited that she sent out an e-mail about it. I can show you if you'd like."

"Sure, I'll take a look at the e-mail," Coletti said as the manager fumbled with his BlackBerry. "But I'm more interested in knowing what was so special about having Mrs. Wilkinson here."

"She was going to help us with the Gravedigger's Ball."

Coletti nodded slowly. "I've seen the banners. What is the ball, exactly?"

"It's an annual event that raises funds to help maintain the cemetery," the manager said as he continued searching his BlackBerry for Clarissa's e-mail. "This year it's taking place at Tookesbury Mansion, less than a mile from here in the park."

"Is the ball some kind of tradition or is it something new?"

The manager stopped scrolling through his e-mails and looked at Coletti, his beady eyes deadly serious. "It's a tradition that began with a gravedigger who worked here during the Civil War," he said. "Ironically, the incident that started the ball was pretty close to what happened today."

"What do you mean?"

"The gravedigger's job was burying Union soldiers' remains, so you can imagine there was always work for him to do. Well, one day, when there were literally dozens of bodies lined up and waiting for burial, the gravedigger didn't show up for work. People were annoyed, but nobody thought much of it at the time. Rumor had it that he was a bit of a drunk. He'd disappeared on binges before. This time was different, though. He wasn't in any of the taverns or flophouses he usually frequented, and he never showed up at home that night. Eventually, they gathered a search party to check the cemetery. Shortly after that, they found him crumpled in a freshly dug grave. His neck was broken. There were those who said he fell in because he was drunk, but most people didn't believe that. Most people thought he'd been murdered.

"The evening after they discovered him, a few neighbors got together to raise money for his widow to give him a proper burial, but the night they were supposed to bury him, his body disappeared. No one ever saw him again, and legend has it he was never really dead at all."

Coletti thought of the man he'd seen in the cemetery, dressed in clothes from a time gone by. "What did this gravedigger look like?" he asked.

"There weren't any pictures of him, unfortunately, but they say he was short, red-faced, and scruffy. The kind of man you might find on skid row. Why do you ask?"

"The man I saw here earlier . . . I was just wondering if the gravedigger . . ." Coletti was about to go on, but he thought better of it. "Never mind."

The manager laughed. It was a squeaky, high-pitched sound. "Of course, none of us believes the legend of the gravedigger, if that's what you're thinking. There aren't any ghosts at the ball. It's usually just a fancy dinner with a hundred or so history buffs who like national historic landmarks. This year, with the economy being what it is, the ball's a little more important. If it flops, we're going to have to make some hard choices."

The manager went back to scrolling though the e-mails on his BlackBerry. "Here's the message from Mrs. Bailey," he said, handing the device to Coletti.

The detective read it and was about to hand the Black-Berry back when he noticed Mrs. Bailey's signature line.

"What's this acronym by her name—DOI?"

The manager looked at it. "It means she was a member of the Daughters of Independence. It's one of the groups that maintain mansions and other landmarks in Fairmount Park."

"Do you know who the other members are?"

"There were only three, maybe four. Unfortunately I don't have their names."

"That's okay, I'll find them." Coletti fished a card from his pocket and handed it to the manager. "If you can forward me that e-mail from Mrs. Bailey, that'd be a big help."

"No problem," the manager said, twitching his nose.

Coletti walked toward the spot where the body had been found, but as he watched the crime scene cops work in and around the grave, taking pictures and dusting for prints, it was clear that they hadn't found much beyond the dirt in Mrs. Bailey's mouth. Coletti had more than that. He had Lenore Wilkinson, and he didn't plan to let her go just yet.

He found her exactly where he'd left her, standing near the crime scene tape and waiting for the body to be lifted out of the grave. When he came alongside her, Coletti could see the grief on her face morphing into a sort of numbness. He knew that she was shocked by what had happened, but shock didn't exclude her as a suspect.

"Come on," Coletti said as he guided her away. "You don't have to stand here. You can wait in the car."

"I want to get out of here," she mumbled.

"I'm sure you do. But I'm going to have to ask you a few questions first."

"Then ask them."

"It might take a while," Coletti said smoothly. "I think we'd probably do better down at headquarters."

There was an uncomfortable pause. "Does that mean you think I was involved in this?"

"Sometimes people can be involved in things and not even know it."

They stopped at the car and she turned to him as the numbness in her eyes gave way to fire. "I think I'd know if I were involved in a murder, Detective Coletti."

"I know you would. That's why you're coming back to headquarters. We're going to find out exactly what you know."

"Oh really?" she said with muted anger. "Well, here's what I know. I know I don't have to talk to you if I don't want to. I know I can call my husband and have a lawyer down here in five minutes, and I know that I didn't have anything to do with what happened here. But I'll answer whatever questions you have, because I know one more thing." She stared at him in the same way she'd done at her sister's grave. "I know you don't trust me."

"I don't trust anybody," Coletti said as he opened the door to his unmarked black Mercury and gestured toward the backseat.

Lenore searched his face carefully. "I know you don't. That's why you've been alone all these years."

She got into the car and looked up at him with a calm that was almost frightening. She'd spoken her piece, and it was neither opinion nor assumption. It was simply the truth.

"You don't know anything about me," Coletti said, sounding more certain than he felt. "But before this is all over, we're gonna find out all about you. I promise you that."

"Good," Lenore said defiantly. "When you figure out who I am let me know, because that's what I came here to find out."

Coletti was about to press her, but before he could say anything more, a familiar voice spoke up from behind him.

"Am I interrupting something?" asked Detective Charlie Mann, his dreadlocks draping over his hoodie as he craned his neck to get a better look at the woman in the car.

There was silence as Coletti and Lenore stared at each other. "No, you're not interrupting anything," Coletti finally answered. "But I do need to talk to you in private."

Coletti closed the car door, turned around, and took his young partner by the arm. Then he walked him across the cemetery to the spot where workers from the medical examiner's office were about to remove the body.

"What's wrong with you?" Mann asked as he examined Coletti's sweaty face. "You look like you've seen a ghost."

Coletti looked back toward the car, where Lenore sat watching them intently. "Maybe I have."

Mann glanced at the woman as she sat in the car and made a call on her cell. "You mean *her*?"

Coletti nodded. "Her name's Lenore Wilkinson. She's Mary Smithson's sister."

"Yeah, right," Mann said with a chuckle.

When Coletti didn't respond in kind, Mann's laughter faded. He glanced at the car, and when he saw Lenore's eyes staring back at him, his expression changed.

"You're serious, aren't you?"

Coletti nodded.

"Have you had a chance to talk to her?"

"Not as much as she's talked to me," Coletti said. Then he paused. "She, uh, seems to know things about me. I don't know if it's some kind of parlor trick or if she talked to her sister more than she let on, but it's strange. It makes me wonder what kind of things she knew about Mrs. Bailey. Or what Mrs. Bailey knew about her."

The two detectives stood there for a moment before Coletti took his notepad from his pocket and handed it to Mann. "We found a piece of paper near the body. I copied down what it said. Does it ring any bells for you?"

Mann looked at the notepad. Then he took out his iPhone. "Deep into that darkness peering . . ." he said as he typed the words into a Google search. A second later, the results popped up. "It's a line from 'The Raven,' by Edgar Allan Poe."

"I gotta get me one o' those phones," Coletti said.

"I *bought* you one two months ago. Where is it?"

"I've got it somewhere," Coletti said, sounding like a school kid telling a lie. "Besides, my old phone still works and I can send texts and get e-mail on it, so . . . anyway, what does the line from the poem mean?"

Mann stared at Coletti for a few seconds. "I can't believe you lost that phone," he said, shaking his head. Then he looked at the phone's screen, and a look of recognition swept over his face. "What did you say Mary's sister's name was?"

"Lenore."

When Coletti said it, the storm clouds darkened, sucking the very sound from the air. Just as he'd heard almost nothing but his own breathing when he was searching among the cemetery's crypts for the killer, Coletti could only hear a few sounds now. One of them was Mann's voice, reading the next line of Poe's masterpiece.

"But the silence was unbroken, and the stillness gave no token, and the only word there spoken—"

Mann's voice was drowned out by the roll of thunder and the patter of the rain against granite headstones.

The two of them walked quickly to Coletti's car, where Lenore was waiting. When they got in, an alert tone came over the radio.

"Cars stand by," the dispatcher said. "Nine two one two, what's your location?"

Five seconds of static followed.

"Car 9212, report."

Again, there was static, and with it, an almost palpable sense of dread. Coletti and Mann looked at each other, then at Lenore. A moment later, the radio crackled again.

"This is 9210," a cop said gravely. "I got 9212 near Reservoir Drive. The car's running, but he ain't in it."

* * *

The dispatcher called for an assist—the highest priority in the department. It meant that a cop was in trouble, and this assist was much like any other. Once the call went out, chaos reigned.

The radio was clogged with the voices of cops falling over each other to respond. The streets were filled with police cars flying recklessly through the park. The air was thick with the electric pulse of cops who were out for blood.

They blocked Kelly Drive and brought civilian traffic to a standstill. As they did so, they tried to do the impossible—fight against the unspoken yet prevailing feeling that time had already run out.

As rain poured from dark clouds that made the morning feel like night, the police used everything at their disposal to search for their comrade. There were K-9 units and SWAT teams, uniformed and plainclothes, and when word of the cop's disappearance hit his former district—the ninth—a steady stream of police sped to the area from downtown.

Lieutenant Sandy Jackson was among them. With cinnamon-brown skin and a beauty that belied her toughness, Sandy commanded officers in the sixth district. She'd served most of her career in the ninth, however, and the cop who'd disappeared was one of the few who'd helped her along as a rookie.

As she whipped her car around Kelly Drive and past the Philadelphia Museum of Art, Sandy glanced out the window at a golden statue of an armor-clad Joan of Arc and thought of her own days on the battlefield.

She remembered how she'd fought to get promotions. She remembered how she'd battled sexism in the department. Most of all, she remembered that the officer who was now missing was one of the few male cops who'd helped her as she struggled for equal treatment.

When her crass colleagues would leave pornography out at roll call to harass Sandy and the other female cop on the squad, it was Smitty who stepped up to make them stop.

He never won any popularity contests because of it, and he never tried to do so. He simply did his job, and most of the time, he did it well. That was what led to his proudest moment—the arrest of two college boys who'd run a major meth operation out of their Center City apartment. On appeal, it all came crashing down when their parents hired the city's top defense attorney to get their convictions overturned.

When the smoke cleared, Smitty was portrayed as the bad guy, and by the time the media finished with him, the commissioner had no choice but to get him out of the limelight. Sandy watched sadly as he was transferred from the ninth district to the park, but she consoled herself with the belief that the new assignment took him out of harm's way. Her belief was wrong.

Her memories of Smitty were set aside as Sandy maneuvered around police cars and wagons at the scene. Her thoughts turned to Charlie Mann. He was, after all, the man who mattered most to her, and it had been that way since they'd begun seeing each other three years before.

He'd made her smile when others couldn't. He'd become someone with whom she could see a future. But things had changed between them since Charlie's last case, right after he shot and killed a murder suspect and a serial killer. Though both shootings were justified, Charlie had become withdrawn and introspective, and while he never said it aloud, Sandy felt as if a piece of him had died that day as well.

Parking her car, Sandy donned her cap and raincoat and tried to put Charlie out of her mind. That wasn't so easy.

When she got out of the car, however, and saw the scene before her, any thoughts of the man she loved disappeared in the urgency of the moment.

There were barking dogs and shouting voices along with the steady hiss of rain. Flashlight beams stabbed through the darkness between the trees. Yellow raincoats and blue jackets moved in every direction, frantically searching the woods for any sign of life.

A hundred yards in front of her, in the middle of the winding road that ran along the edge of the woods, there were hastily erected barricades. Beyond them were news vans and cameras, satellite dishes raised high on hydraulic lifts, and reporters fighting for space on the rain-soaked tarmac.

Information was still scarce, but the media knew two facts for sure. They knew that Clarissa Bailey, one of the richest women in Philadelphia, had died at the Fairgrounds Cemetery in what could very well be a homicide. They also knew that a police officer had disappeared in the woods while searching for the suspect in Mrs. Bailey's murder.

Even as Sandy watched them, bits and pieces of information were posted online, and in minutes, the news went international. "Cop Missing in Search for Heiress's Killer" was the lead story on Yahoo. "Fairgrounds Cemetery" became the most searched item on Google. "Cemetery Ghoul Kills Socialite" made its way onto AOL. But the one that stuck was the headline that was posted on TMZ.com: "Gravedigger's Ball Starts Early." It was linked on Twitter and tagged on Facebook, and while Internet sites repeated every rumor, the conventional media struggled to catch up.

TV reporters at the scene did stand-ups in the pouring rain. Cameramen pressed against the barricades in an attempt to get past the police. Writers shouted questions at every commander within earshot. All of them hoped to be the first to report whatever the cops brought out of the woods.

Sandy could see that it would take more than a few cops to handle the media contingent, so she got on the radio and directed sixth district officers toward the barricades. That was when she saw the commissioner arrive.

He was all broad shoulders and stern demeanor, and even in the rain, she could see the stress in his eyes when he got out of his car.

Kevin Lynch had already lived through more than his share of dead cops, with a string of them killed on duty in the past year. He wasn't looking forward to experiencing it again, and he was in no mood to answer questions. As he watched his officers engage in a frenzied search for one of their own and listened to the media shouting queries from beyond the barricades, Lynch's brown face clouded over.

"Commissioner, what's the next step after the officer's body is recovered?" shouted a reporter from a national news Web site.

The assumption that Smitty was dead angered Lynch, and when he turned to the freckle-faced reporter and saw the young man grinning sarcastically, the commissioner felt himself poised to explode. Then Lynch saw Sandy looking pointedly at him, her eyes begging him not to be goaded into a confrontation. That look said that the reporter wanted him to lose it, to yell, to give in to his most base instincts. That look said that Lynch mustn't do that, lest he give that reporter the chance to portray him as hotheaded and inept.

That look was right.

Lynch took a deep breath, held in the obscenities that were perched on his lips, and walked across the wet, winding road to talk to Sandy.

He'd come to know her during the search for the Angel of Death, and he'd learned to admire her instinct and toughness. Sandy, after all, was much like himself—a cop who had faced all manner of naysayers both inside and outside the department. Like him, she'd managed to survive—to thrive, even—in a job where the brightest stars had to dim their own lights in order to avoid flaming out.

"I'm glad you didn't say what you were about to, Commissioner," she said when he was close enough so only the two of them could hear.

"I'm glad you stopped me," he said, smiling quickly

and humorlessly before his sad, angry expression returned. "Did you just get here?"

"Yes, sir," she said as sadness flashed across her face. "Smitty was—I mean, Smitty *is*—one of my favorite guys in the department. We go way back."

She looked embarrassed at her flub, but Lynch knew as well as she did that she was probably right to speak of him in the past tense.

"Let's hope he's all right," he said, feeling as disingenuous as he sounded.

As Lynch spoke, the captain of the ninety-second district walked slowly toward them, his eyes vacant and his face devoid of color. He didn't have to say a word. The grief on his face said it all.

"They found him," the captain said, his voice barely audible in the rain.

Neither Lynch nor Sandy responded. They simply waited for him to finish.

"He was, um, in a hole maybe two hundred yards into the woods. We probably would've missed him, except his gun was close by and the rain washed away the leaves that had been brushed over the hole." The captain sighed and shook his head, the grief on his face rapidly giving way to anger. "I'm no expert, but from the looks of it, I'd say he was buried alive."

"Okay," the commissioner said, turning to look at the media contingent. "Lieutenant Jackson, get me a few more cars from the sixth to secure those media barricades."

"Yes, sir," Sandy said.

The commissioner looked once more at the bank of cameras. Then he started down the hill that led into the woods.

"Where are you going, Commissioner?" asked the captain from the ninety-second.

"If one of my men is dead," Lynch said with smoldering eyes, "I'm going down to see him for myself."

Mann and Coletti never made it to the assist. They couldn't with Lenore in the car, so they drove back to headquarters, listening to the radio transmissions that ended with the discovery of Smitty's body.

Lenore heard it all, and as she sat in the backseat, watching Coletti cast furtive glances in the rearview mirror, she knew, just as they all did, that the murders of Mrs. Bailey and the officer were connected. Lenore's senses told her something more than that, though. They told her that Coletti was right; sometimes people can be involved in things and not even know it.

Coletti called the office to find out if anyone had been able to reach Mrs. Bailey's husband. They hadn't, so he turned his attention back to Lenore, who was busily dialing her cell phone to leave a message for her own husband.

When they arrived at the police administration building, Coletti and Mann escorted her into the oddly shaped figure eight known locally as the Roundhouse. They walked her down a series of curved halls and into a quiet interview room whose pale fluorescent light made most people look sickly. They marveled that it didn't seem to do that to Lenore.

With the exception of a scraped knee from hitting the ground after the gunshot, she looked as if she'd just stepped out of a magazine. Her cashmere scarf was draped over her shoulder and held in place with a diamond brooch. Her lamb's wool skirt was accented by Italian leather boots, and when she sat in one of the rickety chairs and crossed her legs, they could see a hint of her thigh. It was smooth and supple.

Her hair, blond and shoulder-length, was pulled back in a simple coif that highlighted her eyes and cheekbones. Her skin was flawless except for a sprinkling of freckles. Even in this light, she was stunning, and while she closely resembled Mary, Lenore was a much more beautiful version.

She sat at the battered metal table in the middle of the room, examining the chipped paint on the cinderblock walls and the broken clock above the two-way mirror.

With stale air being piped in through the vents and the smell of sweat lingering from past interrogations, the room felt stuffy and crowded. Coletti liked it that way. It helped to temper the uneasiness he felt about Lenore.

"Can I get you some water or something?" he asked her as Mann looked on.

"No, just ask your questions," she said, sounding as annoyed as she looked.

"Actually, I don't think we're going to ask many questions," Coletti said. "You're a witness, so we just need you to give your version of today's events."

"Including the murder of the police officer?"

Coletti looked at her with a stone-cold expression.

"How could you know anything about that? You were with us when it happened."

"But that isn't stopping you from suspecting me, is it?"

Coletti paused. "For now, let's forget what I suspect. We just need to know what happened in the time leading up to Mrs. Bailey's death."

"And if I tell you that, will you change your opinion about my involvement?" she asked, more curious than afraid.

"I don't have an opinion yet."

She looked at him, and her mouth curled up in a smirk. "Yes you do."

The two of them stared at each other, sizing each other up. Then Mann jumped in.

"I'm going to tape this," he said, placing a small digital recorder on the table. "It'll make it easier to transcribe it later. Now, if you'll just state your full name, age, occupation, and address, we can get on with it."

She looked at Coletti for a few seconds more, her eyes filled with intense curiosity. Then she turned to Mann and smiled pleasantly before she spoke.

"My name is Mrs. Lenore Wilkinson. I'm twenty-nine years old, and I don't have an occupation. I'm married to John Wilkinson, so my job is finding causes and events where our money can best be used. That's part of the reason I was at the cemetery this morning."

Mann and Coletti exchanged knowing glances. Like everyone in America, they'd heard of John Wilkinson. He was a Manhattan real estate magnate and one of the wealthiest men on the East Coast. In their minds, that made Lenore a trophy wife who spent her days by the pool and her nights being ravished by a husband twice her age.

"Have you spoken to Mr. Wilkinson today?" Coletti asked.

"I've left several messages for him," she said, shifting uncomfortably. "He had a business trip to London, but I'm sure we'll talk soon."

Lenore saw the skeptical looks on their faces. There was a moment of uncomfortable silence. She told herself she didn't care.

"Why don't we get back to how you came to be at the cemetery this morning," Coletti said, sensing the tension in the air.

"Of course," Lenore said, smiling nervously. "Mrs. Bailey reached out to me about six months ago. She knew about the fund-raisers I'd run in Manhattan, and she needed a generous sponsor who could raise the profile of the Gravedigger's Ball. I didn't respond at first, because I didn't know her, and frankly, a fund-raiser to save a cemetery—even a historic one—just wasn't on my to-do list."

"So what changed your mind?" Coletti asked.

"You did."

Both Mann and Coletti looked confused, until she began to explain.

"In the days after my sister died, there were all kinds of reports about the awful things she'd done. The murders in the churches, the boys she strung out on heroin, the priest she set up for the Confessional Murders. And the thing that struck me in all those stories was that they said she did it to punish you, Detective Coletti. She blamed you for everything that ever went wrong in her life, but after she died, you never said a word against her, no matter how many times they asked you to.

"Mary's mother and my father, on the other hand, did interviews with every network and disowned her in front of the world. I couldn't blame them, I guess. Every time they showed Mary's picture on the news, or showed the bodies in the churches, or interviewed the victims' families, I disowned her a little bit, too. I'd never met her in real life, so I got to know her through those stories, and from what I could see, she was a monster.

"Then I saw a story about her burial. It was just a two-paragraph sidebar to a *New York Post* article that rehashed the things she'd done. And in that little sidebar, it said someone had anonymously paid to have her buried in the Fairgrounds Cemetery.

"I knew her family didn't do it, and I knew she didn't have any friends, so I called Mrs. Bailey and asked if she could tell me the name of the person who'd paid for Mary's burial. She said she couldn't give me a name, but if I'd agree to come to Philadelphia and talk about the ball, she'd try to arrange for me to meet my sister's benefactor."

Lenore paused as Mann turned to look at Coletti, who was staring into space, as he often did when Mary's name was mentioned.

"Maybe it was a coincidence that I chose today to

visit," Lenore said. "Maybe it was chance that you were standing there when I asked Mrs. Bailey to show me where Mary's grave was. But whether it was chance or not, I know I was meant to meet you today, Detective, because I needed to see that there was at least one person who loved her. The only thing that surprised me was that person turned out to be you."

Coletti took a few moments to gather himself, and when he was able to look her in the eye, he spoke.

"I don't know if it was chance that you were there today, either," he said as he looked at Lenore. "You seem to know a lot about me. Why don't you tell me about yourself?"

There was a long silence as Lenore prepared to talk about the subject she hated most—herself.

"My identity's always been wrapped up in someone else," she said softly. "Even after I left Dunmore and went to Princeton on scholarship, I never felt like I was my own person. I was always Sean O' Hanlon's daughter, or Mary Smithson's sister, or John Wilkinson's wife. I was never just me, and I guess I was always more comfortable that way, because it's scary being me."

She looked from Coletti to Mann and back again. "I've always known things about people that they don't know about themselves. I look at them and the truth just comes to me. Sometimes I share that truth, but mostly I don't. I've learned that people don't like to hear the truth."

"So where does this ability come from?" Mann asked skeptically.

"I don't know," she said. "My mother used to tell me I

was born with a veil over my face, so if the old wives' tales are true, I guess that veil meant I was a seer."

"Did you see what was coming today?" Mann asked.

"I don't know—I don't think so. When Mrs. Bailey and I talked last week and arranged for her to meet me at Thirtieth Street Station, the only thing I saw was that I needed to be here. I didn't know why, but I didn't question it. I just did what I knew I had to do."

"So you felt like you had to be here?" Mann asked.

"Yes."

The detectives looked at each other. Then they stared at Lenore. From the expressions on their faces, she could tell that their suspicions had deepened.

"Run us through the timeline of your morning with Mrs. Bailey," Coletti said.

"My train came in at eight fifteen, and she met me in her own car—a gray Honda, I think. We were at the cemetery by eight thirty-five. I remember, because I looked at my watch when she pulled into the driveway off that street by the river. I think it's called Kelly Drive."

"What did the two of you talk about?" Coletti asked.

"The Gravedigger's Ball, mostly. She wanted me to serve on the event committee this year and replace her as chair next year. She felt like the event needed new blood with new ideas—and new money, of course—and when we got to the cemetery, she walked me around the graves so I'd know what the money was for."

"And what would that be?" Mann asked.

"The money? It's for upkeep and maintenance. At a

historic site like Fairgrounds Cemetery, repairs or restorations have to meet certain standards so the site can maintain its designation. That increases costs considerably. In fact, from what I understand, it's not unusual for repairs on one mausoleum to run into the hundreds of thousands of dollars. Multiply that by a dozen repairs a year and you suddenly have a budget that runs into the millions."

"Maybe Mrs. Bailey's death had something to do with those millions," Mann said, thinking aloud.

Coletti agreed that money was always a possible motive, but a cemetery budget didn't point to an obvious suspect. He thought to himself that there had to be something else, or someone else, that tied Lenore to Mrs. Bailey.

"Did you see anyone or anything that seemed unusual or suspicious?" Coletti asked.

"No, because there wasn't anyone else there. We walked and she talked and when we stopped at the last grave I saw you. That's when I asked her where Mary was buried, and she pointed to that evergreen tree. When I started to walk over to the grave, she told me to hurry back because she had something she wanted to tell me— something that would explain why it was so important for me to work with her on the ball."

Lenore felt a chill at the thought. She folded her arms across her chest and squeezed herself tightly. "That was the last thing she said to me."

Mann and Coletti looked at each other as Coletti pulled out his notepad and placed it on the desk. "Do you remember this poem?" he asked.

She looked at it and nodded. "That's what was written on the paper we found near the grave. Why?"

"Because this might be what she wanted to talk to you about," Coletti said. "The lines are by Edgar Allan Poe. They're from a poem called 'The Raven,' and the next stanza contains a name that shows up eight times in the poem."

"What name is that?" she asked.

"Lenore."

CHAPTER 3

It was 11:30 A.M., a half hour after the stream of police officers going in and out of the woods had slowed to a trickle. The radio transmissions had lost their urgency. The commanders were closemouthed. The police officers guarding the media barricades were tense.

The gaggle of reporters was abuzz about the murderer, to whom they'd affixed a moniker—the Gravedigger. As excited as they were about the gruesome story, they'd stood in drenching rains for nearly two hours, and they were growing increasingly unruly, having been promised a statement more than once. Most of them were from national news outlets. They had no choice but to wait.

Kirsten Douglas was from Philly. She didn't wait for anything. The crime beat reporter from the *Philadelphia Daily News* had already called nearly every source she had in the police department, and all of them were mum. Kirsten guessed they'd been told to say nothing. That meant she had to get her story the old-fashioned way. She had to dig for it.

With brown eyes that were kind but intense and a round, welcoming face, Kirsten looked more like a mother than a crime reporter. Her brown curly hair was unruly. Her clothes were earth-toned and frumpy. She looked every bit of her forty-five years, and still, people found her attractive. Not because of how she looked, but because of her willingness to listen. That quality made people want to talk to Kirsten Douglas. That was what made her so good at her job.

Packing her notebook and pen into the oversized pockets of her old raincoat, Kirsten broke away from the pack and walked toward the park's exit.

"Hey, where you going?" an *Inquirer* reporter shouted after her.

"I'll be back," Kirsten said. "I've gotta get something out of my car."

She walked for three minutes, though it seemed like forever, passing by the front of the golf driving range as she exited the park. Police cars blocked traffic from entering the park, and police cars and vans darted up and down nearby streets. But as the rain poured down in ever-thickening sheets and Kirsten turned right on Thirty-third Street, she decided that she would somehow get around them.

Walking along the border of a struggling neighborhood known as Strawberry Mansion, she looked across the street at abandoned houses and refurbished ones that shared the block with a garage. One of those houses had once belonged to jazz great John Coltrane, and its ramshackle appearance starkly contrasted the shiny state historic marker out front.

Kirsten had seen such neighborhoods many times during her years as a crime reporter. Along the way, she'd won accolades and national awards while filing stories on everything from street gangs to the mob. Her skills had won her the grudging respect of cops and criminals alike, but it had also earned her enemies. Kirsten didn't care. She was much more concerned with finding the truth than making friends, so she walked along the gate that separated the driving range from the street, and when she found her way in, she took it.

Ducking through a hole in the fence near the rear of the driving range, she made her way toward the line of trees. Once she walked into the forest, she felt as if she'd entered a different world.

She could still see the swirling dome lights and yellow barricades in the distance, but it was dark behind those trees, and the lack of light made her feel all alone. It also made her feel something she'd never experienced in all her years of dealing with thugs and murderers. It made her feel fear.

Swallowing hard, she began the difficult trek through slick leaves, fallen tree trunks, and thick brush. Thankfully, there were paths cut through the forest to accommodate the disc golf course, but those paths were empty now, and the terrain was made more difficult by her unfamiliarity. She walked up muddy slopes, stepping on planks that had been placed along parts of the path like crude bridges.

She leaned against fallen trees, pulled on hanging vines, and cut her hands on the ends of errant branches.

For fifteen minutes, she walked through the forest, doubling back more than once and passing a tree that bore a heart with the words "Tom and Jean forever." When, finally, she figured out how to move through the forest by following the paths along the empty disc golf course, the clouds overhead thickened, the woods got darker, and Kirsten was forced to depend less on her sight than on her other senses. She could smell the wet leaves and the pungent urine of animals that had marked their territory. She could smell the moss on the trees and the alcohol in discarded beer bottles. Mingled somewhere beneath those odors, she could smell herself. She was sweating.

Kirsten leaned against a tree to rest as the rain began coming down harder. It was now close to impossible to see where she was going. That frightened her, so she took a deep breath and closed her eyes in an attempt to calm herself. Then she listened as a wind gust swept through the trees, increasing in volume until it sounded almost like a jet engine roaring to life. Kirsten's eyes snapped open when she heard it, and she looked around frantically for something to reassure herself. Unfortunately, there was only the rain.

It fell in a steady drumbeat that stabbed at her consciousness until her nerves were frayed. The sound of it made everything seem large and imposing, including the tree she was leaning against.

Suddenly, she felt that tree move, and she looked up,

expecting to see someone bearing down on her. Instead, she saw two squirrels chasing each other down the trunk.

She felt her heart beating wildly and her breath coming faster. Placing her hand on her chest, she leaned against the tree once more and tried to keep her imagination in check.

"Get it together, Kirsten," she whispered in a quaking voice.

A moment later, she heard the sound she'd been seeking since making her way into the trees. She heard the crackle of police radios.

Leaning forward, she listened intently and traced the sound to an area beyond a knoll fifty yards to her left. She moved toward it, but the sound, instead of growing louder, seemed to fade. As she stopped and looked around, trying once more to get her bearings, she heard something behind her. It sounded like footsteps.

Kirsten whipped her head around in time to see a pasty white face near a tree just twenty yards to the rear, but when she looked again, the face was gone. Kirsten told herself that it was an animal of some sort. She told herself that a cop had followed her into the woods. She told herself that it was one of her media colleagues. But when she heard the footsteps moving once again, she told herself to run.

Weaving between the trees, she moved quickly toward the knoll where she'd heard the radio chatter. She turned around once and saw a black coat. She turned around again and saw staring eyes. She didn't turn a third time, because she knew that if she did so, he'd be upon her.

Kirsten ran, her body screaming out as she tried to

shake the feeling that her pursuer was only a few steps away. She ran, ignoring the pain in her legs and the burning in her lungs. She ran, heeding the only sensation that mattered now—fear.

Scrambling up the knoll, she heard the police radios once again. She tried to scream, but she couldn't, because she was out of breath. She tried to run faster but slipped on a pile of wet leaves. Digging her hands into the muddy embankment, she struggled to the top and felt something touch her ankle.

Gasping for breath, she kicked with all her might while pulling herself up and over. Seconds later, she slid down the other side, saw police officers in the distance, and stumbled toward the thicket of trees where the cops milled about.

Quickly, she looked around for the white face and black coat she'd seen on the other side of the hill. When she saw neither, she tried to convince herself that she'd imagined it all, but deep down she knew what she'd seen.

She continued toward the officers and was about to call out to them, but then she saw what they were doing, and her reporting instincts overtook her fear.

Kneeling by a tree to catch her breath, she saw a section of the woods sealed off by crime scene tape. Beyond that tape were ten supervisors, including Commissioner Lynch. Eight more officers were from the crime scene unit. Four were guarding the scene. None of these cops were the ones who interested her, however. The others were the story.

She watched as two patrolmen carried a plastic body

bag toward the middle of the group. Two more joined them to hoist a muddy corpse. She glimpsed the body before it was zipped into the bag, and she saw that it was covered with thick red mud. As the rain poured onto it, the dirt was washed away, revealing a blue uniform shirt and a face frozen in fear. Kirsten had seen that man in many news reports about the meth case two years before. Now she was seeing him again, only this time, he was dead.

Quickly, Kirsten grabbed her cell phone from her pocket and snapped a picture. Then she texted the picture to the paper's Twitter account, along with the words, "Gravedigger 2? Officer Frank Smith pulled from shallow grave."

It took a few seconds for the text to go through. When it did, Kirsten began dialing her editor's number. That was when she felt someone standing over her. Slowly, Kirsten looked up from her phone. When she saw his chalk-white face, with his crooked, brittle mustache and coal-black eyes, all hell broke loose.

Her scream was so loud that the air ripped in two. Everything else ripped, as well. The media horde she'd left behind pushed against the barricades while police fought to hold them back.

Down in the woods, things were even worse. As the rain poured down, ten cops ran toward the sound of her scream. The officers carrying Smitty's body slipped in the mud. The ones collecting evidence tried to keep the scene from being compromised in the confusion. The chaos was almost complete. Then Lynch assumed control.

"Get a detail together now and secure the area!" he shouted to a lieutenant from the crime scene unit. "Nobody gets beyond the tape!"

The lieutenant moved to obey the order, and Lynch removed his Glock from its holster. With a series of hand signals, he directed two groups of cops to circle around from both sides and move in the direction the scream had come from. Lynch himself moved straight ahead, and Sandy and two others went with him.

"This is Car 1," Lynch said into a handheld radio as he moved slowly through the woods. "What have we got?"

There were a few minutes of radio silence before one of the cops spoke up. "This is 9215. We found her. She's a little shaken up, but she's fine. She's about twenty-five yards in front of you, sir."

Lynch saw a group of officers huddled around a tree. Then he saw a woman stand up. Even as one of the cops draped her shoulders with a poncho to shield her from the rain, she looked deathly afraid. That was odd to Lynch, because the closer he got to her, the more clearly he saw her face. He'd never seen Kirsten Douglas afraid of anything before.

Holstering his gun, he walked up to her. "Forget about what you're doing down here," he said, his brow furrowed in annoyance. "We'll get to that later. What did you see?"

She looked up at him with a mixture of fear and confusion, as if she were unsure how to explain. "There was a man," she began, but she stopped mid-sentence as a chill ran through her body.

"What did he look like?" Lynch demanded. "Which way did he go?"

She tried to answer, but she felt very cold. The rain seemed to have soaked through to her very bones. It wasn't the rain that made her cold, however. It was what she'd seen, and more than that, it was what she hadn't seen.

"He was white," she whispered. "Too white. It was almost like he didn't have any blood at all. And he was wearing a black coat—a coat like you'd see in an old war movie."

"Okay," Lynch said, turning to his men. "That's the same description from the cemetery. I want these woods searched and I want him found. He can't be far away."

The officers began to fan out, and Kirsten watched them with curious resignation. She knew they wouldn't find what they were looking for, but she was afraid to tell them that. Not out of fear for her safety, but because she was afraid for her sanity.

"Did he hurt you?" Lynch asked.

Kirsten shook her head slowly from side to side, her eyes unfocused and staring straight ahead.

"Then why did you scream?"

She took a deep breath and tried to compose herself. After a few seconds, she looked up at the commissioner.

"I came through these woods, hoping to see why you were taking so long to give us information about the missing officer," she said. "But along the way, I thought I saw someone behind me, so I ran the last twenty or so yards until I got to this spot. I probably should've just kept running, but when I saw your men moving the body, I guess my reporter's instincts took over. I stopped, took a picture, and posted it online. When I turned around, the man who'd followed me was standing right next to me."

"And that's when you screamed?" Lynch asked.

She nodded.

"Where did he go after that?"

Kirsten shook her head and sighed. "He went up," she said, not sure if she believed it herself.

"What do you mean, he went up?" Lynch asked. "Did he climb a tree? Did he run up a hill?"

Kirsten looked into the distance and spoke as if she were in a dream. "You know, Commissioner, I've spent my entire professional career dealing in facts. Who, what, when, where, and why. Every time I wrote a story I could ask myself those questions, along with the other ones I learned in journalism school. Is it timely? Is it unusual? Is it news? And for more than twenty years, I could always answer all those questions, but not now. Not here. Not today. For the first time in my life, I'm not sure that what I'm dealing with is fact. And that scares me, Commissioner. It scares me more than some man standing over me in the woods."

"What are you saying, Kirsten? What did you see?"

Kirsten looked at Lynch, and the officers around the commissioner edged closer, especially Sandy Jackson. Sandy knew what it was to see something that her mind couldn't explain. It was a helpless feeling, one that generated its own special fear. Sandy had experienced it when she saw the Angel of Death. She wondered if it would be the same for Kirsten.

"He was so close to me that I could smell him," the reporter said as Sandy looked on. "It was an odd smell, almost like the stench of something that had been buried. When I saw him standing there next to me, I thought that I was about to be buried, too, so I screamed. Then I closed my eyes and told myself that if he was going to kill me, I wasn't going to watch him do it. A second later I felt this breeze, and I heard something like flapping wings. When I opened my eyes, he was gone, and there was a black bird flying away. It was a raven, Commissioner, and as crazy as it sounds, when that raven flew away, I think that man might have flown away, too."

At eleven forty-five, Coletti and Mann walked into homicide with Lenore, and the room was nearly empty. Almost every cop in the city was on the street looking for the man who'd killed one of their own. Of the three detectives who remained in the office, two were on their way out the door, and the third was busy shuffling papers.

The three detectives stopped what they were doing when they saw Lenore. They'd heard that Mary Smithson's sister had been at the scene, but hearing about her and seeing her were two different things.

Coletti and Mann tried to ignore their stares. Lenore did, too, but as they walked through the room, Lenore's presence filled everyone's minds with recollections of Mary, and the memories were anything but good.

Coletti pulled out a chair for Lenore next to his battered desk. Everyone was so quiet that the scrape of the metal legs against the floor sounded like an earthquake. He booted up the ancient desktop he refused to relinquish and checked for Clarissa Bailey's e-mail that the cemetery manager had promised to forward to him. It wasn't there.

Mann sat down at his desk, as well. He turned on his laptop and plugged his digital tape recorder into the USB port. As he fiddled with the mouse pad, a voice spoke up from across the room.

"She looks just like her," one of the detectives whispered as he looked at Lenore, but as quietly as he tried to say it, the words were like a shout against the silence.

With those five words, he had reaffirmed the history between Mary and Coletti and had caused every detective in the office to replay it. They could still remember Mary coming into that very room just two months before and cracking Coletti's tough exterior with brash talk and blue eyes. She'd confronted him about his attitude toward Mann and forced him to backtrack. No one had ever made Coletti back off of anything. That was how his colleagues had known, even before it happened, that Coletti's and Mary's fast friendship would develop into something more. What they didn't know was that the woman who seemed so genuine was really something else altogether.

They'd watched Coletti lose when he gambled on loving her, and though most of them would never say it aloud, their hearts broke with his when Mary betrayed him. Because Lenore was Mary's sister, they viewed her through the prism of those memories, and, fairly or not, at least one of them believed that Lenore would eventually prove herself to be just like Mary.

Lenore tried to keep her focus straight ahead as she watched Coletti fill out the incident report from that morning's shooting, but it was hard to do so with everyone staring. She occupied herself by making a call on her cell. When there was no answer, she disconnected and put the phone in her bag. Soon after, one of the detectives—a biker type who'd transferred from northwest detectives just three months before—came over to Coletti's desk.

"I guess you heard they found Smitty," he said to Coletti while continuing to stare at Lenore.

Coletti felt uncomfortable. He'd never worked with this new guy, but he didn't like him. He was tactless in the squad room and reckless in the streets. Guys like that were accidents waiting to happen.

"Yeah, we heard about Smitty," Coletti said with a sigh as he continued to write. "It's a shame what happened to him, but right now we're trying to work through Clarissa Bailey's case. Has anyone reached her husband?"

"We've sent a couple cars by the house, but no luck yet," the detective said, still looking at Lenore. "We haven't talked to Smitty's wife yet, either, but maybe it's for the best."

Coletti looked up at the detective, his eyes warning the man to stop. The new guy either didn't get the hint or didn't want to.

"I'd hate to have to be the one to tell Smitty's wife he was buried alive," the detective said as he glared at Lenore.

"I'd never want her to know that they pulled him out of the mud with his mouth wide open like he died gasping for air."

Lenore tried to be strong, but the image brought tears to her eyes. She quickly reached up and wiped one of them away, but that tear was immediately followed by another.

Coletti saw her crying and stared at the detective with a look that carried bad intentions. "Mrs. Wilkinson's been nice enough to cooperate. So if you care so much about what happened to Smitty, why don't you run along and find his killer instead of harassing my witness?"

"Maybe I've found the killer's accomplice right here," the detective said, his eyes glued on Lenore.

"Or maybe you haven't," Coletti said slowly. "Now leave."

"Or?"

"Or somebody'll be doing paperwork on *you*," Mann said, standing up and looking him in the eye.

The detective's eyes shifted from one man to the other. Then he raised his hands in mock surrender. "Okay," he said, backing up with a smirk on his face. "I'll hit the street. Just remember what happened last time you brought a lady in here, Coletti."

Coletti jumped up to go after him, but Mann held him back.

"Ignore him," Mann said as the detective left with his partner. "It's not you, it's him. He doesn't know how to handle what happened to Smitty."

Mann was right. When a police officer was murdered, it made each cop consider his or her own mortality. It let them know that each day could be their last, and for many, that realization was quickly followed by anger. Both Mann and Coletti had seen it often after the deaths of numerous officers in recent months: enraged police beating suspects in the streets; cops' wives enduring violence at home; and officers walking around like ticking time bombs, their tempers ready to flare at any moment.

Smitty's death was just another in a line of on-duty incidents that dredged up the underlying danger in the job. Every officer handled the pressure differently, but most handled it, nonetheless. Coletti preferred to work through it, while others liked to play.

The detective who'd stayed behind waddled over to Coletti's desk, his large belly pointing the way. "I'm Tommy," he said to Lenore, who wiped her eyes once more before reaching up to shake his proffered hand.

"Nice to meet you," she said with a sniffle. "I'm sorry about the tears. It's just that I've never seen anyone die, much less have someone try to blame me for it."

Tommy put down the papers he was carrying and leaned his ample butt against the side of Coletti's desk. "If my colleagues aren't treating you right, my dear," he said with a ridiculous, Jim Carrey–like smile, "I will."

"You finished, Tommy?" said an irritated Coletti.

"Not quite." Tommy turned his attention back to Lenore. "I just want you to know that I like horseback riding, walks in the park, and listening. And I know it might not look like it, but I'm into weightlifting and mixed martial arts, too. Call me."

He winked and dropped his card on the desk.

Lenore chuckled. "I'm afraid I'm married, but thank you. I'm flattered."

Tommy reached down, grabbed her hand, and kissed it. "I don't care how great you think your husband is, honey. Once you go fat, you never go back."

Lenore laughed. Mann did, too. Coletti smiled in spite of himself. "Now you see what happens when the captain isn't around," he said. "People start losing their minds."

"Actually, we *use* our minds," Tommy said with a grin. "You'd see that if you checked out those papers I put together for you when I heard about Mrs. Bailey's untimely demise."

Coletti picked up the documents Tommy had placed on his desk. As soon as he began to thumb through them, he saw that they told a story all their own.

"Excuse us for a minute," he said to Mann and Lenore as he beckoned for Tommy to follow him into the captain's adjacent office.

They went inside, and Coletti closed the door behind them. "So, how long ago did her husband file for divorce?" Coletti asked as he looked through the petition.

"I think he served her with the papers about a month ago."

Coletti grunted as he looked at Ellison Bailey's signed affidavit. "Loss of companionship, huh? That means she stopped sleeping with him."

"Yeah," Tommy said, "but I think that's probably because he was a bum." He pointed to a section in the divorce petition that listed Ellison Bailey's occupation. "Says here he's a visiting lecturer at the University of Pennsylvania. I'd be guessing, but I'd say he doesn't make a mint doing that."

Coletti nodded. Then he flipped through the rest of Ellison's divorce petition, which requested, among other things, alimony payments from his wife, who served as CEO of Bailey, Inc., a publicly traded jewelry firm with a billion dollars in assets.

"I see she filed a counterclaim," Coletti said as he went through the rest of the papers.

"Yeah, she not only denied that there was any loss of companionship, she was apparently going to fight him on the alimony, too. And take a look at this."

Tommy showed him paperwork from two six-year-old civil suits that had been filed against Ellison Bailey by women in Florida and California. Suddenly, the picture became clearer.

"Thanks," Coletti said, snatching the door open and quickly crossing the floor to his partner and Lenore.

"Charlie, we've gotta track down Clarissa Bailey's husband," he said. Then he looked at Lenore. "I hope you're going to stick around."

"I'd already reserved a room at the Loews. I planned to stay for a few days anyway," she said. "It's like I told you earlier, there's something I need to do here. I'm not leaving until I find out what it is."

Coletti's cell phone rang. He looked at the number and saw that it was Kirsten Douglas, the reporter from the *Daily*

News. He pressed ignore. A moment later his desk phone rang. He picked it up, ready to scream at the reporter for harassing him, but it wasn't Douglas. As he listened to the voice on the other end of the line, his mouth pressed together in a pale thin line. He jotted down some notes on his pad.

"Thanks," he said before hanging up, a troubled expression on his face.

Both Mann and Lenore looked at Coletti, waiting for him to explain.

"We'll have someone take you over to your hotel," Coletti told Lenore. "And we'll assign you a security detail until we can make some other arrangements for you."

Lenore looked from Mann to Coletti with fire in her eyes. "I can take care of myself," she said defiantly. "I don't need protection."

"I'm afraid you're wrong," said Coletti. "That was the crime scene unit on the phone. They found a handwritten note stuffed in Mrs. Bailey's mouth along with the mud that killed her."

"What did it say?" Mann asked.

Coletti looked at them both before reading the five words from his notepad. "It said, 'I'll be back for Lenore.'"

CHAPTER 4

By noon, the rain had stopped, and the raven was perched high in a tree that loomed nearly six stories over Sedgley Woods. Most of the tree's dead branches had fallen off long ago, but the trunk remained. It was split in two, like a divining rod stretching toward the sky.

But unlike the rods men used to detect trinkets in the ground, the tree was used by the raven to detect power in the air. Most men didn't believe in such power. Oh, they said they believed, even wrote of it in their most holy scriptures, but only something that lived in the air could see it.

The raven was such a creature. He spent his life in the air, stretching his wings and gliding on gusts that carried with them all the good and evil in the world. He lived in the air, where words of love and hate escaped the lips of men and floated skyward, coming apart and releasing themselves into the universe.

There was power in words. The raven knew that intuitively, but men did not. That was why the raven's master needed him. The bird could go beyond finding the power in words. He could unleash that power.

Perched on the tree, standing two feet tall, his eyes filled with intelligence and his neck feathers fluttering in the breeze, the raven himself looked powerful. His wings, which spanned four feet across when he was in flight, were pressed tight against his body. His claws, sharp and strong, sunk deep into the tree's damp wood. His sturdy bill looked more like a weapon than a mouth. In fact, his entire body was a weapon. It was set off by a word that held more power than most. "Lenore."

That word was the reason for the raven's existence. It was the task for which he'd been trained. It was the thing that had driven him back to Fairgrounds Cemetery time and time again. That word was nothing less than his destiny.

For a year, the raven had been trained to recognize that word and the woman to whom it was assigned. He was taught to identify her face, her walk, her scent, and her voice. He was starved each time he failed and rewarded with treats of bloody lamb hearts each time he triumphed. The meat fed the raven's need for flesh, and the bird's resultant obedience fed the master's lust for power.

The two of them now depended upon each other. The man, for his part, was the raven's provider, and the raven was the man's enforcer and protector. He was an extension of the man himself.

The raven watched from the top of the tree as the scene in Sedgley Woods took shape. He saw Kirsten Douglas, still shaken, being led from the woods by police. He saw the media contingent, their ranks swollen by bloggers, You-Tubers, and curious passersby. There were flashing lights and angry voices, aggressive cops and determined reporters, all scrambling forward for a glance, a video clip, or a snapshot of Officer Frank Smith's body being carried to a waiting police van.

The raven could see the confusion taking shape below as one cameraman, then two, broke through the barricades to get shots of the spectacle. Police pushed back and a brief melee ensued, but even after it was quelled, there was an undercurrent of unrest among the media and a feeling of anger and grief among the police.

Cops darted in and out of the streets surrounding the park, searching for the man who'd wreaked havoc that morning. The cars moved in fits and starts, and the men and women who drove them did so with their heads on swivels. There was something inherently aggressive in their posture. The raven saw all of it, but he didn't see the woman he'd come to find. His master, who watched from afar, couldn't locate her, either, but what he saw through his live satellite feed was enough to pique his interest.

As he sat in a dank chamber with rats squealing and scurrying on the dirt walls and floors, the man closed his coal-black eyes and allowed his laptop's azure light to wash over his face. When he opened his eyes and the secure connection revealed what the satellite filmed from overhead, the man smiled at the sight of police scrambling around the park. He wondered what they'd do if they knew he was watching.

The man sat back, his black coat draped over his rickety wooden chair. Like his hands, shirt, and tie, the coat was encrusted with the soil he'd used to choke his victims to death. His mind, however, was clear. He knew his purpose, he knew his goal, and he didn't care how many people he had to kill to achieve it.

If it meant spending the night with filth and vermin, he was willing to endure it a thousand times. The treasure that lay beneath Fairgrounds Cemetery was more valuable than anything the world had to offer, and he was going to find it, no matter what it took.

There was a buzzing sound in the pocket of his greatcoat. The killer reached in, extracted a phone, and looked at the screen. There was a simple text message that read, "Proceed to phase 2." The killer read it with a measure of resentment. He didn't plan on taking orders from anyone, no matter how much money they offered to pay.

He pocketed the phone and opened another window on his laptop so he could switch from the overhead view of the park to a live feed from CNN. He watched closely as the police commissioner and a group of commanders approached a bank of microphones near the media contingent. The reporters pressed closer and hoisted their cameras high in the air. The raven left his perch and landed twenty yards from the microphones. The killer sat in his dank hiding place, hoping to see or hear something in the anger and angst of the moment that would tell him when and where to resurface.

As everyone pressed forward to listen, Lynch took a deep breath and began to speak.

"Today, a woman was killed at Fairgrounds Cemetery," Lynch said, pausing as the boisterous crowd grew silent. "Though her identity has already been revealed by several media outlets, we won't be sharing her name publicly until we can notify her next of kin."

Looking around at the assembled media, the commissioner tried to be businesslike, but it was clear that he was agitated. "Here's what we know so far. Shortly after 9:00 A.M., one of our detectives was already on the scene when a gunshot was fired at the Fairgrounds Cemetery."

"Who was the detective and what was he doing there, Commissioner?" asked a radio reporter.

"We can't comment on either of those questions right now, as the answers might compromise the investigation. But we can say that shortly after the detective heard the gunshot, he spotted a man in the area where the victim's body was found. The detective gave chase, and when the suspect eluded him, the detective put out a description. We believe the man he described, a white male with black hair and a mustache who was dressed in black and white clothing, may have been involved in the victim's death."

"So is this male you described the same man who's been identified informally as the Gravedigger?" the reporter pressed. "And are you treating the death in the graveyard as a homicide?"

Lynch glared at him for a long moment. "We won't be commenting on the name, and we'll have no comment on the manner of death until we see the coroner's report, but I will say this." Lynch locked eyes with several reporters before continuing in an angrier tone. "After that description was broadcast, Officer Frank Smith responded, and he did so with the same sense of urgency that he would if someone had found one of you dead in that cemetery. Whatever folks in the media had to say about Frank Smith in the past, I know one thing beyond a shadow of a doubt. He went into those woods because he had enough respect for his badge to do his job. And just like all the other officers who've been killed in the last year fighting crime in this city, Frank Smith did that job well."

Lynch paused, his jaw working furiously as he ground his teeth in an effort to calm himself.

"I've already seen a picture of his body online, and I haven't even had the chance to meet with his family," Lynch said with a stony stare. "That's wrong. It's disrespectful, and I think some of you agree with me, so if you're covering this story, do all of us a favor. Give Officer Smith the same respect he gave to that victim and this job, because the bottom line is, he lost his life in an effort to protect yours and mine."

There was a slight pause. Then a reporter from the *Inquirer* spoke up. "Does that mean you're placing some kind of gag order on the media, Commissioner Lynch?"

"It means there won't be any more pictures of this officer's body posted on the Internet for his wife and children to see," Lynch said with smoldering eyes. "Not one more."

The reporters looked around at each other, unsure if they'd just heard a request or an order. Lynch didn't care what they thought. He had one more message to deliver, and the media were going to deliver it for him, whether they liked it or not.

"And to the person who fled the scene this morning, you know who you are, you know what you've done, but you need to know this: we don't let our officers die in vain in Philadelphia, and we don't take our justice lightly."

"So you're promising retribution?" yelled a reporter from CNN.

Lynch turned his withering stare on him, and both the reporter and the rest of the crowd grew quiet. "I'm promising that wherever this man is, we'll find him. No matter how far he runs, we'll get him. No matter how good he thinks he is, we're better. So if he's out there listening, he should know that he better not stop, he better not sleep, he better not blink, because if he does, we'll be there waiting. I promise you that."

Lynch walked away from the microphones to the sound of shouted questions, and when the raven flew away, the man Lynch was looking for snapped shut his laptop and took a sharp knife to his mustache. After he'd shaved it, he changed the clothes he'd worn for the killings, and smiled at the name they'd given him.

The Gravedigger. He liked the sound of that name. It fit what he was about to do.

Ellison Bailey awakened to the sound of the brass knocker pounding the oak door of the Society Hill brownstone he shared with his wife. The sound always startled Ellison, especially when he was sleeping, and this afternoon, he was sleeping more soundly than usual.

For what seemed like days, he'd repeatedly heard the knocker along with the sound of ringing bells in his dreams. His mind had incorporated the sounds into a story of bombs and air-raid sirens. This was the first time since he lay down that morning that he realized the knocking was real.

Slowly, he opened his eyes and looked toward the ten-foot ceiling, blinking as a shaft of sunlight knifed between the drapes in his study. He raised his hand to block the light and squinted at the leather-bound volumes of Frost, Thoreau, Dickens, and Poe that lined the bookcases on the other side of the room.

Peeling himself off the couch, Clarissa Bailey's husband smacked his lips and rubbed the sleep from his eyes. Then he sat there with his head in his hands, trying to wake up.

The knocking came again, more insistently this time, and Ellison cursed under his breath before crossing the room and turning on his laptop to make it look as if he'd been working on his never-ending novel.

"I'm coming!" he yelled as he walked down the winding staircase and through the cavernous rooms and hallways that led to the front door of the four-story, thirty-room home.

The knocking became more persistent. It was annoying, just like Clarissa. The sound reminded him of why he wanted to be rid of her. By the time he arrived at the door, he was downright angry, and it showed when he snatched open the door and yelled in his clipped British accent, "What is it!"

He was greeted by an outstretched hand holding a badge. "Detective Coletti, Philadelphia Police. Are you Ellison Bailey?"

Ellison nodded, looking at the detective and the officer who stood at the bottom of the steps, near a parked police car with another cop in the driver's seat.

"We've been trying to reach you all morning, Mr. Bailey. It's about your wife."

"What about her? Is she all right?"

Coletti paused to look at Ellison Bailey, whose sprayed-on tan and dyed brown hair starkly contrasted the two-day growth of gray stubble that lined his wrinkled face. Dressed in driving loafers, jeans, and a slept-in designer shirt, Ellison appeared to be fighting a losing battle against age.

As they stood there looking at each other, several of the Baileys' neighbors peeked out their windows and doors.

"Maybe I should come in, Mr. Bailey," Coletti said, nodding toward the patrol officer. "It might be a little more private."

"Oh, of course," Ellison said, standing aside. "We can talk in the den."

Coletti told the officers to stay outside. Then Ellison led Coletti through a labyrinth of halls and rooms that were lined with prominently displayed sculpture and paintings. They passed through the living room, with luxurious furnishings and Fabergé eggs strategically placed beneath banks of recessed lighting. They passed through the drawing room, with rich oils by impressionist masters encased in ornate frames. The dining room was equipped with a marble table whose velvet and silk runner was a deep royal purple. The den was appointed with plush wingback chairs, earthtoned African carvings, a giant flat-screen television, and most importantly to Ellison, a bar.

"Please sit down," Ellison said as he mixed himself a martini and took a sip. "Can I get you anything?"

Coletti had neither the time nor the inclination to socialize, so he got to the point quickly. "Your wife's dead, Mr. Bailey."

Ellison stopped in mid-sip. There was no grief, no shock, and no joy. There was only acceptance of the grim news. A moment later he gulped down the martini and mixed himself another.

"How did it happen?" he asked as he popped an olive into the glass and fell into a chair directly across from Coletti.

"Someone pushed her into a grave and stuffed her mouth with dirt. We think she choked to death."

"Really?" Ellison asked, sounding surprised, but not grieved. "That's dreadful."

Coletti knew what it was to lose a woman he loved, and what he saw from Ellison Bailey didn't compare to the grief he felt each time he thought of Mary. The question came out of his mouth before he could stop it. "You didn't care about her at all, did you?"

Ellison took another sip of his martini. "We were in

the midst of a divorce, Detective. At least, I was. She wanted to fight to keep the marriage intact so she wouldn't have to pay."

"So you stood to gain financially from the divorce?" Coletti asked.

Ellison looked at him. "I suspect you already know the answer to that, so let's cut to the chase, shall we? My wife was rich and I'm her sole surviving relative. In your eyes, that makes me a suspect, right?"

Coletti smiled in spite of himself. He appreciated Ellison's bluntness, if not his attitude. "There are a lot of things other than the money that make you a suspect, Mr. Bailey, including the fact that you were trying to divorce your wife."

"Lots of people have marital problems, Detective. There's nothing unique about that."

"But it's unique for a man with no steady source of income to be married to a billionaire."

"Yes, aren't I the lucky one?" Ellison asked sarcastically.

Coletti's cell phone buzzed, and he took it out and looked at the message. It was the e-mail Clarissa had sent out announcing Lenore's visit. The cemetery manager had finally forwarded it, as promised. There were five addresses in the "to" line. Four of them had names attached. One of them didn't.

Ellison took another sip of his martini. "Is everything all right, Detective?" he asked. "Do you need to make a call?"

Coletti's instincts told him not to share the e-mail with Ellison. He quickly put the phone away. "No, I don't need to make any calls," he said. "But I do need to know a little more about your relationship with your wife. How did the two of you meet?"

"We met five years ago at the Borrowers Ball," Ellison said. "It's a black-tie gala to benefit the Free Library of Philadelphia."

"And you were on the guest list?"

"Yes," Ellison said, taking another sip of his drink. "I once wrote a book on the history of Mayan civilization, and somehow, through serendipity or dumb luck or whatever you want to call it, my book became a Hollywood film. The genius who directed it decided to make the movie without dialogue. It flopped, and after that, no one would touch any of my books with a ten-foot pole. I was forever relegated to being a featured author at literary events, and it didn't take me long to go broke."

"You sound bitter."

"On the contrary," Ellison said. "I'm grateful that the library invited me. I felt like I'd turned the tables on Cinderella, and for once, the prince got to be the one to crash the ball."

Coletti smiled at Ellison's sardonic wit.

"Clarissa was at my table that night," Ellison continued. "She took a liking to me. And when I told her I was working on a novel about a nineteenth-century writer who's involved in a murder, she was actually rather intrigued. A few weeks later, she invited me over to, um . . . look at her etchings. She showed me hers, I showed her mine, and six months later, we were married."

"I see," Coletti said. "If you don't mind my asking, how old are you, Mr. Bailey?"

"I'm eight years Clarissa's junior. She was fifty-five when we met. I was forty-seven. It was quite the scandal on the society page. Still is."

Coletti looked around at the trappings of wealth that surrounded them. "Scandal or not, banging old broads for a living pays well, doesn't it?"

"I beg your pardon?" Ellison said sharply.

Coletti stood up and walked over to the chair where Ellison Bailey was sitting. "You said you wanted to cut to the chase, Mr. Bailey, so let's do that. Clarissa wasn't the first older woman to take care of you, was she? There was the woman you lived with in California who sued after you ran through her fortune. Then there's the woman you lived with in Florida who sued after you drained the bank accounts the two of you shared. But they were lucky, weren't they? They didn't end up dead."

"I had nothing to do with anyone's death, including Clarissa's," Ellison said nervously.

"Maybe not, but you've got a pattern of defrauding old women, and Clarissa would've been your biggest victim. You couldn't afford to fight her in divorce court, so the next best thing would've been to kill her. As her husband, you would get everything. So you see, Mr. Bailey, you're the perfect suspect, and the way I see it, you've got two options. You can go get a lawyer and try to delay the inevitable, or you can talk before I track down the rest of the old ladies you scammed and see who else ended up dead."

Ellison stared at Coletti for a moment. Then he gulped the rest of his martini and looked down into the empty glass. He seemed to be fighting a battle with himself, and from the expression on his face, he was losing. When finally he spoke, it was with a quiet humility that hadn't been there before.

"I've never killed anybody or arranged to have anyone killed, including Clarissa. I was here sleeping all morning, just like I do most days. I'm sure if you check with Clarissa's friends, they'll verify that I'm the laziest man they've ever seen. They kept telling her to just grant me the divorce and move on, but Clarissa was much too kind for that. That's why I cared for her so much."

"If you cared for her why did you file for divorce?"

Ellison got up, walked over to the bar, and made himself a third martini. "You've already told me what you think of me, Detective, and, sadly, you're right. I'm a failed writer who takes money from old women and leaves them worse off than when I found them. I'm not proud of that, but I accept it. That's why I couldn't stay with Clarissa. She deserved much better than me."

"Why?" Coletti asked skeptically. "What made her any different from the others?"

"Trite as it might sound, she was a good person," Ellison said, as he walked toward an oil painting of Clarissa that hung on the far wall. "She funded nurseries for crack babies, shelters for alcoholics, and a million other little causes for people nobody else cared about. She loved humanity, Detective . . . almost as much as she loved history and the arts."

Coletti joined him in front of the portrait. "If she was such a saint, why would someone kill her?"

"I'm afraid I don't know much about why people kill," Ellison said. "I create things. I'm not into death."

"But your wife was into death," Coletti said. "She was heavily involved in fund-raising for a historic cemetery called Fairgrounds."

Ellison walked slowly to his seat and sat down. He looked concerned. "Is that where it happened—at the cemetery?"

"Yes. Does that mean something?"

Ellison sighed and shook his head. "As I told you, my wife loved history and the arts—writing, especially. She was involved with Fairgrounds Cemetery because she believed it was connected to one of her favorite nineteenth-century writers."

"You mean Edgar Allan Poe?"

Ellison looked surprised. "How'd you know that?"

"We found a line from 'The Raven' near your wife's body when she died." Coletti pulled out his notepad and read it. *"Deep into that darkness peering, long I stood there, wondering, fearing . . ."*

Ellison's face turned ashen, and Coletti stopped reading.

"Are you all right, Mr. Bailey?"

Ellison started mumbling. "I told her to let it go, but she wouldn't listen."

"What are you talking about?"

He looked at Coletti, unsure how much he wanted to reveal. "Our divorce was about more than just money, Detective. It was also about Clarissa's insistence on dabbling in things I thought were dangerous. Things she thought were revealed in that poem."

"What do you mean?"

"Certain scholars believe Edgar Allan Poe was a seer who stood between life and death and saw something that regular people couldn't see—some sort of secret that would literally change the course of mankind. Those scholars believe that's what 'The Raven' was really about. And some of those scholars—men like Irving Workman at Penn—believe the place where Poe stood is somewhere at Fairgrounds Cemetery."

Coletti remembered that Workman was one of the names on the e-mail Clarissa sent regarding Lenore's visit. He asked his next question while jotting down Workman's initials. "Do you know Irving Workman?"

"I met him once or twice when I was lecturing at Penn, but Clarissa was friends with him," Ellison said with disdain. "Workman had Clarissa convinced that Poe discovered his gift of sight here in Philadelphia. He even took Clarissa and her friends to the house where Poe lived."

"And where's that?"

"Seventh and Spring Garden."

Coletti wrote down the location. "So why did you think it was dangerous for your wife to listen to Workman?"

"Because he kept telling Clarissa that there was another seer—a woman who could decipher what Poe found at the cemetery. Clarissa was obsessed with that woman, almost to the point where she'd do anything to find her. If a reasonably stable person like my wife could get so lost in Workman's teachings, I figured there were those who would give their very lives for those beliefs, or worse, take the lives of others."

Ellison shook his head sadly. "Turns out I was right."

Coletti's cell phone rang as Ellison stared down into the last few drops of his martini. When the detective took the phone from his pocket and saw the number, he answered immediately.

"Okay," he said after listening to the voice on the other end. "We'll be right down."

Ellison looked on as Coletti disconnected the call.

"That was the medical examiner's office," Coletti said solemnly. "They've found something on Clarissa's body."

With every passing second, Kirsten Douglas realized just how fortunate she was. Unlike Clarissa Bailey and Officer Smith, she'd seen the Gravedigger face-to-face and survived. Kirsten was the only one other than Mike Coletti to do so. It was that distinction more than anything else that landed her a guest spot on CNN.

In less than a minute, she'd be on the air, and she was sweating profusely. Sitting in the studio at VideoLink for her first television appearance in twenty years as a crime reporter, with Philadelphia's skyline superimposed on the greenscreen backdrop, Kirsten was nervous. Not only were the lights intense in the tiny room, but the air-conditioning seemed to be broken. And while the satellite technology was impressive, the squiggly wire attached to her earpiece was tickling her.

In the hours since she'd sneaked past the police barricades and taken the only picture of Officer Frank Smith's mud-covered body, Kirsten had become a national figure. She'd talked to the police commissioner. She'd generated millions of Internet hits. She'd sparked a fierce debate on media ethics, but she still couldn't get a call back from Mike Coletti.

As she waited for the interview to begin, a bead of sweat trickled down her face. She reached up and dabbed it dry with a napkin. Fortunately, her face was devoid of makeup except for a bit of lipstick. Studio makeup was apparently reserved for the truly important. Despite her instant fame, Kristen was not yet among them.

"Five seconds." The director's voice came through the earpiece as she stared at the square camera in front of her.

She reached up nervously to adjust her hair and took a last look at the notes she'd jotted down in front of her. Then suddenly the host's voice was in her ear, and she forgot about her talking points and points of emphasis and everything other than the truth.

He recapped what she'd done and who she was, and as Kirsten tried to focus on what he was saying and what she would say in response, she somehow heard the host welcome her to the show.

"Thanks for having me," Kirsten croaked, clearing her throat and trying to smile while staring into the camera.

The host spoke a few more words about the murders and asked Kirsten for her impressions on the investigation thus far.

Kirsten took a deep breath and tried to remember that the camera was supposed to be the audience. Then she stared straight ahead and talked until the slight tremor in her voice went away.

"Honestly, I don't have any real thoughts on the investigation at this point, because I can't get any of my sources in the department to return my calls. But I do want to say before I go any further that my condolences go out to the victims' families. I think that's kind of been lost in all this discussion about media ethics and privacy and everything else. I'm a human being and I can't help feeling for the families, especially since I'm lucky that I made it out of those woods alive."

The host stared into the camera with a serious expression. "And for our viewers who don't know, Kirsten, what exactly happened when you went into those woods?"

Kirsten paused to gather herself. Then she said things she'd never expected to come out of her mouth.

"I think going into those woods changed me in ways I still haven't quite figured out. Initially it was just about getting the story because I felt like we were being stonewalled by the police. And as you know, sticking to traditional approaches means getting our butts kicked by online outlets that have a no-holds-barred approach to reporting, and—"

The voice in her ear interrupted her. "Does that mean you don't believe you did anything wrong?"

"It means newspapers, including mine, are threatened with being shut down because our news is old before we even go to press. I'm not saying it's right. I'm just saying it's reality."

"So what do you mean when you say you were changed in those woods?"

"I mean, I went back there initially just to get the facts, you know? But sometimes the story goes way beyond just facts. Things aren't always black and white. Sometimes, they're gray, and even though my training as a journalist tells me to reject that type of subjective thinking, what I saw in those woods today changed my mindset. In fact, I think it changed everything about me."

"Wow," the host said. "What did you see?"

"Well, I think it's more important to establish what I didn't see," Kirsten said. "I didn't see any trails or markings at first, which is odd, since it's not like I was going into the Amazon back there. The part of Sedgley Woods I walked into is pretty tame. There's a disc golf course back there, so while there are some areas that are pretty dense with fallen trees and vines and the like, I should've seen fairly well-traveled paths and markers."

"And you didn't?" the voice in her ear asked.

"Not at first," Kirsten said, looking down at her hands and trying to stop them from shaking. "It was almost like they weren't there one minute, then the next minute they appeared, and then they were gone again."

The camera zoomed in as her facial expression said things her mouth never could.

"So what was real and what wasn't?" the host asked, drawing Kirsten back to the moment.

Kirsten looked up into the camera, smiled nervously, and dabbed at her face with the napkin. "I've been wracking my brain trying to figure out how to answer that without sounding completely insane, but the truth is, those woods seemed to change when I was back there. They got darker and denser. Now, part of it might have been the weather. The rain and the dark clouds made it a lot harder to see, but while I was back there, it was almost like I'd been transported to a different place."

"Are you trying to say—"

"I'm not *trying* to say anything," Kirsten said, growing impatient. "I'm telling you that there was something—no, *someone*—back there behind those trees, but every time I thought I saw him, he melted into the darkness, almost like he'd never been there at all."

"Forgive me for saying this, but people don't just melt away."

Kirsten went from being impatient to being angry. "In twenty years as a reporter I've never had my integrity questioned," she spat, "and I don't plan to have it questioned now. Not by you, and not by anyone else."

"Wait a minute, Kirsten, I—"

"Don't tell me to wait!" she snapped. "You asked me to tell you what I saw, and I'm telling you what I saw! It really doesn't matter to me what you think about it! I'm the one who risked my life going into those woods, not you!"

As Kirsten ranted, the director cut from the single camera to the split screen. The side-by-side image of an embarrassed host and an angry interview subject was riveting.

"Okay," the host said, refusing to be shown up on his own show. "Do you have a picture of this person you supposedly saw in the woods?"

"No," Kirsten said, "and frankly, I resent the implication that I might not have seen him. I know what I saw."

"Well, why don't you share what you saw with the rest of us?" the host said, his voice growing louder.

"I saw a man, okay?" Kirsten said, leaning forward in her chair and pointing into the camera. "He was pale, he was tall, and he was wearing a long black coat that looked like something out of the eighteen hundreds."

"Did you get video?"

"No."

"Then how are we to believe you saw this man in the woods? How do we know you didn't just listen to the police description and claim you saw him? Why didn't you take his picture?"

"I was too busy running!" she shouted as the camera zoomed in on her face. "The man I saw in those woods wasn't interested in having a chat. He was stalking me, and I'm convinced that if I didn't keep running, he was going to kill me. Do you understand that? He was going to—"

Kirsten's voice broke. She covered her eyes with her hand, and tears fell down her cheeks as her shoulders began to shake with sobs.

"Kirsten?" the host said as the camera captured every captivating moment. "Kirsten?"

"I'm all right," she said, sniffling and wiping her eyes with the back of her hand.

"Kirsten," the host said, his voice much gentler than it had been just seconds before. "How did you get away?"

She looked into the camera, her face a portrait of the fear she'd experienced while running through those woods. "Honestly, I don't know. He was behind me and I ran until I came to a hill. I slid down and tried to run again, but I fell near a tree. A second later, he was right there, almost on top of me. That's when I screamed. And when I opened my eyes again, the man was gone, and the only thing I saw was a huge black bird flying away."

"What kind of bird was it?" the host asked.

Kirsten dropped her eyes before staring into the camera once more. "It was a raven."

"So after this harrowing experience, what's next for Kirsten Douglas?" the host asked.

She smiled sadly. "I'm going to keep following this story. Not just for me, but for the victims and their families. I feel like I owe them that much."

CHAPTER 5

The reality of his wife's death began to hit home for Ellison Bailey as he got dressed for the trip to the ME's office. He'd spent years avoiding anything that even remotely resembled responsibility. Yet here he was, the only one who could speak on Clarissa's behalf, because he was the only family she had. The feeling that came with that realization wasn't one that Ellison relished. It was one that he dreaded.

He'd fought Clarissa for months for the ability to leave and take part of her fortune with him. Now that she was dead and he stood to gain everything he'd sought from her, he didn't know if he could handle receiving it this way.

Coletti had sensed Ellison's change in attitude as soon as he got the call from the morgue. Now, as Coletti sat waiting, he wondered if Ellison's change of heart came from a sense of guilt. He'd have to wait and see.

Coletti's phone buzzed. He looked at it and saw that it was another call from *Daily News* reporter Kirsten Douglas. Coletti pressed ignore. Then he called Charlie Mann.

"Are you getting a bunch of calls from Kirsten Douglas?" Coletti asked when his partner answered.

"Yeah, she's calling everybody. I guess she's upset because nobody's talking. Somebody said she was even on CNN saying we were trying to stonewall her. Did you see her?"

"No, but it's just as well. Did you get the e-mail I forwarded you? It's the one Clarissa Bailey sent out right before Lenore visited."

"Yeah, I got it. What do you want me to do with it?"

"Can you see if you can trace that fifth address—the one without a name attached to it?"

"I'll see what I can do," Mann said.

"How's our witness?"

"She's fine. We've got a two-man detail over at the Loews with her, and we should have the safe house ready in a little bit. How's things over there with you?"

"Clarissa's husband is chock-full of information," Coletti said. "We're about to head to the ME now. I'll fill you in later."

Coletti disconnected the call just as a freshly scrubbed Ellison came back with two cups of coffee in his hand.

"Would you like a cup, Detective?"

Coletti begged off. Ellison needed it much more than he did, although the fact that he would have to actually look at his dead wife was far more sobering than coffee could ever be.

Ellison gulped down both cups, and a few minutes later the two of them emerged from the house for the ride to the ME.

"I need you guys to follow us," Coletti said to the two cops who were parked outside in the cruiser. He didn't say why. He didn't have to. They all knew that Ellison was a suspect.

Ellison knew it, too, and he looked troubled as he got into Coletti's car.

"You all right?" Coletti asked.

Ellison nodded. Then he looked out the window as the streets of Society Hill flew by in a blur of bricks and branches. It was funny how beautiful the city could be when one's senses weren't dulled by alcohol. It reminded him of the way Clarissa looked when his mind was clear.

Physically, she'd never been alluring. She had wrinkles and sunspots and a face that was unremarkable, but just like the city with its grime and old age, Clarissa was lovely beneath the surface.

Ellison's mind went back to the way she loved him in spite of himself. She cooked him gourmet meals and smiled as she watched him eat. She rubbed his temples on the days when he was gripped by writer's block. She told him he was talented although they both knew it was a lie. She cared for him even when he didn't care for himself.

Now Clarissa was dead, and Ellison was in a police car with a detective looking at him as if he were somehow involved. In truth, Ellison didn't blame him. He understood why he was a suspect.

In a few minutes, Coletti rounded the bend on Walnut Street and arrived at the building where the medical examiner's office was located. With the Veteran's hospital across the street and Penn's campus just a few blocks away, the gray concrete building, with its flat structure and straight lines, seemed out of place. A gate in front shielded the ramp where the bodies were delivered: most people who drove by had no idea that this place was home to so much death.

Coletti turned into the asphalt driveway and rolled down the ramp to the loading bays. When Ellison looked around at the black vans with the words "Medical Examiner" written on the sides, his face paled. And when he and Coletti got out of the car and walked up onto the platform leading to the back entrance, he was downright afraid.

Coletti watched him carefully. He'd purposely brought him this way instead of taking him to the front of the building. He wanted to see how Ellison would respond to being on a bloodstained platform where the mingled scents of congealed blood and formaldehyde flooded the air.

"The first thing we're going to do is have you identify her," Coletti said as they stood on the concrete platform. "Then we'll talk to the investigator and the doctor about whatever it was they found. You ready?"

Ellison's face was turning a pale shade of green. The sickening stench was turning his stomach. There was something like grief in his eyes as well. Coletti was relieved to see that. It meant that Ellison had feelings.

The detective rang the bell, and one of the autopsy technicians opened the steel double doors. He was bald and black and had been there for twenty years. He'd seen everything there was to see, including every body that had come in during the Angel of Death case. He was happy to see Mike Coletti.

"What's up, Old Man?" the technician said as Ellison followed the detective inside. "I thought they'd send that young guy down here again."

"No, you're stuck with me, Simon." The two of them shook hands. "This is Ellison Bailey. He's here to identify his wife's body and look at her personal effects."

"Okay." The technician went into the small office near the door and took out the book where they documented personal effects. He scrolled down to a number in the second column and wrote it on a slip of paper. A few seconds later, the medical examiner's investigator came down on the elevator.

"How are you?" the investigator said to Coletti as the technician handed him the paper containing the number.

"I'm fine," Coletti said, turning to Clarissa's husband. "This is Ellison Bailey."

The investigator spoke with practiced sympathy. "I'm sorry to have to meet you under these circumstances, Mr. Bailey, but I'm going to need you to step over here and look up at the monitor when you're ready."

Ellison took a deep breath and did as he was asked. A second later, the technician turned on the screen. Clarissa's face appeared. Her hair only partially covered the stitching around her forehead from one of the autopsy incisions. The other stitching down the middle of her chest was clearly visible. She was lying flat on a gurney, and her gray, mud-flecked hair was spread out around her head. Her face was so white it looked almost blue, and her lips were smeared with black dirt. Ellison felt his legs buckle slightly, but Coletti reached out to steady him.

Clarissa's husband stared at her dead face for a few seconds more. "That's her," he croaked before turning away from the screen.

Coletti watched him carefully. He had seen murderous husbands before, and Ellison Bailey didn't fit the bill. There was clearly something bothering Ellison, though, and it was more than just the smell of formaldehyde.

After Ellison ID'd the body, the investigator went into the office and beckoned for Coletti to join him. The autopsy technician took Ellison into a smaller room where a television was tuned to a Nicole Kidman movie.

The investigator closed the door and turned to Coletti. "Listen, I don't know how much you want the husband to know, but when the doctor examined Mrs. Bailey, he found gunpowder residue on her right sleeve and some bruising on the webbing between her thumb and index finger."

"So are you saying . . ."

"I'm saying that if anybody fired a gun this morning at the cemetery, it probably was Clarissa Bailey."

Coletti looked confused. "But the crime scene guys didn't find a gun or bullet casing at the scene."

"The doctor didn't find a bullet in her body when he did the autopsy, either," the investigator said. "All he found was the dirt stuffed down her throat. This is going to be declared a homicide, and the official cause of death will be asphyxiation."

"No big surprise there," Coletti said.

"We were surprised by one thing, though," said the investigator. "Hold on a minute, I'll get the doctor to show you."

The investigator went to the back of the room, unlocked a door, and went inside to open the safe where the clothing from homicides was kept. When he returned with Clarissa's belongings in a paper shopping bag, he gestured for Coletti to follow him.

They left the office and walked down the hall to the back of the building, passing the freezer where the freshly dead shared space with bodies frozen in varying states of decomposition. They passed the autopsy rooms with their stainless-steel tables and scalpels and bone-cutting saws. They walked down the hall with its spotless floors and bright lights, and still, Coletti marveled at the smell of death lingering in the air.

"Come this way," the investigator said, ducking into a room that was filled with computers, cameras, and state-of-the-art software.

When Coletti went in, the coroner was sitting in front of a Mac with a double monitor. He'd been waiting for them.

"Dr. Aronchik, you know Detective Coletti," the investigator said.

"Of course," the doctor said. "How are you, Detective?"

"I'm fine. What've we got?"

Dr. Aronchik opened a picture on the computer screen as Coletti and the investigator came and stood behind him to look over his shoulder.

"This is a photograph of the victim's face," he said, zooming in on her eyes and nose. "If you look closely, you can see some bruising along her temples, and her nose appears to have been under intense pressure just before she died. From the alignment of those markings—the thumb on the left temple and the four fingers on the right side of her face—it looks like someone with very large hands held her down with his left hand, and probably shoveled dirt into her mouth with his right."

"Were you able to get any prints from it?" Coletti asked.

"No, we weren't," the doctor said, clicking through a number of other pictures as he spoke. "But we did see something unusual when we lifted her hair and looked at the back of her neck."

He clicked on an image that appeared to be a single green line with four short spaces in between. "These markings, which are about a quarter-inch high and two inches in width, were tattooed onto the victim's neck. We know they're recent because the skin is inflamed in the area, and there appears to be some kind of salve that's been applied to it."

The doctor enlarged the picture to six hundred percent. "When we looked closer, we saw that it's more than just lines. It's actually letters and numbers. We have no idea what they symbolize, but if the victim made the effort to have them tattooed there, I would think they meant something to her."

Coletti squinted and looked closer. It looked like a serial number that read: H20Z18G 1G 20S5 V22V18T18V5M 2I5V.

"Can you print that picture for me, Doctor?"

"I already have," he said, handing Coletti five copies.

"Did you find anything else unusual on the body?" Coletti asked as he looked at the picture.

"No," the investigator said, donning latex gloves and opening the bag containing the victim's clothing and personal effects. "We did find this, though."

He took out a well-worn book with yellowing pages and placed it on the table in front of Coletti. It was a collection of Poe's poems. Coletti pulled on a pair of gloves and opened it to the pages containing "The Raven." The section they'd found next to Clarissa's body had been torn out.

"There is one more thing," Dr. Aronchik said as the investigator bagged the book and handed the bag to Coletti.

"What's that?"

"We examined Officer Smith's body just before you came in."

"And?"

"We haven't done the postmortem yet, but he had some injuries indicating that he may have been beaten before he died."

"Do his injuries tell us anything about the assailant?"

Dr. Aronchik opened another folder on his computer screen and brought up a photo of Smitty's arm. "His ulna is broken in his left arm. It looks like a defensive injury, as if he was trying to fend off a blow." He clicked another picture of the officer's face. "His left cheek is also badly bruised from what looks like a blow from a large fist. If you look closely, you can see three bruised areas that are fairly close together. Those marks could have come from someone's knuckles, and just like in Clarissa Bailey's case, the assailant was probably right-handed."

"So can you say conclusively that they were both attacked by the same man?"

"I'll have to see what we find in Officer Smith's autopsy, but I can tell you that both of their attackers were large, strong, and right-handed. Does that mean it was the same person? I can't say that for sure."

Coletti looked through the bag containing Clarissa's belongings. Besides the book, there was a purse, her clothing, her wallet, and a phone. Coletti picked up the phone and tried to turn it on, but the battery was dead. He placed it back into the bag with the rest of her belongings.

"So I'm assuming it won't be long before it's publicly announced that you've declared Mrs. Bailey's death a homicide," Coletti said.

The doctor looked up at a small television mounted on the far wall. "No, Detective Coletti," he said as he watched the commissioner step out of police headquarters. "It won't be long at all."

Kevin Lynch moved toward the bank of microphones, and all he could think of was how much he hated dealing with the media. He hated the repetition, hated the callous questions, and hated the sense of entitlement that the reporters brought to their work.

If Lynch had his druthers, he would lose himself in the drudgery of policing and leave the media to find their own way. But in today's world, the media couldn't be left to themselves. That's how pictures of dead cops ended up on Twitter.

He'd tried to avoid making this latest appearance, but a call from the mayor's office had forced his hand. The extensive coverage of the murders had transformed this into a political issue, and in the new media landscape, where every phone was a camera and every keyboard was a voice, politics meant visibility, and the public equated visibility with action.

So it was that Commissioner Kevin Lynch was forced to lay aside his disgust with the media circus and make his second appearance before them; this to make official what they already knew.

Before Lynch could speak, he had to endure the pronouncements of those whose presence was required in the age of camera-phone journalism. He stood outside police headquarters with the rest of the brass, flanking the mayor and the district attorney as they each made the requisite tough-on-crime pronouncements.

As their words blurred together in a series of meaningless sounds, the wind outside the police administration building swirled in a figure eight, blowing discarded hot dog wrappers and potato chip bags into the air.

Lynch watched absently as the trash climbed almost as high as the black bird circling overhead. His eyes followed the bird for the next few seconds. Then his gaze shifted to the assembled reporters. He saw Kirsten Douglas standing at the edge of the crowd, her eyes locked on the bird and her mouth open wide in a mixture of shock and fear. It was then that Lynch knew the story Kirsten had told about the raven in the park was true. He watched her for a few seconds more, and when she felt him looking at her, the two of them locked eyes, and the commissioner almost forgot why he was there.

A deputy tapped Lynch on the shoulder when the mayor was finished speaking, and Lynch stumbled toward the microphones with his mind still on the raven that had since flown away.

He reached for one of the microphones and raised it to his lips as a radio reporter ran up to the podium and placed a digital tape recorder in front of him. Clearing his throat, Lynch stared out at the media, who were waiting for their next bloody morsel. Then he looked at Kirsten Douglas once more and delivered the news he'd been given.

"We've positively identified the person who died this morning at Fairgrounds Cemetery as Mrs. Clarissa Bailey of Society Hill. An autopsy was performed this afternoon, and while we're still awaiting some DNA results and other lab tests, the medical examiner's office has been able to determine that Mrs. Bailey's death was a homicide."

The press exploded, shouting questions that all centered on one person.

"Are you any closer to finding the Gravedigger?" yelled a blogger from MSNBC.

"Has the Gravedigger been in touch with the department?" asked a reporter from the AP.

"Has anyone gotten a picture of the Gravedigger?" a radio reporter shouted.

Lynch stood there in the crisp autumn air, the stars on his shoulders gleaming. He raised his hand, and the reporters fell silent. The only sounds that remained were those from nearby traffic and the occasional pop of a flashbulb.

"We're following every lead in the case, and we're particularly interested in speaking with a white male who was spotted near the scene this morning. As you know, there was another death shortly after Mrs. Bailey was killed. One of our officers, Patrolman Frank Smith, was found dead in Sedgley Woods. The medical examiner has not yet completed an autopsy on Patrolman Smith, so we'll have no further comment on his death at this time, other than to say that our investigation is ongoing, and we're using every resource at our disposal to solve this case quickly. Again, as in the case of Mrs. Bailey, we are very interested in speaking with the male who was spotted in the area around the time of both deaths. We'll give further updates as information becomes available, but that's it for now. Thank you."

Lynch turned away from the podium to go back inside police headquarters. The press hurled questions after him but quickly settled down when the mayor stepped into their midst and began to speak about the importance of keeping the city safe.

While the rest of the media were preoccupied with the mayor, Kirsten stood off to the side, still gazing at the sky and waiting for the raven to return. Lynch stopped at the door in the hope of getting her attention, and when she looked in his direction again, he beckoned for her to follow him inside.

Kirsten looked around self-consciously before ambling toward the door. Four other reporters saw where she was going and attempted to follow her, but when they got to the door, Lynch stopped them. "I need to talk to Ms. Douglas about what she saw this morning," he said.

They tried to protest, but Lynch was firm.

"It's a police matter, not a media matter," he said, glowering at them. "Please back away from the door. I don't want to have to ask you again."

They did as they were told, and the deputy commissioners who were walking with Lynch hustled Kirsten inside.

Lynch moved quickly toward the elevators, forcing her to run to catch up.

"First CNN, then you make a bird appear. That was an interesting display back there," Lynch said as he arrived at the elevators and jabbed the up button.

"I don't know what you're talking about, Commissioner."

"I'm talking about the raven. That *was* the same one you saw in the woods, wasn't it?"

"Yes, I believe it was," she said, trying her best to sound confident.

The elevator doors opened, and Lynch looked at his deputies. "Gentlemen, I need to talk to Ms. Douglas alone for a few minutes. Can you catch the next one?"

The deputies backed off, and Lynch stood aside to let Kirsten get onto the elevator first. When the doors closed, he pressed the button for the fourth floor and looked up at the numbers as the elevator went up. "I should've locked you up when you pulled that crap this morning," Lynch said. "I doubt that I'll ever forgive you for doing that."

"I doubt that I'll ever expect you to," Kirsten said. "So now that we've got that out of the way, what do we do?"

"We talk." The elevator doors opened at the fourth floor and Lynch got off with Kirsten hot on his heels.

"Hold my calls," Lynch said as he walked into the department's executive offices.

"Yes, Commissioner," said his secretary.

Kirsten followed him into his private office, and he closed the door. Then he took off his jacket and sat down behind his desk.

She walked toward the far wall, looking at the framed newspaper articles that lined the wood paneling. There was a column about the murder of a previous police commissioner and a front-page story that had run after a mayoral assassination. There were drug dealers and preachers, a corrupt council president and her streetwise niece. All the stories prominently featured Kevin Lynch, and each of them was written by Kirsten.

"I didn't know you were paying attention to my work," she said as she sat down across from him.

"But I always knew you were paying attention to mine."

"I still am," she said with a smirk. "But with this case

it's a little harder to do that. I've been calling cops all morning. Nobody'll talk to me."

"Tell you what," Lynch said. "I'll answer your questions if you'll answer mine."

Kirsten started to take out her notebook.

"Off the record," Lynch said.

"But Commissioner—"

"Take it or leave it."

She stared at him to try to gauge whether or not he meant it, but she'd learned over the years that Lynch was always serious. With a sigh, she put away her notebook and sat back in her chair.

"Is Coletti working on this case?" she asked.

"Yes he is."

"Don't you think that's a little too close for comfort?"

"What do you mean?"

"My sources tell me that the woman at the graveyard with Mrs. Bailey was Mary Smithson's half-sister," Kirsten said. "Since Mary tried to kill Coletti, having him on this case might present a bit of a conflict."

"I know where you're going, but I don't see it that way."

"What if Coletti finds that Mary's sister was involved in the murder? What if he takes the opportunity to carry out some kind of vendetta?"

"We don't do vendettas here, Kirsten. We solve crimes."

"Tell that to the guy who was shot by the off-duty cop after an argument over water ice. Or the guy whose son was locked up on trumped-up charges because his girlfriend's dad was a cop."

"Those are isolated incidents. Coletti's a thirty-one-year veteran who's never been involved in anything like that, and frankly, he's one of the best I've got. I need him on this case."

"Even if departmental policy says he can't work a case where he has a personal stake?"

"Technically, this is a separate case from what happened with Mary Smithson, and we're going to treat it that way. That means Coletti is going to stay on this case until I decide he shouldn't be on it anymore."

"That's a slippery slope, Commissioner."

"Maybe so," Lynch said. "But at the end of the day, I'm the one who has to live with my decision. I'm comfortable with that."

The two of them looked at each other across the desk. "Do you have any more questions?" Lynch asked.

"Just one," Kirsten said with a weary grin. "What do you want from me?"

"What makes you think I want something?"

"I've been a crime reporter for twenty years. This is the first time I've ever been in the commissioner's office. You want something," she said flatly.

Lynch got up from his chair and sat on the edge of his desk. "I want your help."

"I'm a reporter, not a cop."

"You're also the only one besides Coletti who saw the murderer close-up. I know you told us what you saw this morning, but if we're going to catch this guy, we need more than that."

"I don't have more to give," she said. "He was big, he was pale, he was scary. That's all I know."

"What about the raven?" Lynch said.

Kirsten's eyes grew fearful as she thought of it. "The only thing I can tell you about the raven is that it's tied to this somehow. I don't know how to explain it or if I should even try. The last thing I need is for the police commissioner to think I'm crazy."

Lynch smiled. "Crazy? I don't think you're crazy. Reckless? Yes. Foolish? Sometimes. But in all the years I've seen you cover crime in this city, I've never thought you were crazy, Kirsten. Not by a long shot."

She looked at him, and a tiny bit of trust showed up in her eyes. "Then you know what I saw was real—as real as that bird that was circling over us a few minutes ago."

"Of course I know it was real," Lynch said. "That's what I'm worried about. If you saw that bird after Smitty was killed and Coletti saw it after Mrs. Bailey was killed—"

"Wait. So Coletti saw it, too?"

"Yes," Lynch said, locking eyes with Kirsten. "And if the pattern holds, seeing that bird here could mean someone else is about to die."

"Maybe so," Kirsten said in a small, still voice. "Or maybe the next victim's already dead."

Coletti left the medical examiner's office and loaded the bag containing Clarissa's belongings into the trunk of his car as Ellison Bailey slid into the passenger seat.

Ellison's cavalier attitude was gone, replaced with a sort

of shock that permeated his every movement. He appeared older, slower, more reserved.

"We're going to have to hold on to your wife's belongings as evidence," Coletti said as he got in and started the car.

"That's fine," Ellison said quietly and with a nervous smile. "Let me know if you need anything else."

Coletti pulled out of the parking lot and looked in the rearview mirror at the patrol car that was following them. Then he glanced at Ellison, who seemed lost in the moment. "Are you all right, Mr. Bailey?"

"I'm fine. It's just hard to get the picture of Clarissa out of my head. I've never seen a dead body before, let alone someone I cared about. It's sobering."

"I'm sorry you had to see that, but I appreciate you coming down," Coletti said, pausing slightly. "I did want to ask you something, though."

Ellison turned to him expectantly.

"What was your wife's usual routine?"

"For the past few months she'd been leaving around nine every morning to go to Tookesbury Mansion. She'd swing by Fairgrounds Cemetery. Then she'd come home around four and go upstairs."

"Did she seem nervous or afraid lately?"

"In the years we were together, I never really saw Clarissa get nervous or afraid about anything. Why? Did they find something to make you think she was afraid?"

"They found traces of gunpowder and other signs that she might have fired a gun today."

Ellison looked surprised. "Clarissa? She despised guns. She wouldn't even allow a gun in the house for protection."

"Are you sure?"

"Let me put it this way," Ellison said. "In order for Clarissa to even come within sight of a gun, she would've had to be in fear of losing her very life, and as far as I could see, she wasn't."

"Maybe she didn't tell you about it. I mean, you *were* trying to divorce her."

"That's true," Ellison said, his tone pensive. "We didn't share much these days. Some things she simply tried to hide."

"Such as?"

"Oh, I don't know. She seemed to spend a lot of time online doing some kind of research. Whenever I'd come in, she'd close the page she was looking at. I found that odd, because she'd never tried to hide things before."

"Was there anything else strange about her behavior?"

"Well, there was the trip she took a few days ago."

"Where did she go?"

"Somewhere in upstate Pennsylvania. I found her hotel reservation the day before she left. When I asked her about it, she told me she was going to see some friends, but she never told me who they were."

"Do you remember the name of the place?"

"Of the hotel? No. But maybe where it was located—it was a unique little name," Ellison said, closing his eyes as he tried to recall it. "Had a small-town ring to it."

Coletti's mouth went dry, and his heart began to beat faster. He knew the name of the town before Ellison Bailey even spoke it.

"She went to Dunmore," Coletti said.

"Yes, that's it. How did you know?"

Coletti glanced at him. "I had some friends there once, too."

He drove in silence for the next few minutes and thought of the stories Mary had told him about the town. He thought of the bad memories of Dunmore that Lenore had shared with him. He thought of the people he'd heard so much about, and of the ones about whom he'd heard nothing. Coletti thought of Clarissa, and he realized that if she'd gone to Dunmore, she'd gone to great lengths to find out what she could about Lenore.

"Had you ever noticed any kind of tattoos on Clarissa's body before?" Coletti said.

"Tattoos? No."

"The ME found one on the back of her neck when he examined her," Coletti said. "It looked like it was done fairly recently—maybe even in the last few days."

"A tattoo of what?" Ellison asked, sounding bewildered.

"A series of letters and numbers. Could've been a code of some sort."

"I can't imagine Clarissa doing anything like that."

Coletti glanced at Ellison and surmised that he was telling the truth, primarily because Ellison's grief now seemed to be genuine. Coletti thought that Clarissa's death was probably the first thing in a long time that Ellison had been forced to feel.

"Mr. Bailey?" Coletti said as they pulled up in front of the house.

Ellison was looking out the window, his mind in another place as he tried to process his sorrow.

"Mr. Bailey!" Coletti repeated, louder this time.

Ellison snapped out of it. "Yes, Detective?"

"I think we're going to need your help with the investigation."

"Whatever you need. Just let me know."

"I need Clarissa's computer and her phone charger," Coletti said. "And while we're at it, I'll need your computer, too."

Ellison seemed to hedge a bit. "How am I supposed to write?" he said.

"You weren't doing much writing anyway, Mr. Bailey."

Ellison thought about all the porn sites he'd visited in the past year. He wasn't sure he wanted the police seeing that.

Coletti saw the wheels turning. He didn't want to give Ellison time to think. "I could get a warrant if you prefer," Coletti said. "It's up to you."

Ellison sighed heavily. "That won't be necessary," he said. "Believe it or not, I want Clarissa's killer caught as badly as you do."

"Good," Coletti said.

As he and the two cops who'd followed them went

into the house to take out Clarissa's and Ellison's laptops, Coletti hoped that whatever he found would help piece together the last few days of Clarissa's life. Experience told him that a victim's last few days always told a story, and the story, more than anything else, always solved the crime.

CHAPTER 6

Sandy Jackson drove from the park and headed to police headquarters while trying to clear the image of Smitty's dead body from her mind. She told herself she was going to headquarters to drop off paperwork. In reality, she was going to see Charlie Mann.

She hoped he could say something that would help her stop thinking about how closely this case resembled that of the Angel of Death. She wanted him to make her forget how another murderer in black had changed their lives for the worse, but deep down she knew that Charlie could do nothing to erase the images from her mind. He was coping with demons of his own.

As Sandy turned onto Race Street and made her way to the Roundhouse, she thought of how the Angel of Death had come to her in dreams on a night she'd hoped to spend with Charlie. She still remembered falling asleep and dreaming of jogging on Kelly Drive, the road that wound along the western edge of the cemetery. In that dream, she had jogged beneath a bridge and watched in horror as geese turned to vultures and the river turned to ice. Then she had awakened and found messages from the killer in her house. Those messages frightened her at first. Then they made her angry. She had used that anger, along with her penchant for finding the truth, to help bring a killer to justice.

It seemed like years had passed since then, but it had only been two months. A lot had changed in that short time, but as Sandy pulled into the parking lot of police headquarters, she realized that certain things were starting to resemble old patterns.

Instead of walking into homicide with Mary Smithson, Charlie and Coletti had driven Mary's younger, prettier sister back to the office. True, she was a witness in the latest set of murders to rock the city, but Sandy didn't want her man to spend too much time around her; not without a reminder of the woman he already had.

Parking her cruiser near the back of the parking lot, Sandy teased her hair, fixed her makeup, and thought of all that she and Charlie had been through together.

She remembered how she'd met him three years before, after stopping him for a traffic violation. She recalled how he'd badgered her for a date after that, and how, when she finally gave in, their every interaction seemed like magic.

In their first few months together, she glowed like a candle in his presence. Her voice went from wool to velvet when she spoke to him. Her brown eyes brightened each time they focused on his. As time went on, the magic was tempered by the reality of their lives and careers as police officers in a department where secrets were hard to keep. Still, they loved each other enough to settle their arguments in private and, to the extent that they could, leave their personal lives at home.

In the two months since the Angel of Death investigation, Charlie seemed to be the same on the outside: warm and gregarious; funny and charming; smart and loving. In quiet moments, however, he would sometimes withdraw to a place where Sandy couldn't reach him. In those moments she would simply hold his hand and tell him they could talk when he was ready. At times like those, Sandy cursed the name of the woman who was there both times Charlie had to kill, because killing had damaged Charlie in ways Sandy had never expected.

Sandy couldn't blame Mary Smithson for all their problems, though. Just as Charlie had changed, Sandy was changing, too. She was a lieutenant now, and while that didn't affect who she was in private, it changed who she was in the department. Charlie sensed that, and it made him more distant than he used to be.

As Sandy put the final touches on her makeup and prepared to get out of the car, she tried to clear all that from her mind. She just wanted to see him and whisper that she loved him.

Coletti wanted to see Charlie Mann, too, but as he pulled into the space next to Sandy's, love was the last thing on his mind.

Coletti got out of his car with a paper bag in his hand. Sandy looked at it and knew from the way the numbers were arranged that it was an evidence bag from the ME's office. Two more cops pulled up next to Coletti in a patrol car. They got out carrying plastic bags.

"I see you've been busy," she said as she got out of her car and followed the three of them into the building.

"Somebody's gotta work while you're hanging out in the parking lot," Coletti said with a hint of sarcasm.

"For your information, I came to drop off some paperwork," she said, looking away so he wouldn't see her eyes.

"Yeah, right." Coletti smiled as he walked through the door to headquarters and was buzzed in by the sergeant behind the glass. He started down the hall toward homicide.

Sandy tried to act as if she was going the other way, but Coletti stopped and looked back at her, winking and nodding his head in the direction of the office. Sheepishly, she followed him.

They walked in and saw that the office was virtually empty. Only a few detectives were there. Lenore was nowhere in sight, and Charlie Mann was on the phone wearing the frustrated expression of a man caught in automated phone system hell. He waved at them while mouthing a silent hello.

Coletti looked at Sandy and saw that he'd guessed right about her reason for coming. "I've gotta go log this evidence in," he said. "Why don't you two chat until I get back? I've got a lot to tell you."

Coletti beckoned for the two uniformed police to follow him to the evidence room as Sandy sat down at Charlie's desk.

Mann put his hand over the phone's mouthpiece and whispered to Sandy. "Hey honey," he said, smiling weakly as he listened to yet another automated voice telling him to press two.

She returned the halfhearted smile.

After following prompts and pressing numbers for the next five minutes, Charlie slammed the phone into the cradle.

"That good, huh?" Sandy asked with a forced smile.

"I'm trying to find the owner of an e-mail address," Charlie said. "It would've been easy if the e-mail had been sent from the address, but it wasn't, so I had to call the hosting company and try to get to a live human being. That's like trying to get water from a rock. But enough about me. How's your day going?"

"It's been a tough one," she said with a sigh. "Smitty was one of the few guys in the department I really respected. It's hard knowing that he died the way he did, and even harder knowing we almost had the guy who did it."

"Are you gonna be okay?"

"I will if I get a piece of Smitty's killer," she said, her eyes smoldering with barely concealed anger. Then she looked at Charlie, and her eyes softened. "It's hard losing one of my friends like that—almost as hard as watching someone I love slip away."

He immediately understood what she meant, but this wasn't the place to get into it. "Maybe we can get together in the next few days and talk some things over," he said. "I know it's been a while since we've done that."

"It's been a while since we've done a lot of things," she said plainly.

"I know. I've just been really busy with work and—"

"How 'bout this?" Sandy said. "When this is over we can take some time, just the two of us, to work on something other than homicides." She looked at him suggestively as she spoke. "I've got a lot of work for you to do."

Charlie licked his lips and thought of all the images she'd packed into those words. Then he looked into her honey-brown eyes and thought of how fortunate he was to have her. She was sexy and self-assured. She had curves that the uniform couldn't hide. Her face was so pretty it glowed, and at thirty years old, she was wise enough to provide counsel when he needed it. With all she had to offer, he wasn't sure why they were drifting apart. He just knew that they were, and like Sandy, he didn't know what to do.

Before he could respond to her, Coletti walked in. "I've got some goodies for you," he said as he deposited Clarissa's laptop and phone on Mann's desk. Both items had been bagged and tagged.

"I'd better go so the two of you can talk," Sandy said.

"I'd rather you didn't," Coletti said. "We might need you."

Sandy glanced at Charlie Mann, wishing he would say he needed her. But wishing couldn't make their relationship right. If it could, both she and Mann would've wished things back to normal a long time ago.

"What've you got?" Mann asked Coletti.

"There was gunpowder residue on Clarissa Bailey's clothing. The ME's pretty sure that the shot I heard this morning was fired by Clarissa, not her assailant."

"So where's the gun?" Mann asked. "Where's the shell?"

"Your guess is as good as mine," Coletti said. "But from what her husband says, it would've been really strange for Clarissa to carry a gun. She hated guns."

"So do you think she knew someone was going to try to kill her?" Sandy asked.

"She knew something," Coletti said. "I'm just not sure what it was. Which reminds me, Charlie, were you able to find out who that e-mail address belongs to?"

"No," he said. "Maybe the guys in IT might have better luck. Or we could get a warrant and make the hosting company give up the information."

"We don't have time for that," Coletti said as he donned latex gloves and plugged in Clarissa's phone using the charger he'd gotten from Ellison.

He handed Mann a pair of gloves and the phone. Mann put them on and scrolled quickly through Clarissa's contact list, then through the numbers on her "recent calls" menu.

"Looks like she hadn't placed any calls home in a while," he said as he examined the numbers. "In fact, almost all of these calls are to the same three people: Violet, Lily, and this third one with the 570 area code. Where's 570?"

"My guess is Dunmore," Coletti said. "Clarissa's husband said she visited there a few days ago."

Mann dialed the number on the phone and an answering machine came on. He put the phone on speaker so all three of them could hear.

"You've reached Sean O'Hanlon," said a voice that sounded hollow through the phone's cheap speaker. "Please leave a message at the sound of the tone."

Mann disconnected the call and looked at Coletti. "That name sounds familiar."

"It should," Coletti said. "Sean O'Hanlon is Mary and Lenore's father."

Commissioner Lynch knew, someplace deep down, that there was something dark about this case—something that he felt, but couldn't explain. He'd seen it in Kirsten Douglas's eyes. He'd witnessed it in the raven's presence. He'd sensed it when he stood in the woods and saw the dead officer who'd been pulled from the ground.

But it didn't matter if the style of the killer was unconventional or if the reason for the killings was beyond his understanding. Kevin Lynch was a cop. His job was to solve the crime, and he was going to do that, no matter what it took.

He couldn't help replaying Kirsten Douglas's comments in his head. Even after she left his office promising to share whatever she could find that would help them, Lynch kept thinking of the raven circling above them. He remembered the way the bird soared effortlessly, as if it were taunting them for their inability to act or, worse, daring them to do something more than talk. Whatever the reason for its presence, Kirsten was right about one thing. Not only did the killer show up when the raven did, bodies showed up, too.

Lynch called the homicide captain and told him to put together a meeting. Ten minutes later, when the commissioner walked into homicide with the captain on his heels, his footsteps echoed through the room like thunder. There was purpose in his gait, and everyone inside knew it. Coletti, Mann, and Sandy stopped fiddling with the laptop they were trying to access, and the two other detectives who were toiling away in other parts of the office pretended to work harder.

Both of them acknowledged the commissioner's presence with mumbled words of greeting, but Lynch wasn't there for them. He was there for Coletti and Mann, and though he hadn't come for Sandy, he was glad to see her, because he wanted her in the meeting, too.

"I need the three of you in the captain's office now," Lynch said as he and the captain breezed by them.

When all five of them were inside, Lynch told Mann to shut the door and looked around at the four chairs in the office. He hadn't been down to homicide in at least two months, but not much had changed. The offices were still ragged, and there still weren't enough chairs.

"Sit down wherever you can," Lynch said, opting to stand.

Sandy and Mann sat in chairs while the captain sat at his desk and turned on his computer. Coletti leaned against the wall and suspiciously eyed his commanders.

"I called you all here so we could get on the same page,"

Lynch said. "I know you're out interviewing witnesses and gathering evidence, and all that's great, but anytime we cordon off neighborhoods, shut down schools and businesses, send cops door-to-door, and still come up empty, something's wrong. Either we need to change tactics, or we need to rethink who or what we're chasing."

"What do you mean?" Coletti asked.

Lynch walked around to the front of the captain's desk, leaned against it, and folded his arms. "I just had a talk with Kirsten Douglas."

"Good, maybe she'll stop calling me," Coletti mumbled.

Lynch glared at Coletti before continuing. "When I talked with Kirsten she was still petrified from this morning. It wasn't just about the killer, either. It was about the raven."

"She saw the raven?" Coletti asked, sounding surprised.

"Yes, and it was just like when you saw it," Lynch said. "The body showed up and the bird wasn't far behind. That's why Kirsten's convinced that the raven is somehow tied to this whole thing."

"Do you think she's right?" Coletti asked.

"I know she is," Lynch said, pausing slightly. "Because I saw the raven, too."

There was silence as the commissioner's admission sunk in.

"Of course, knowing the raven is linked to these murders and acting on that knowledge are two different things," Lynch continued. "But if we're going to act on it, we need to know it's more than just a hunch."

"It's definitely more than that," Mann said. "You don't

get this many connections by accident, especially when you think back to the poem."

"What poem?" Lynch said.

" 'The Raven,' " Coletti explained. "It's a poem by Edgar Allan Poe that Clarissa believed was tied to a message at Fairgrounds; a message that only Lenore Wilkinson could find. The killer apparently believed the same thing, because he left a note saying he'd be back for Lenore."

The captain, who'd sat quietly at his desk listening, began to type on his computer as the commissioner tried to wrap his mind around the connections.

"So if the killer's doing this based on some legend in a poem, where does an actual raven fit into the equation?" Lynch asked.

The room fell silent as they all searched their minds for answers. Then the captain looked at his computer monitor and read the first few facts he'd found while researching ravens online.

"Death," the captain said as he scrolled through the information. "That's what ravens represent, so if the killer's trying to tell us there's more death to come, the raven is the perfect messenger. But he'd have to be a patient man to deal with one, because ravens are smart, cautious, and they don't take kindly to people. According to this, it's almost impossible to completely control ravens, so it probably would've taken months, if not years, for him to train one. That tells me he's taken plenty of time to plan this whole thing."

"But if he's operating according to a plan he must've done more than just train a raven," Sandy said.

"That's true," Mann said, "and I think this whole 'Gravedigger' persona is part of his preparation. For all we know he's already dug dozens of other graves back there in those woods."

"I doubt it," said the commissioner. "We searched every inch of Sedgley Woods this morning. We didn't find anything else like that. Besides, why would he dig dozens of graves in advance?"

"Maybe he's planning to kill dozens of people," Mann said.

"Could be," said Lynch. "But the note he left about Lenore means he's after a specific person."

"I think all your points are valid," the captain said. "But we still need to answer a very basic question: Where did he go?"

They were all silent. None of them had the answer. It was the commissioner who spoke first.

"We might not know the where, but we know the why. He killed because of Lenore, which means we need to figure out what's so special about her."

"We already know what Lenore claims is special about her," Coletti said. "She says she knows things other people don't."

"What do you mean?" the commissioner asked.

Coletti was hesitant to tell him. But he'd brought it up, and now he had to at least attempt to explain. "She thinks she has a . . . sixth sense," he said haltingly. "She believes she can see the truth about people. Don't ask if I believe it yet because I'm not sure."

The captain looked skeptical. Commissioner Lynch looked intrigued. Coletti felt like this was his only chance to convince them, so he went on. "Lenore believes she's what they call a seer—someone who has dreams or visions or just the natural ability to know things instantly. Now, I'm not sure that we can deal with that in a conventional sense. That's why I was going to request that you permanently reassign Lieutenant Jackson to this case. Based on what she was able to do in the Angel of Death murders, I think she could be helpful here."

Sandy turned around and looked at Coletti. "You've lost your mind, haven't you?"

"No," Mann said as he thought about the idea. "No, I think he's right. You're a lot like Lenore Wilkinson claims to be. You see things in ways other people can't."

Lynch and the captain saw the look that passed between Mann and Sandy. Coletti did, too. He smiled to himself, but he knew that a single glance couldn't heal whatever was wrong between them. Lynch knew it, too.

"If you want me to start reassigning people, I need facts."

"You want facts?" Coletti said, taking out the pictures he'd gotten from the ME's office and handing each of them a copy. "Here's fact one."

They all looked at the pictures as Coletti spoke. "The coroner found this when he examined Clarissa's body. It's a cryptogram—a kind of code that Poe used in some of his writings. She had it tattooed on the back of her neck."

They looked at the strange arrangement of numbers and letters that read: H20Z18G 1G 20S5 V22V18T18V5M 2I5V.

"Did anybody bother to try to find out what it means?"

"I called a buddy of mine in the State Police," Coletti said. "He ran it through a program that decodes cryptograms and it came up with gibberish. But we're still working on it."

"Okay," Lynch said. "What other facts do you have?"

"Clarissa Bailey placed several calls to Lenore's father in the days leading up to her death."

"And?"

"I don't know yet. I haven't been able to get in touch with him. But whatever Clarissa was dealing with in recent days obviously scared her, because she went out and got a gun. In fact, she's the one who fired the gunshot in the cemetery this morning."

Lynch looked at the captain. Then he looked at Coletti and the others as he sat on the edge of the desk and folded his arms. "Lieutenant Jackson, I'm gonna call your captain and tell him you're being reassigned, effective immediately. You'll work with Coletti and Mann until we close this case. Coletti, I'm assuming that laptop I saw when I came in belonged to Mrs. Bailey. Am I right?"

"Yes, Commissioner. Her husband turned over two laptops and a phone."

"Okay, get all that stuff to IT. They should be able to dump the hard drives and give you whatever's there pretty quickly. Mann, you'll be responsible for following up with IT."

"Yes, sir."

"Coletti, you got any interviews lined up?" Lynch asked.

"I'm going to Penn to talk to the man who got Clarissa to believe in this whole thing about Poe."

"Penn?" Mann said. "I might know the guy."

"I almost forgot you went there," Coletti said. "His name is Workman. You know him?"

"I think he taught in the English department," Mann said. "Kind of intense. Elbow patches. I never had him, but everybody thought he was way too serious about literature."

"That's good to know," Coletti said. "Speaking of literature, I wanted to see if you and Sandy could take Lenore over to the house on Seventh Street where Poe used to live. If Lenore's really some kind of seer she should be able to sense something there that could be useful."

"No problem," Mann said. "We'll pick her up from the Loews. I've got a detail there with her until we can transport her to a safe house."

"And when will the safe house be ready?" Lynch asked.

"Should be within the hour, Commissioner."

"It better be. I want her under lock and key right after you leave the Poe house. Once that's done, I want the three of you to interview everyone who was sent that e-mail from Clarissa Bailey. I don't care how you do it, just get it done.

"Coletti, before the day is out, I need you to go to Dunmore and find out who Clarissa Bailey spoke to there. What did she learn? When did she learn it? That type of thing.

"Finally, we need to know how this raven ties in to all

this, and why it matters to the killer. Lieutenant Jackson, you'll be responsible for that. The captain here will give the three of you whatever support you need. And I'll be checking in throughout the day. I want this killer caught, I want him caught now, and I don't want to hear any excuses. You're dismissed."

The three of them walked out with their marching orders, and Coletti stopped to get the computer and cell phone off Mann's desk.

While Coletti was gathering the items to take them up to IT, Lynch came out of the office and spoke to his old friend so only he could hear. "There was one other thing I wanted to tell you, Mike."

"What's that?" Coletti said as he finished wrapping the items.

"I need you to talk to Kirsten Douglas."

"Why?"

"She questioned why you were working the case after what happened with Mary. I told her you don't have a personal stake in it, but we both know Kirsten. She's not gonna let it go."

"She shouldn't talk to me, then, 'cause if she questions my integrity I won't be nice about it."

"No, you *will* be nice about it, Mike, because I promised her you'd talk to her."

"Why would you do that?" Coletti asked in disbelief.

"So you can find out what she knows before the paper does, and get this killer off the street."

Coletti sighed.

"Whatever you tell her doesn't have to be for attribution. You can be an unnamed source with knowledge of the investigation. Besides, she just wants a few exclusive tidbits. I don't see any harm in giving her that. Make her think she's getting more than she's giving. Who knows? She might like it. You might, too."

Coletti looked at the commissioner and shook his head. Then he walked out of the office and saw Mann and Sandy in the hallway. They were standing together near the front door. Mann was on the phone placing a call to the Edgar Allan Poe house. Sandy was trying not to let her personal feelings show. From what Coletti could see, she was failing miserably in that effort.

Mann waved at Coletti and then turned back to Sandy as his partner made his way upstairs. "We're set for the Poe house," Mann said to Sandy. "And Lenore Wilkinson's ready to be picked up."

Sandy was quiet because she didn't want to be anywhere near Lenore, and she wasn't even certain she wanted to be bothered with Mann. Sandy wanted to tell him that she had to supervise her officers, or that she had duties in the district office, or that she had to go back to check on the scene in the park. But the commissioner had given his orders, and Sandy was bound to comply.

"You ready?" Mann asked as he prepared to leave.

Sandy nodded.

Mann walked out, but Sandy lagged behind, so he stopped to wait for her. "You seem preoccupied," he said when she caught up to him.

"I *am* preoccupied. I want to find Smitty's killer."

"I was hoping you wanted to find more than that," he said, turning to her with a forced smile.

"Don't play with me, Charlie. You know you don't mean that."

"Yes I do."

"Then show me," she said, her tone a mix of skepticism and frustration.

They stopped and looked at each other, each of them hoping that Charlie Mann had rediscovered the thing that he'd lost two months ago. After a few seconds, however, it was apparent that he hadn't, so he dropped his gaze, knowing that he wasn't quite ready. Sandy knew it, too, but she liked that he was trying.

"I'll meet you at the Loews," Charlie said as he turned and walked to his car.

Sandy watched him and thought of what she'd come to headquarters to say.

"Charlie?"

He turned and looked at her.

"I love you," she mouthed silently.

For the first time in a long time, he had to force himself to respond. "Me, too," he said with a grin.

Sandy wanted to believe what he'd said, but there was no life in his words, no emotion in his voice, and no joy in his smile. Sandy knew he couldn't possibly love her. The look in his eyes said he didn't even love himself.

CHAPTER 7

Lenore Wilkinson looked out the window of her hotel room and stared at the city below. The Loews building that formerly housed the Philadelphia Savings Fund Society had once been one of the tallest buildings in the city. Though it had long since been dwarfed by the likes of One Liberty Place and the Cira Centre, it still provided a bird's-eye view of everything that made Philadelphia tick.

She could see the traffic crawling along Market Street, and the towers of City Hall. She could see the people below, like dots moving along the sidewalks. It all seemed so insignificant from up there. No one seemed to matter any more than anyone else.

Lenore knew appearances could be deceiving, however. There were distinctions between the dots she saw moving below. The one on the corner of Thirteenth Street who sat on the sidewalk in utter defeat, his arms outstretched for a coin or a morsel, was less significant than the one stepping into the cab a block away. The one whose Bentley was stopped at a Market Street traffic light was vastly more valuable than the bike messenger dipping in and out of traffic.

Lenore knew that this was the way of the world, because this was the life that she lived. Her beauty had vaulted her far beyond her own humble beginnings and had taken her to the higher echelons of society. She'd paid a price for that, of course. It was a price that she was no longer willing to pay.

She thought about how she had met John Wilkinson. It was a year after she'd graduated from Princeton with a bachelor's in philosophy. She was enrolled in a master's program at NYU and still living on a budget with a teaching assistant's job that paid a small stipend. Five days a week, Lenore traveled back and forth from Princeton, New Jersey, to Manhattan on the cheap. One day she decided to splurge and take Amtrak instead of Greyhound, and there was a charming older man doing what everyone does on Amtrak—trying to find two empty seats so he wouldn't have to sit next to anyone. The train was crowded, though, so he ended up next to Lenore.

She was surprised at first that he didn't behave like most older men. He didn't ogle her. He didn't make silly conversation. He didn't offer her the world on a silver platter. He simply took out his laptop and went to work on a proposal.

Lenore was relieved that she wouldn't have to find a way to nicely rebuff his advances. But then, when he got off the train at Penn Station, he left his briefcase behind. Lenore didn't know much about high fashion, but she knew that a

Louis Vuitton briefcase could be two thousand dollars or more, so she opened the briefcase and found his business card inside. Then she took the day off and set out to return it to him.

When she did finally find his company's headquarters, high up in an office building on Fifth Avenue, she walked into the lobby and saw a veritable shrine to John Wilkinson. There were framed magazine covers sporting his face, including *Money*, *Fortune*, *Forbes*, and *Newsweek*. There were pictures of him with various dignitaries from around the world. There was a young secretary who looked Lenore up and down as if she were the competition.

Lenore often thought of that moment—the moment when she had a chance to turn around. It was at that moment that John Wilkinson stepped out of his office to tell his secretary something, and for the first time he looked at the young woman whom he'd sat next to on the train.

Because he was so accustomed to having gold diggers throwing themselves at him, John was taken with the innocence of a woman who would actually take the time to return one of the trappings of his wealth. He asked her out, and she refused at first, which made him want her all the more.

He took the time to learn her every interest, to study her tendencies as if he were chasing yet another business deal, and when he finally was able to make his way into her heart, he wooed her with the same simplicity that he saw in her personality. By the time he finished, she was putty in his hands. Two years into their relationship, they were married.

But as John's business empire expanded, his once encyclopedic knowledge of Lenore's interests waned. She began to complain that they no longer spent time together, and he threw money at the problem, giving her every material thing she could possibly want. Still, Lenore realized that the chase for her was over, and he was now chasing his true love—money. While doing so, he relegated Lenore to the status she'd tried so hard to avoid. She was a trophy, and John was never there for her, not even in the moments when she needed him most, like right now.

She dialed his number once again on her cell phone. It was her third call in an hour. She knew that he was returning from Europe on business, but that was no excuse. John traveled in private planes where calls got through. If he hadn't answered her by now, it wasn't because he couldn't. It was because he chose not to do so. When the phone rang for the fifth time and there was no answer, Lenore declined to leave another message. She simply hung up the phone.

As she gazed out her window at the people below who looked so insignificant, she realized that she was just like them. The distinctions that separated rich from poor were of no consequence if the money couldn't buy happiness. In Lenore's case, it couldn't even buy satisfaction.

There was a knock at the door, and she turned from the window. "Come in," she said.

"Mrs. Wilkinson, Detective Mann is on his way up," said the uniformed officer who was posted at her door. "We'll be ready to move you in a few minutes."

"Thank you," she said with a grateful smile.

She went to the mirror and teased her hair into place. Then she put on some lipstick and tried not to look as sad as she felt. She told herself that she was finally doing something that she wanted to do. She was finally out to learn who she really was. That was why she was going to stay to find the answers that had eluded her for a lifetime. It wasn't about John, or her father, or her sister, or anyone else but herself. Knowing that would have to be enough.

There was another knock on the door, and Lenore pasted on a smile. "I'm ready," she said, walking out of the room to meet Charlie Mann and the two officers who'd been detailed to her.

"Right this way," Mann said, walking down the hall as the uniformed cops followed them.

Mann looked at Lenore when they got on the elevator. "We're going to make a stop before we go to the safe house," he said.

"You're just full of surprises," Lenore said absently.

When they reached the lobby and walked out the door, Lenore saw yet another surprise. Sandy was sitting in her patrol car, watching as she came out the entrance. At first, the look on Sandy's face was friendly. But when Sandy looked at Lenore, her friendliness turned to something else.

Sandy got out of her car and walked across the sidewalk as Mann opened his car door for Lenore, about whose looks Sandy had heard much. When she was close enough to get a good look at the woman in Charlie's passenger seat, Sandy's posture changed even more, and though Sandy tried to hide it, everyone within thirty yards of them could see.

"Lieutenant Sandy Jackson, this is Lenore Wilkinson," Mann said as Sandy stuck her head in his car window.

"It's nice to meet you," Sandy muttered. Then she turned to Mann and kissed him on the cheek.

Mann was surprised by the gesture. There were no public displays of affection while in uniform. But Sandy was more than a cop now. She was a woman—*Charlie's* woman—and she wanted Lenore to know it.

"I'm going over to the Poe house," Sandy said before glancing at Lenore once again. "I'll meet the two of you there."

Poe's stoic face stared out from a colorful mural on the side of the housing project on Seventh Street. The painting was the Housing Authority's feeble attempt at making the development blend in with the nearby red brick house where Poe had once lived. The effort was a failure.

The writer's sullen image looked on with disapproval at the way the land around his former house had gone from country meadows to a mix of mean streets and hastily constructed new development. To add insult to injury, the man who'd invented the modern detective story was now at the center of one, and from the look on the mural's painted face, he was none too pleased.

Sandy pulled up within sight of Poe's staring image. She parked her cruiser and looked at the corner where the National Park Service, which ran Poe's former house, vied with the neighborhood for control. Judging by the broken glass and tiny red plastic baggies that littered the ground near the national historic site, the neighborhood had fought the government to a draw.

She looked at the mural and the housing project that had thus far survived the neighborhood's gentrification, and she realized that she was now part of the fight to hold that corner. Having transferred from the ninth district to become a lieutenant in the sixth, she was still learning her new environment. From what she saw, it was a world apart from the other side of Center City.

In her five years in the ninth, Sandy had gotten to know the beggars and security guards, shopkeepers and salespeople in the high-end shopping district on Rittenhouse Square. She'd learned the rhythms of the skyscrapers that loomed within walking distance of City Hall. She'd come to recognize those faces that belonged downtown and those that didn't. Moreover, she'd recognized her place in it all.

She was the mediator—the one who knew the district better than it knew itself. As such, she was required to adjust her persona to fit the needs of the moment, and she did so to great effect. She was reassuring to the rich and a counselor to the downtrodden, a disciplinarian to the recalcitrant, and a supporter of her subordinates. More than any of those things, she was a lover to the one who made her rough edges smooth—Charlie Mann.

But she wasn't in the ninth district now. She was in the sixth, and things had changed. Her job was different, her location was different, and as she watched Mann pull up at the corner with another unmarked car following closely behind, she realized that her relationship was different, too.

That grieved her, but Sandy had watched too many women stifle themselves and the men they purported to love simply because they refused to let go. Sandy didn't plan to be one of those women.

She got out of her car just as Mann walked over to meet her.

"You all right?" Mann asked. "You left the hotel pretty fast."

"Let's just get to work," Sandy said, her face fixed in the serious expression she wore when she was in cop mode.

Mann glanced at her once more. Then he signaled to the uniformed officers who'd followed them there from the hotel. One of them helped Lenore out of the car, walked her to the door of the Poe house, and stood guard outside. The cop wasn't the only one on post. A black, wrought-iron raven hovered against the south wall of the sturdy brick house. It stared into the distance as the four of them walked in and were greeted by a thin woman with inquisitive eyes and short, auburn hair. She was wearing the green uniform of the National Park Service.

"You must be Detective Mann," she said. "I'm Ranger Franklin. I'm the one who took your call."

"Pleased to meet you," Mann said. "This is Lenore Wilkinson and Lieutenant Jackson. We appreciate you setting this up on such short notice."

"No problem. I got the last tour out as quickly as I could so you'd have the house to yourselves. What exactly is it you're looking for?"

"We were hoping to learn something about the woman

who was killed at Fairgrounds Cemetery this morning," Mann said. "I understand she'd visited here before."

"Yes, we knew Mrs. Bailey well," the ranger said, her voice tinged with sadness. "She was here a lot over the past few months, trying to find some clue about Poe that she hadn't already learned."

"What kind of clue?" Lenore asked as she walked past the ranger and toward the interactive exhibits.

"We never knew," the ranger said with a sad smile.

Lenore looked at the pulley-driven balloon for children and the television screens for adults. Then she peered around a wall and into a room whose tables and red-cushioned chairs were arranged into what Poe described as a manifestation of good taste. Mann and the others looked at the room, too, and saw that its bookcase and mantelpiece were painted onto the walls.

Lenore wandered out of that room and stopped at the wall whose cracked plaster and exposed wooden slats led to the actual area where Poe lived.

"What did Clarissa learn here?" Lenore asked, speaking as she ran her hand along the walls.

"Nothing she didn't already know, I'm afraid," the ranger said as they all followed Lenore into the back room. "We tell specific stories about Poe that we know are factual. Mrs. Bailey wanted more than that. Unfortunately, we couldn't help."

The ranger looked at Lenore. "Would you like to see the rest of the house?" she asked.

Lenore smiled. "Yes. I'd like that very much."

The ranger walked them all into the living room area. It was small by modern standards, perhaps twelve feet across. The walls were blotched and speckled. The wooden floors were painted brown. Lenore looked at every detail while the rest of them watched her curiously.

"Did Poe own this house?" Lenore asked.

"No, he rented it with a hundred dollars he won in a writing contest," the ranger said. "He lived here for about a year with his wife and mother-in-law. His wife was very sick at the time."

Lenore walked into the small kitchen and stared at the space where the stove had been. There were holes in the walls for gas lines, and a walkway leading to a back porch. The ceilings were low, and there was a narrow staircase leading to the upstairs.

"They must've been small people," Sandy said as she looked at the cramped kitchen and low ceilings.

"Yes, they were," the ranger said. "Poe was about five eight. Of course, a lot of people in the eighteen hundreds were short by today's standards."

They walked up the rickety stairs to the second floor and saw private rooms with closets and shelves that once held the belongings of Poe; his sickly young wife, Virginia; and his domineering mother-in-law, Muddy.

Lenore and the others looked through windows whose views once showed similar houses across the street but now showed two-story rows of public housing and the building that housed the German Society.

A few minutes later, they climbed creaky steps to the

third floor and listened as the ranger told stories of Poe's tragic life, filled with abandonment and death, disappointment and poverty. In the midst of her stories about Poe's exploits as a magazine and newspaper man, she said something that piqued Mann's interest.

"He was writing for a newspaper—one of several he worked for—and he challenged readers to send in cryptograms so he could solve them," she said.

"Did anyone keep any?" Mann asked anxiously. "Are they in a museum somewhere?"

"I'm not sure," she said. "But you can find one of Poe's cryptograms in a story called 'The Gold Bug.' It's about three men who find buried treasure on an island off South Carolina."

"Do you have a copy?"

"I'm sure I can dig one up."

Lenore looked at Mann curiously. "Is there something important about cryptograms?"

Mann looked to Sandy, who took out her copy of Clarissa's tattoo and showed it to Lenore. "Do you recognize this?" she asked gently.

Lenore stared at the picture, touching it with her fingertips and squinting. "No," she said, her voice filled with uncertainty. "Well, other than the fact that it's a tattoo."

"Yes, but is it anything else?" Sandy prodded. "Is it more than a tattoo to you?"

Lenore gazed at the picture for a few minutes more, trying to see something, anything other than dead white skin that had been pricked with ink-tipped needles. Try as she might, she could see nothing more than letters and numbers that made no sense together.

"It's okay," Sandy said, nodding to the ranger. "Let's finish the tour."

The ranger led them down a newly built set of back stairs, and they walked into the dark basement whose tiny windows shed shafts of light on dark alcoves, brick floors, and stone walls. The ranger told them that Poe had set the horrors of his short story "The Black Cat" in that basement. From the dangerous wooden steps and the openings to secret passages, the ladders set against bricks and the beams in the low ceiling, it was easy to see how fear could live in such a place.

Mann watched Lenore carefully as she ran her fingers against the lime and plaster on the basement walls. Sandy watched, too, waiting to see when Lenore's supposed gift would reveal itself. But there, in the darkest room in the house, where spirits seemed to lurk in shadows, Lenore didn't feel anything more than what she'd felt while looking at the cryptogram.

Standing on her toes, she looked out one of the narrow basement windows at the backyard. "I bet it was beautiful back there when Poe was alive," she said.

"Yes, it was," said the ranger. "Poe's mother-in-law planted flowers and did her gardening back there in the spring and summer."

"Can we go out?" Lenore asked.

"Sure."

The ranger led them to the back door, and they followed her outside. The grass had already shriveled and faded with the change of seasons. The area that had been home to brightly colored flowers in the summertime was now filled with dirt and mulch.

None of this interested Lenore. She was taken with the wrought-iron raven that stood on stilts with its wings spread out and its beak open wide as it permanently soared over the yard.

"There was a bird like this one in the graveyard this morning," Lenore said in a faraway voice. "It flew away right after Detective Coletti found Clarissa's body."

The ranger looked at Lenore with those inquisitive eyes. "Are you sure it was a bird like this?" she asked. "Ravens are pretty rare around here. Maybe you saw a crow."

"No, the bird was bigger than a crow," Lenore said as she stared at the sculpture. "Smarter, too."

"Why do you say that?" Mann asked.

"After we heard the gunshot this morning, Detective Coletti chased the killer and lost him. That's when he found Clarissa's body. The strange thing about the bird is that he stayed there in that tree, watching the whole thing. And even with all that commotion—a gun going off, a chase through the graveyard—the bird never moved until the killer got away. It was almost like the bird was standing guard."

Mann and Sandy both recalled what the commissioner had said about the raven. Lenore hadn't been there for that conversation, and yet she'd come to the same conclusion that Lynch had. The raven was somehow connected to the case, and to the killer.

"Maybe that's what the raven was doing when the killer chased Kirsten through the woods this morning," Sandy said as she thought through Lenore's scenario. "Maybe it *was* standing guard."

Lenore looked at Sandy with gratitude. Then she looked at the ranger with questions. "Was Poe's raven like the one we saw at the graveyard today?" she asked. "Was it a guardian?"

"Depends on how you look at it," the ranger said. "Ravens have always symbolized death, and the raven in Poe's poem is no exception."

"What exactly is the poem about?" Lenore asked.

"It's about a man grieving his dead lover," the ranger said, looking her in the eye. "A woman whose name is Lenore."

They all looked at Lenore, and she looked inside herself. There, she saw a kindred spirit to the man whose life was filled with one tragedy after another. In a strange sense, she felt as if she understood Poe. She could relate to his pain.

"In the poem, this grieving man is sitting in his study," the ranger continued. "His grief is slowly driving him mad, and as he wrestles with the fact that he may never see Lenore again, the raven tortures him with a single word: 'nevermore.' So, to answer your question, the raven in Poe's poem isn't a guardian. If anything, it's a symbol of hopelessness—a symbol that Poe later describes as a tool to reveal the human tendency for self-torture."

"But what does it mean?" Sandy asked impatiently. "When you strip away all the academic analysis, what did Poe see when he wrote 'The Raven'?"

The ranger sighed and looked around at all of them. They stared at her eagerly, waiting for some tidbit that would take them beyond the normal narrative.

"This isn't the story I would usually tell, but since you're here about Clarissa, I feel like I should share it," she said, looking up at the wrought-iron bird that hovered over them. "Some people look at 'The Raven' as evidence of Poe's ability to see into places that others couldn't. The people who interpret it that way focus on the stanzas about opening doors, looking into darkness, and dreaming dreams. They also focus on the name Lenore, and they believe that this Lenore, like Poe, can see things. As you probably know by now, Clarissa was among those who believed that. But what you might not know is that there are others who believe it, too. Sometimes they come here, just like Clarissa did, looking for proof that Poe's visions are actually true."

"Can you identify any of them?" Mann asked.

"Now that you mention it, there was one man who was coming pretty often up until about six months ago. Then all of a sudden he just stopped."

"Do you think we can access your surveillance video from that far back?" Mann asked. "Maybe we can identify him."

"We might be able to do that," the ranger said. "I'd

have to check with headquarters, but I don't know how quickly we could get it to you."

"Do you remember what the guy looked like?" Sandy asked.

"I couldn't forget if I wanted to. He was white, fairly young, and tall, with dark eyes and hair. I used to tease him sometimes about all that dark hair. I told him he looked just like the raven."

A chill went through the room as they realized that the description fit that of the man who'd killed twice that day.

They only hoped they could stop the Gravedigger from killing again.

Sandy had to get away. Standing there in that house, walking through those rooms, and hearing those stories hadn't awakened her intuition. It had awakened her independence, because being that close to Charlie at a time when she wasn't sure he wanted to be close to her had reminded her of who she was.

She was whole. She had always been whole, and she would be whole whether Charlie ever came around or not. Sometimes, as a cop, she needed to remind herself of that. She was so accustomed to working within a structure and being part of a team that she sometimes forgot that teamwork could only get you so far.

Born in West Philly at a time when the Junior Black Mafia rolled in custom ragtop Volvos, slinging drugs and killing competitors, Sandy understood survival better than most. She'd seen people rise as teams, but when a team stopped working together, she'd seen those same people drag each other down.

Sandy wasn't willing to gamble on the team anymore. She'd much rather hold on to the sure thing, and since Sandy was the only sure thing she knew, that meant holding on to herself.

If she was going to help solve this case, she couldn't do it while keeping one eye on the evidence and the other on her man. She couldn't worry about Lenore either, because in truth, Lenore was no threat to her, and Sandy felt silly for even thinking that way. Lenore was in the midst of a firestorm that, by all indications, someone else had created. If Sandy and Lenore were anything to each other, they were kindred spirits, not enemies.

As Sandy walked into the sixth police district, which was nestled on a small block halfway between the Poe house and police headquarters, she received mumbled greetings from the desk sergeant and a few of the others who were there. They'd heard about her temporary reassignment to homicide and most of them weren't happy about it. They felt abandoned, as if she'd been waiting for a better deal someplace else. That couldn't have been further from the truth, but Sandy didn't have time to explain that now. She had too many thoughts swirling through her mind, not the least of which was the thought that the case wasn't as impossible to solve as it seemed.

She went into the locker room and gathered her things in a Louis Vuitton Speedy. Then she changed into the uniform most popular in the streets of West Philly.

As she stepped out of the locker room in snug jeans, a T-shirt, and a paper-thin, form-fitting leather jacket, the desk sergeant nearly fell out of his chair. He'd never seen a lieutenant who looked like her. Sandy knew that, and it gave her great pleasure to know that the curves beneath her jacket and jeans were leaving a lasting impression.

"Hold down the fort while I'm gone," she said. Then she put on a pair of Chanel sunglasses and walked out the front door wearing a hint of perfume and a self-assured grin.

A few officers did double takes as they passed her in the parking lot. She didn't respond—not outwardly, at least—but on the inside, she was thinking what every beautiful woman knows instinctively. If her man wouldn't give her what she needed, there were plenty of others who were more than willing to fill the void.

Sandy got into her black Dodge Charger and checked her hair and makeup in the mirror. Then she rumbled out of the parking lot with her mind switching back into cop mode. She thought about the man who'd killed so easily in the cemetery that morning and then killed her friend in the woods. She thought of the task the commissioner had given her—to learn how the raven was connected to the killer—but she didn't know where to start. In cases like that, Sandy always went back to the beginning, and this was no exception.

She swung her car around and headed back to Seventh Street, slowing as she rode past the Poe house, and parking there to look once more at the place where Clarissa and the black-haired man played out their obsessions with "The Raven."

She sat there and imagined what it must be like to return to the same place again and again, looking for something that simply wasn't there. Then she smiled and remembered how many times she'd asked Charlie to open up, to let her in, to let go of the past, to move forward. Sandy knew exactly what it was like to return to the same thing again and again. She'd been doing it for the past two months.

She got out of the car and looked at the house, then she looked at the streets, and before she knew it, she found herself walking, trying to put into order the thoughts that were swirling in her mind.

Clarissa had come to the house on multiple occasions, looking to find something that the ranger couldn't give her. The black-haired man had done the same. The ranger said they both believed that Poe had hidden something at Fairgrounds Cemetery. Why, then, would they keep coming back to the house? Why wouldn't they just go to the place where the knowledge was supposed to be hidden? It didn't make sense to Sandy.

As she walked north on Seventh Street, she passed by the public housing she'd seen earlier. It was getting cool out, so there were only four men outside to whistle and yell at her. When she gave them a perfunctory hello and kept walking, one of them hurled an insult. Sandy ignored him and continued on her way.

She walked by a building that had been converted to

condos during the housing boom and was now up for sale. As she continued walking north, she saw signs that the neighborhood was teetering between success and failure. There were townhouses for young couples and a new apartment building for seniors, alleys for drug addicts and vacant lots for dealers.

When she crossed Girard Avenue and walked past the corner where Xanax and Vicodin and Valium were sold to refugees from nearby outpatient drug rehabs, everyone on the corner went silent. They knew she looked good. They knew she wasn't from the neighborhood, and they knew she was a cop, because only a cop would be bold enough to walk there alone.

Sandy had everyone's attention now, though no one would say it aloud. No one that is, except for the old man wearing a dirty, rumpled ski jacket with several layers of clothing underneath. He was a bum, but you couldn't tell him that.

"You shouldn't be out here by yourself," he said, coming alongside her with a friendly grin. "This ain't no place for a lady."

"Thanks, but I'll be fine," Sandy said, noting that the drug dealers across the street were rapidly closing up shop as she approached.

"I know you will," he said reassuringly. "But my mom taught me to never let a lady walk alone if I could help it. So if you don't mind, I'll just tag along to make sure nothin' happens to you."

She looked at the old man with a smile of genuine gratitude. "You're a rare breed," she said. "An actual gentleman. I thought they were extinct."

"We still around," he said. "We might disappear for a while, but we always come back."

Sandy thought about what he'd said as she looked at the brick houses that stood between trash-strewn, weed-filled lots. Everyone on the block pretended to continue what they were doing as she and the old man passed by, but they were all watching her, waiting for the backup they assumed was on the way.

Sandy smiled at a few of the children. Then she saw an old woman amble out to the street and drop breadcrumbs on the asphalt. A group of pigeons swooped in. The old lady watched along with Sandy and her escort as the birds pecked away at their treat. A car came flying past and the birds scattered. A second later, they came back to finish what they'd started.

"Pigeons somethin' else," the old man said as he continued to walk with her. "They just survive off whatever's there. They don't care where it comes from or who put it there. They're survivors, and they'll still be here a long time after we gone."

Sandy looked at the man and then at the birds. "Does that lady drop those breadcrumbs here every day?"

"Like clockwork," the old man said. "And I swear those same four or five pigeons wait for it. They know where the treasure is, and they come back every day to get it."

Sandy immediately thought of what the captain back

at homicide had said about the raven. He was smart, and just like the pigeons, he knew where his treasure was supposed to be. It stood to reason that he would keep coming back to find it. When that thought crystallized in Sandy's mind, she knew exactly where she should look.

CHAPTER 8

As he drove to the University of Pennsylvania to meet with Professor Workman, Coletti's mind was filled with Lenore. He tried not to allow those thoughts to consume him, but he was fighting a losing battle.

He thought of the things she'd told him about himself, and of her resolve in the face of danger, and of the zeal with which Clarissa believed in her. Even if nothing else happened, Lenore had already proven that there was something special about her. Coletti hoped that the next few hours would reveal what that something was.

Of course, Coletti knew old-fashioned police work got more results than hope did. When his efforts to contact Lenore's father continued to fail, he had arranged to interview Workman.

On his way to meet the professor, Coletti realized that he hadn't eaten all morning. This was one of the small ways in which police work got tough. He turned onto Walnut Street while reaching into his glove compartment for a half-eaten piece of beef jerky. Peeling off the plastic, he bit down hard, bending the tough, dry meat until it broke off in his teeth and filled his mouth with the taste of salt and old gravy.

Coletti knew he should eat better. His cholesterol had been in the two hundreds for years. Still, he'd managed to avoid the doctor's repeated attempts to medicate him by promising to diet and exercise. At fifty-eight, he'd figured it out: having a doctor was no different from being in a relationship. You lied to keep things intact, because lies were easier to stomach than the truth.

Coletti had chosen to believe the lies with Mary Smithson. He'd ignored the fact that she shouldn't have wanted him, *couldn't* have wanted him, even in his wildest dreams. He told himself that she was different from the women he'd managed to drive away with his caustic style and refusal to commit. But that was all in the past now. At least, that was what he told everyone else. Deep down, he knew that it would be years before the scars would heal, if in fact they ever healed at all.

Still stuck on Walnut Street, Coletti took a look at the heavy downtown traffic in front of him and flipped on his lights to try to move it into a single lane. It didn't work. Armored cars, UPS trucks, and FedEx vehicles were parked in the inner lanes, delivering money and inventory to the banks and high-end stores near Rittenhouse Square. Slow-moving buses clogged the outer lane.

Coletti figured the traffic would clear up when the street widened from two lanes to three, but while he was waiting, he turned on both the car radio and the police radio. It had taken him years to learn to listen to both at once, but it was particularly easy today, since the topic was the same no matter which station he chose.

KYW Newsradio ran an endless series of recaps and updates from the morning's events, with periodic reports from the scenes where the bodies had been found. A so-called expert spoke about the possibility that the killings were part of a satanic ritual, while another surmised that the killings weren't connected at all. Meanwhile, police radio featured snippets of conversation centering on the search for the suspect.

Officers in the park and at the cemetery remained on their posts, sealing off the nearby roads from all vehicle and foot traffic. Officers outside the park were busy making car and pedestrian stops, trying desperately to find someone who matched the description.

Commanders worked with school district and transit police to cordon off every school within a five-mile radius. Homes and businesses were searched. Informants were questioned. But while Coletti knew that everything they were doing was necessary, he was sure that most of it was in vain.

Based on what Ellison had told him, Coletti had a hunch that Clarissa Bailey's murder was connected to something much bigger than money. If indeed it was related to a set of beliefs, it could prove to be particularly dangerous. Coletti had seen people killed in the name of beliefs before.

The traffic thinned out when he reached Twenty-second Street, and as Coletti sped around the cars that had blocked his path, he wondered if Workman could shed light on Clarissa's beliefs. More importantly, he wondered if Workman could identify others who shared them.

Coletti turned off Walnut Street on University Avenue and parked near the small walkway where the Kelly Writers House was located. The Tudor-style cottage was a work and social center for Penn's writing community. When Coletti knocked on the door, a deep voice called out from the parlor.

"Come in," Workman said, walking into the living room to greet the detective.

Coletti reached out to shake Workman's hand, noting that the professor was a man of average height, with the rumpled look of an intellectual and the kind eyes of a grandfather. He was balding and wrinkled, but his movements were spry.

"I was so sorry to hear about Clarissa," the professor said, shaking his head sadly. "She was a dear friend."

"I'm sorry for your loss," Coletti said, noting that the professor's grief appeared to be sincere.

Workman locked the front door and drew the blinds before leading Coletti to a seat in the parlor. "Tell me how I can help."

"Well, I spoke with Mr. Bailey—"

"And you didn't lock him up?" the professor said, his face still pleasant but his tone deadly serious.

"I take it you're one of the friends he mentioned—the ones who didn't like him."

"You don't have to be Clarissa's friend to dislike Ellison. Not even her worst enemy would wish him on her."

"Why?"

"Because he's a lazy fraud who never had her best interests at heart," the professor spat. "We tried to tell her not to marry him, but Clarissa wouldn't listen. She saw something in him that the rest of us didn't."

"Who do you mean when you say 'the rest of us'?"

"I mean her friends. The people who cared about her, like Violet Grant and Lily Thompkins—the other two women in the Daughters of Independence."

Coletti thought for a moment. "The manager at the cemetery mentioned that she was a member of that organization. They deal with historic preservation, right?"

"I don't know how much of an organization it is at this point," the professor said with a wan smile. "There's only Violet and Lily now, but yes, historic preservation is part of what they do. They maintain the Tookesbury Mansion in Fairmount Park, and they've become more involved at Fairgrounds Cemetery. They were trying to create stronger links between some of the city's most important historical locations. That's why the Gravedigger's Ball was going to take place at Tookesbury this year. But now, with Clarissa gone . . ."

The professor didn't need to finish. Both he and Coletti knew that the mansion, located in Fairmount Park, near the sites of both murders, might not be the best location anymore.

"You said historic preservation was only part of their mission," Coletti said. "What else do they do?"

"They believe," the professor said with a grin. "They

believe in Philadelphia, its history, and the people who made it. People like Edgar Allan Poe, who lived here for six of the most productive years of his writing career."

"Clarissa's husband said those beliefs came from you."

The professor chuckled. "Yes, they did, and Ellison hated that. He shuddered to think that another man might be influencing Clarissa, but I never sought to recruit Clarissa or the others. I shared my theories, and they thought they were interesting. When Clarissa talked to Ellison about it, he told her she was stupid to believe me. Of course, Ellison doesn't understand how Poe changed the way we see ourselves and our fears. He doesn't understand what Poe saw."

Coletti smiled. "You seem to know a lot about the conversations Clarissa had with her husband. Did she talk to you often about her marriage?"

Workman raised his hands in a "stop" gesture. "I know where you're going, and I assure you I was merely a listening ear for Clarissa—nothing more. Our friendship was platonic. She didn't want anything from me, and I didn't want anything from her."

Coletti took note of Workman's defensive posture. The professor quickly tried to conceal his discomfort, but it was too late. Coletti had found a weak spot.

"So, as Clarissa's *friend*," Coletti said, "can you tell me what it was about your theories on Poe that came between Clarissa and her husband? I mean, I'm no expert, but from what I've read, Poe was a drunk who spent most of his life broke."

The professor's eyes flashed angrily, just as Coletti knew they would. People spoke most truthfully when they were angry, and Workman was no exception.

"If you knew anything at all about Poe, you'd know that he was much more than a drunk," the professor said indignantly. "He was a seer, and he drank because the things he saw were beyond human comprehension. They were horrible, frightening things, and whenever he saw them, he drank himself into a stupor so he wouldn't have to see them anymore."

"How do you know what he saw?" Coletti asked skeptically. "He died a hundred years before you were born."

The professor looked at Coletti with a smug expression. "I've spent my life poring over every word Poe ever wrote. I've written a thousand-page dissertation on his life and career, and what I'm telling you is that Poe lived with visions that horrified him. That's why he loved poetry so much. In poems he could forget the pictures in his mind and paint a world where everyone could see the frost on a wave as it came in from the sea, or the dew on a flower in the morning. Unfortunately, Poe realized that the world didn't want beauty. The world wanted horror, so Poe unlocked the unspeakable things he'd seen in his mind, and he shared them with a world that was all too happy to receive them."

"So you're saying Poe was crazy?"

"I'm saying he was troubled," Workman said. "And it's no wonder. His father left when he was too young to remember. His mother died when he was two. He was taken in by family friends, but when he grew up to be a gambler and a drunk, he fell out of favor with his stepfather, dropped out of college, and got himself kicked out of West Point. He drank and wrote and failed repeatedly, and when he was twenty-seven, he married his thirteen-year-old cousin and moved in with the girl and her mother. So you're right, Detective. He was a drunk who spent most of his adult life broke, but Edgar Allan Poe was nothing less than a genius."

"What does any of that have to do with Mrs. Bailey being killed?"

The professor regarded the detective with a knowing smile. "Poe wrote about murder quite a bit. It was the subject he knew best. And when his detractors said he'd copied the German authors of his time by writing gothic tales of beauty and murder, Poe said, 'Terror is not of Germany, but of the soul, and I have reduced it to its likely source.'" Workman stopped smiling and looked Coletti in the eye. "The source of Poe's terror was his mind. It was there that he saw things that frightened him. He wrote about those things in graphic detail. And that has everything to do with what happened to Mrs. Bailey."

"What are you saying, Professor?"

"I'm saying that Clarissa was chasing one of Poe's visions—visions he shared in every horror story he ever wrote. 'The Fall of the House of Usher' was a vision. 'The Black Cat' was a vision. 'The Murders in the Rue Morgue' was a vision. But the vision that made him most famous was the one he saw at Fairgrounds Cemetery, where some believe he worked as a part-time gravedigger when things got lean with his writing. The vision he saw at Fairgrounds was immortalized in 'The Raven,' and that's the vision Clarissa was trying to find."

The professor got up and grabbed a leather-bound volume off a bookshelf near the couch, sat down next to Coletti, and opened the book to a well-worn page.

"Look here," the professor said, pointing to the book. "When he speaks of a chamber door, it's a metaphor for the death chamber. And here, where he talks of peering into darkness, he's speaking of looking into the future. And here, where the raven continually repeats the word 'nevermore,' Poe's saying he'll never see that vision again."

"And what exactly was this vision?" Coletti asked.

"It was a vision about unlocking the power of the human mind," Workman said excitedly. "That's why the raven sat on a bust of the goddess of wisdom. You see, Poe understood, even before science proved him right, that we only use a fraction of our brains. He knew that the human mind, when fully unleashed, could heal sickness, move mountains, even defeat death. Fortunately, Poe knew one more thing. He knew that he couldn't allow that knowledge to fall into the wrong hands, so he hid it somewhere in Fairgrounds Cemetery for another seer to find. Poe told us that seer's name right here in 'The Raven,' when he spoke of his lost love, Lenore."

"Okay, let's say your theory is true," Coletti said, his tone skeptical. "What, besides that poem, makes you think a woman named Lenore is the key to all this?"

Workman went back to the book, flipping through it

as he spoke. "Lenore appears in several of Poe's works, including a poem called 'Lenore.' There, Poe wrote that Lenore was young, beautiful, and rich, and that the friends who claimed to love her really didn't. In 'The Raven,' he wrote about Lenore again, only this time, there was a hidden message."

"So you're saying Lenore Wilkinson knows where this message is?"

"I'm saying that if such a message exists, Clarissa apparently believed that Mrs. Wilkinson was the only one who could find it."

"Suppose, just for argument's sake, Clarissa had already come across a clue that could help Lenore find this message. Would you be able to interpret it?"

"What do you mean?"

Coletti pulled out the picture of the cryptogram. "Clarissa had this tattooed on her neck a few days before meeting Lenore. Call me crazy, but she didn't seem like the tattoo type, which makes me think it's connected to finding Poe's message."

Workman looked at the picture, and the color drained from his face. He seemed to want to say something, but he wasn't quite sure what it was.

Coletti saw him struggling to find an acceptable version of the truth, so he decided to help him along. "You've seen this cryptogram before, haven't you?"

Workman got up and ran his hands through his sparse hair. Looking through the window at the students on the brick walkway outside, he spoke quietly. "Yes, I've seen it before. Supposedly it's an old cryptogram that Poe himself couldn't solve. I showed it to Clarissa and the others on a lark."

"Why do you think she had it tattooed on herself?" Coletti asked.

Workman left the window, sat back down on the couch, and smiled sadly. "Sometimes people get lost in things so they don't have to deal with their reality. With her marriage falling apart the way it was, maybe this thing with Poe became Clarissa's way to escape."

"It was more than an escape. She was so excited about Lenore's visit that she sent you an e-mail about it."

"Actually, she sent it to the manager of the cemetery," Workman said. "I was just copied on it. But clearly Clarissa was excited about Lenore's visit. I was excited, too."

"But not excited enough to be there to see if Lenore was the key to your theory," Coletti said, his eyes boring into him.

"I had departmental meetings this morning. I was planning to catch up with them later."

"Were you really?" Coletti asked cynically. "Professor, if I didn't know better, I'd think Clarissa believed in this stuff more than you do. I mean, for an academic of your stature to have a chance to see his theory proved is the opportunity of a lifetime. But you're telling me you missed it for a staff meeting."

"What I'm telling you is I was going to meet Clarissa and Lenore later," Workman said, sounding irritated.

"Or maybe you were there at the graveyard this

morning," Coletti said accusingly, "in which case you'll either need to get a lawyer or get a few people to vouch for your alibi."

The professor chuckled. "I assure you the entire English department can vouch for the fact that I was in a meeting this morning."

"Then maybe you can help me with something else," Coletti said. "I can account for four of the five people on that e-mail Clarissa sent, but I don't know who the fifth person is. Do you?"

"I can't say that I do."

"But I suppose the people on that e-mail aren't the only ones who believe in your theories about Poe," Coletti said.

"You're probably right. Unfortunately, I couldn't tell you how many believers there are. Could be ten, could be twenty, there might be hundreds."

"Have you ever taught your theories on Poe in a classroom environment?" Coletti asked.

"For the past year my History of English Literature course included a snippet on Poe, but other than that, I haven't done it."

"Is there a way to access a list of the students who took that course?"

"Sure, class registration is computerized, so the registrar has a list of every student who's taken my class over the past four years, along with their ID pictures. You should be able to request that list and get it fairly easily."

"How about people outside your class who might have learned of your theories?"

"My writings on the subject are public knowledge, so I have no way of knowing who else might have read them other than the people I know personally."

"Can you provide me with a list of those you know personally?"

"It's a short list—Violet Grant and Lily Thompkins."

"And do you think either of them would kill to get to the secret first?"

"I doubt it," Workman said. "They're history buffs, not killers."

"How about you?" Coletti asked. "Would you kill to get it?"

"No," Workman said firmly. "But I suppose someone who believed in my theories could've killed Clarissa, then killed Officer Smith to avoid being caught."

"Yes, I suppose they could have," Coletti said thoughtfully. "I guess the only question is why."

"You should study English literature, Detective. Then you'd know there are only a few reasons people kill: love, hate, fear, money, and power. In Clarissa's case, she was seeking the ultimate power, but obviously there was someone who wanted that power even more than she did."

Coletti got up from the couch, fished a card from his pocket, and handed it to the professor. "If you think of anything else, give me a call."

"I will," Workman said, taking the card and handing Coletti one of his own.

"And, Professor?" Coletti said as he walked out the

door. "Stick around. I'm sure I'll have more questions for you later."

Lenore sat silently in Mann's car as they drove away from the Poe house. She was trying to understand how she'd suddenly become so important.

She'd spent more than half her life being viewed as an outcast—the bastard daughter of a man who'd disgraced his entire family. After that, she'd spent four years toiling in college, only to find that academic success didn't fulfill her. Soon after, while in grad school, she met and married a man who had everything several times over, but even that didn't change the way she viewed herself.

For twenty-nine years Lenore had felt like a nobody. Learning that there were those who saw her as the key to a 150-year-old secret was overwhelming. She'd never been anyone special before.

"You all right?" Mann asked, glancing over at her as they turned onto Broad Street.

"I'm fine," she said. "Where are we going now?"

"To the safe house I told you about."

"Is Lieutenant Jackson going to be there?" she asked with a schoolgirl grin.

He shot an annoyed look in her direction, then checked the rearview mirror to make sure the cop in the unmarked car was still following them. "She's going to meet us later."

Lenore was quiet for a few minutes. "She seems to have real feelings for you," Lenore said as she gazed out the window. "I don't understand why you're so distant toward her."

"It's not for you to understand," he said curtly.

"I'm not trying to pry, but—"

"Then don't," he snapped.

"Okay," she said, sitting back in her seat. "I was just . . ."

She let the words trail off as she looked out the window and watched the city go by. She saw smiling college students walking among neighborhood residents whose faces looked worn out by poverty. She saw white-coated doctors in Crocs and scrubs near Temple University Hospital. She saw drug-addled people with hopelessness in their eyes.

Lenore saw a city where poverty and affluence, history and hope were locked in a strange sort of dance, repeatedly switching partners while the music played on. She'd heard once that the sound of Philadelphia was the happy and hopeful chorus of songs like "Love Train." But on trash-strewn streets where the distance between rich and poor looked insurmountable, all Lenore could hear was a dirge.

Suddenly, the silence in the car was broken by the sound of a buzzing phone. Lenore looked at Mann to see if it was his, because it was rare for her to receive cell phone calls. When Charlie didn't make a move, she fished her phone out of her purse.

"Hello?"

The voice on the other end of the line spoke so loudly that Mann could hear it. He glanced at her curiously, but

Lenore ignored him and bent forward as if that would some-how muffle the sound of her husband's shouting.

"Honey, you need to calm down," she said as the yell-ing continued. "John . . . John! John! Stop shouting at me!"

Charlie tried not to listen, but John Wilkinson was screaming so loudly that he couldn't help hearing snippets of the conversation. Apparently John had returned from Europe to find that his wife had witnessed a murder, but rather than asking if Lenore was all right, he was demand-ing that she come home. Charlie didn't understand all of it, but from what he could surmise, it had something to do with international investors who would frown upon Lenore's in-volvement in a murder.

"Listen, John," Lenore said when she was able to get a word in edgewise. "I can't do this right now."

There was more screaming, and when Charlie glanced at Lenore again, she had tears in her eyes.

"Why are you more concerned about your investors than you are about me?" she yelled while her husband con-tinued to rant. "Why can't you, just one time, put me first? Do you even care about what I've been through? Does it matter to you that I could've been killed in that cemetery?"

Lenore knew her husband didn't hear a word she'd said. He was too busy trying to shout her down, just as he always did. But this conversation was different. He'd crossed an invisible line that Lenore had finally drawn for herself.

"Shut up and listen to me, John!" she yelled, and mi-raculously, her husband did as he was told.

Lenore was shaking with anger. Decorum was no

longer the priority, and for the first time in a long time, neither were her husband's desires.

"I've called you five or six times since all this happened, and you ignored my calls, just like you always do."

Her husband tried to interrupt her, but Lenore wouldn't let him.

"No, I'm talking now, John, and you're listening!" she shouted as tears streamed down her face. "I've tried to be a good wife to you. I've never used you, never crowded you, never taken more than I've been given. I've loved you, John, probably a lot more than you deserved. And for you to be callous enough to call me after what I've been through and talk to me about your *investors*—"

Mann could hear him trying to backpedal, but Lenore was having none of it.

"You know, John, I wasn't sure that I should come to Philadelphia. I thought it was selfish of me to come here looking to do something for myself. But you've shown me what real selfishness is. Thanks for the lesson."

She disconnected the call, and in a few moments, the phone began buzzing again. Lenore hit the power button to turn the phone off and threw it in her pocketbook. Then she sat back and looked out the window with her arms folded.

Charlie glanced at her once again. He almost felt sorry for her. "Are you all—"

"It's not for you to understand. Isn't that what you told me?"

"Okay," Charlie said nonchalantly, thankful that he didn't have to talk.

As they turned off Broad at Pike Street and headed north on Germantown Avenue, they both tried to get their minds off their relationships. Mann focused on the road ahead. Lenore stared out the window and wondered what it would be like to live in a place such as this.

There were barber shops and churches, restaurants and discount stores, and women wearing everything from Muslim garb to low-cut blouses. The men were dressed in boots and work clothes. The streets were dressed in discarded trash, and, mixed in amongst the teenage boys with their underwear exposed, there were children.

They laughed as they ran along the sidewalk near the high school football field that bordered Hunting Park Avenue. They jumped rope along the residential strip near the train station called Wayne Junction. They rode bikes and skateboards on cracked, uneven sidewalks. They seemed to live happy lives, even as they frolicked in places where death was always close.

Mann drove through a block of ramshackle houses where a waving American flag looked oddly out of place, and Lenore read the names of drug-war casualties on telephone poles with dingy teddy bear memorials.

They rode farther, and the storefront churches that dotted nearly every block of Germantown Avenue gave way to storefront mosques. A tiny strip mall was surrounded by a low stone wall, and as Lenore stared out the window at the people, the people stared back, curious as to why she was so interested.

"Where's this safe house?" Lenore asked Mann as they passed yet another barber shop.

"You're the psychic," Mann said. "You tell me."

She turned on him with all the attitude she could muster. "What is your problem?"

Charlie Mann glanced at her before returning his attention to the road. "I don't like people who get in my business."

"Well, from the way you treat your girlfriend, it looks like your business is a lot like mine. For that reason alone, I would've thought you'd be a little nicer to me after you overheard my conversation with John."

"And I would've thought we'd all get together, hold hands, and sing 'Kum ba Yah.' But since people keep killing each other, I keep coming to work."

Lenore didn't respond. Instead she looked at him closely for the first time. She saw his rounded nose and chiseled jaw, his ample lips and chocolate skin. She saw something else beneath his handsome face, too. She saw that he was hurt.

"You don't like coming to work anymore, do you?"

He laughed. "Is that one of those broad statements you psychics make so people think you're for real?"

"I don't call myself a psychic," Lenore said. "But I know when I see someone who's hurting."

"What makes you think I'm hurting?"

Lenore didn't answer. Instead, she stared out the window, watching as the neighborhood changed from residential to commercial and back again. They passed Germantown High School and the First United Methodist Church. They passed the Johnson House, a former stop for runaway slaves on the Underground Railroad. And with each historical landmark she saw, Lenore felt the triumph and heartbreak and pain and hope of those who'd traveled this road. None of her feelings were stronger than the ones that took hold of her as they approached Cliveden, a centuries-old estate near the site of a Revolutionary War battle.

As Lenore looked through the wrought-iron gate at the grounds surrounding the mansion, the brilliant light of artillery flashed in her mind. She reached for her temples and squeezed to dull the pain, but the sound of charging horses grew louder as images from the battle filled her consciousness. Muskets flashed. Blood poured. Bodies fell. Then, suddenly, she saw a war of a different type.

The uniforms were black instead of red and blue, and while the soldiers were spurred on by drugs and false belief, the deaths were all too real. A red-haired man lay dead on a train platform. Blood-spattered pews played host to twisted bodies. An angel's wings stretched toward a hundred-foot ceiling. The final image she saw was her sister, falling as a bullet struck her head. A dark face was on the other side of the gunshot. That face belonged to Charlie Mann, and the grief belonged to him, too.

As Lenore fell farther into the cavern that was her

vision, the car stopped with a jolt. Charlie Mann's voice came softly at first, like an echo, but as the cloud lifted from her mind and she came back to the moment, she could feel his hands gripping her shoulders.

"Mrs. Wilkinson!" he shouted as he shook her. "Lenore!"

She heard him, though barely, so Charlie Mann shook her once again. Her shallow breathing became stronger, and the blackness in her mind gave way to a sea of colors, and she awakened feeling as if she'd seen the joy and pain of many lives, including Charlie's.

"Are you okay?" he asked. He had pulled the car over to the curb. "You looked like you blacked out for a minute there."

"No, I just saw something," she said as she looked into his face. "I'm fine."

"Are you sure?" he asked with genuine concern.

She nodded and ran her hands through her hair.

He looked at her again, just to be certain she was all right. Then he pulled back into traffic, with the other car following close behind.

"I never answered your question," she said weakly as they bumped along the cobblestone street.

"What question?"

She closed her eyes and leaned back against her seat. "You asked what made me think you were hurting. Do you still want the answer?"

They both knew he didn't, but after a few seconds of silence, Lenore continued.

"I think you're hurting because you never imagined that being a cop meant you'd actually have to kill people."

Her words catapulted him back to the Angel of Death investigation. He didn't know or care how much Lenore knew. He just wanted her to let it go.

"The department exonerated me for what I did," he said, his tone defensive. "So let's just drop it."

"Dropping it won't erase the fact that you're still looking for forgiveness," she said. "Especially if you can't forgive yourself."

Mann was angry, then defiant, and finally, sad. He wasn't sure how to handle those feelings, or if he wanted to handle them at all. "Your theory's interesting," he said as they sped along the avenue, "but how I do my job is none of your business."

She turned to him with a puzzled expression. "Of *course* it's my business. You killed my sister."

Mann pursed his lips as grief crept up from the place where he'd hidden it from everyone, including himself.

"Do you want to talk about it?" she asked with a compassion Mann hadn't expected.

"I've already talked to a counselor about it," he said quietly. "They make you do that after police shootings."

"And I'm guessing you told that counselor what he wanted to hear," she said. "Then you told Sandy and everyone else that you're fine. But you're not fine, are you? A man like you doesn't just forget about taking a life. He sits in it, hurts from it, and unless he talks about it, he dies a little bit every day."

"What do you mean, 'a man like me'?"

"I mean the kind of man who knows what it's like to lose someone."

Mann's eyes grew vacant as he thought of losing his father to a murderer's bullet. He wondered, each time he thought of what he'd done, if he was a murderer, too. Lenore could sense that, so she tried to give him a measure of peace.

"I need you to know something," she said as he made himself look at the road ahead. "I need you to know that I forgive you for what happened to Mary. I don't know if that'll make any difference in how you feel about it, but I think that's one of the reasons I'm here—to tell you that you're forgiven."

Mann hesitated, unsure how to respond. He thought of the long nights he'd spent with Sandy after the shootings, and how she'd never been able to reach him. He thought of talking to the counselor and never feeling relief. He thought of consulting his mother and not feeling better. And yet, here was this woman he barely knew, speaking the words that caused the weight to slowly lift from his shoulders.

There were only two words left for him to say, and he spoke them in a strong, clear voice. "Thank you."

A few minutes later, they drove past a black gate and into a driveway on a quiet street at the city's outer edge. The tree-lined community was known as Chestnut Hill. It was a haven of sorts, where the people were fiercely liberal and the property values were extremely high.

This community, with its quaint shops, suburban feel, and fairytale dwellings, was the last place anyone would look for a murder witness.

As the cops who'd followed them emerged from the other car and Charlie Mann led Lenore into the house, Mann took extra care to make sure she was properly protected. She gratefully accepted his help.

Their truce was real but tenuous. Mann was thankful that she'd given him some peace, but he was wary of her gift. Lenore felt odd in the presence of the man who'd killed her sister, yet she was strangely drawn to him.

As Mann set her up in the safe house, they each knew they'd have to learn to accept their dependence on each other. Lenore needed Mann for protection, and Mann needed Lenore for truth.

Nearly everything else in their lives was in doubt. They'd both seen enough to know that. But amidst the uncertainty, they were sure of one thing. The killer was out there, and eventually he'd have to surface.

CHAPTER 9

A pale man wearing a Phillies cap over his jet-black hair walked out into the cool afternoon and stood on the curb near a Fairmount Avenue apartment building. The art museum area, which bordered the park, had undergone a tremendous rebirth in the past twenty years. The juvenile jail had given way to plans for a museum. Poverty had been replaced by affluence.

Here, in a neighborhood filled with condos and custom townhouses, colorful shops and cafés, no one questioned the killer's presence on the street. After replacing his nineteenth-century greatcoat with a cap, gray sweats, and worn running shoes, he looked as if he belonged. The neighbors couldn't have known that he'd just left a room carved out from the soil of a graveyard. They couldn't have known that his stony stare was the heartless gaze of a killer. They weren't close enough to know that he smelled of blood and damp earth. They only knew that he appeared to be normal, and that was enough for them.

Standing less than a mile from the spot in the park where he'd murdered Officer Frank Smith after eliminating Clarissa Bailey, he could still see dozens of police cars blocking the entrance to Kelly Drive. But in spite of their presence, the killer stood his ground, because here, he was just one of the anonymous faces that traversed the pristine streets near the Philadelphia Museum of Art.

He thought back to the text he'd received earlier, and he patted his pocket to make sure he'd remembered to bring the phone. As much as he wanted to rebel against the order, he'd spent too much time formulating his plan to deviate from it. He would proceed to phase 2 as planned, and he'd work within the established time frame.

It was odd the way things had come about. The murder of his wife the year before had created in him an unbearable grief. He thought if he could learn about death, if perhaps he could understand it better, the grief would subside. Thus began his morbid fascination with death. He read about it in books, researched it online, and went to a mentor who sat on the Fairgrounds board to ask if he could volunteer at the cemetery. He was given three weeks to do so, and over the course of that time, the grief did anything but go away. In fact, it transformed into outright rage. He didn't know if there was anyone who could understand how he felt. That is, until he found the raven.

It was in a remote area of the cemetery, near a three-story-high piece of rock that stood at least fifty yards from the nearest grave. The bird was standing over its fallen mate, its demeanor defensive and its manner uncertain. Like all ravens, this one had mated for life, and when its mate died, the raven didn't know what to do. The man understood that, and so he took his anger and grief and focused it on a new goal. He would train the raven to live again, and in doing so, the man would learn to live again, too.

He'd heard that ravens had guarded the Tower of London for centuries and that a series of keepers had trained the birds to do so. Knowing that ravens are dangerous carnivores who can pluck out a human's eye if provoked, he researched the trainers' methods and adopted them as his own.

The day after he spotted the raven, the man returned with all manner of food for the bird—from eggs and cow livers to mice. He left the food near the area where the dead mate lay and watched from a distance. The raven refused to eat. The man repeated his trek for a second day. Still, the raven refused to eat. On the third day, the man brought a different type of food. It was the heart of a lamb. The raven ate. From that point on, the raven regained his strength, and it was almost as if he'd been resurrected.

When his time volunteering at the cemetery was completed, the man continued to come back to see the raven. Over the next year, the raven and the man bonded. There were disagreements, as evidenced by the deep gouge the raven had inflicted on the man's left forearm, but over time, they both came to understand what they needed in order to live again. They needed the power to overcome whatever they faced, and when the man recalled Dr. Workman's theory, he trained the raven to help him get that power. He trained the raven to help him get Lenore.

Now, as he stood on Fairmount Avenue, fresh from the execution of the first part of his plan, the man who'd trained the raven placed his hands on his hips and twisted his body, preparing for an afternoon jog. Cars passed by, and their drivers cast perfunctory glances, but none of them was suspicious. In their minds, if the man could afford the luxury of a midday jog in one of the city's most trendy areas, he was above reproach.

As the dome lights from nearby police cars glowed red and blue in the crisp autumn air, the killer continued to warm up for his short jog, bending his neck to the left until the bones cracked loudly, then bending it to the right until they cracked again. Grabbing his left foot, he pulled his leg toward his back, and did the same with his right. Then he bent and touched his toes, holding the pose for a full ten seconds before plucking an iPod from his pocket and sticking the earplugs in his ears.

With another glance at the police cars that were gathered just blocks away, he turned and jogged east on Fairmount Avenue, running toward nearby Eastern State Penitentiary, the long-closed prison whose thick, castlelike walls had once housed Al Capone.

He jogged past the gas station and the water ice stand, beyond the bars and the restaurants, and as the autumn breeze whispered in the air around him, he turned up the volume on his iPod and listened intently to his favorite poem.

"The Raven" had opened the door to a whole new world for him. It was a world where his mind could go beyond any boundaries. It was a world where he could achieve anything he could think. It was a world where he could dominate everything around him. He simply needed to find the woman who would lead him to Poe's secret.

He listened to the poem while he ran, his heart pounding as the reader's voice rose and fell with the cadence of each verse. He listened to the words of love and hate, life and death, good and evil. His breath came faster as he listened to each stanza, and every time he heard the name Lenore, he got excited. Each time he heard the tortured, mournful words of love and loss, he felt energized. Each time he thought of the true meaning of that poem, he moved faster. By the time he reached the final verse, which spoke of souls and shadows, he felt almost as if his own soul had come out from the shadows. He felt almost as if he, like the raven, could fly.

With Poe's words reverberating in his mind, he ran as the sour smell of damp earth emanated from his skin like sweat. The vacant look in his jet-black eyes seemed to harden with each step he took.

He knew Workman's theories intimately. He'd read all the works the professor had written and had followed those who followed him. That was how he knew that Lenore Wilkinson was the seer they'd all sought. Now that she'd come to Philadelphia, he was nearing the end of his race. But Clarissa Bailey and the cop who'd gotten in his way weren't the only obstacles he'd have to clear. There were others, and if he was to have the chance to reap the rewards he so desperately sought, they'd have to be eliminated as well.

For that reason, he ran, unconcerned with the police

who were seeking him. He ran, unafraid of the fate that awaited him. He ran, believing that he could traverse the quarter mile to his waiting car without incident. This whole thing, after all, was about the power of the mind. If he believed in his mind that he could make it, then reality should bend to his will.

As he ran toward the car that would take him to his next destination, he passed the walls of Eastern State, the prison whose history of solitary confinement had been blamed for driving inmates insane. The killer didn't know he was losing his own tenuous grip on reality. He only knew that he was going to find out what he could from the man who'd convinced him to believe.

He looked up in the sky above him and saw a familiar sight, circling and soaring on the autumn breeze. The raven's wings were extended to their full four feet. He circled effortlessly, his wings capturing the power of the air. The man almost smiled at the sight of the raven, watching over him as the man had once watched over the bird. He saw the raven and in that split second, he forgot about the danger he faced in being outside. In the next instant, he was reminded.

A black Ford slowed as it passed by, and the driver cast a long, lingering glance in his direction. Everyone had heard the description by now. The killer was a white man, tall and powerful with jet-black hair and eyes to match. His skin was extremely pale, he had a mustache, and he was dressed in a black coat with the wide lapels and the numerous buttonholes of a time gone by.

The woman in the car was perceptive—too much so. When she saw him, she slowed and took a second look. This jogger seemed to have everything but the mustache and the clothing, so she stopped and looked again. Pulling over and putting the car in park, she looked away from the jogger and reached for the cell phone in her pocketbook on the passenger seat. Before she could pull it out to call the police, her driver's-side door flew open. The man was upon her.

He punched her once, and the bone in her nose crunched into a dozen pieces. Thick maroon-colored blood poured down her face and back into her throat. She was choking on it. Gasping for breath, she reached up to try to fend him off, but he was much too strong. With one powerful hand, he grabbed her throat and squeezed until her windpipe collapsed. Still holding her throat, he pushed her aside and climbed into the driver's seat. With the other hand he closed the door to the car. He pushed the woman down into the space between the glove compartment and the seat, looked up into the sky, and saw the raven dip his left wing into the autumn breeze and fly north.

The killer put the car in drive and turned north as well. He wouldn't need his car after all.

Charlie Mann hung up the phone after placing the last of his calls to headquarters. Then he cracked the blinds, looked out onto the tree-lined street, and watched a breeze blow red and orange leaves toward the car where the cops sat watching the front of the house.

There were only eight houses on the entire block. They were all huge, with winding driveways and expansive lawns, shade trees and two-car garages. There were no white picket fences here. Instead, there were huge black gates that hid abusers and drunks and unhappy wives. Each morning, when the gates were thrown open, the denizens of this street donned the masks they wore in their daily lives and told themselves that everything was all right.

If you could hide whole lives in such a place, it made perfect sense to hide witnesses there, too. The department had done so for years, and today was no different.

Mann shut the blinds after looking once more at the patrolmen who were parked in a car on the driveway. Then he turned from the window and saw Lenore sitting on the couch watching round-the-clock coverage of the murders. He walked across the hardwood floor and sat down on a chair across from her.

"How are you holding up?" he asked.

"I've been better."

"Yeah, me, too," he said, glancing at the television and seeing Clarissa Bailey's face onscreen once more. "Doesn't it bother you to watch that?"

She looked at him and smiled nervously. "I'd be lying if I said it didn't."

"So why are you doing it?"

Lenore sat there for a moment, searching for the words to express what she was feeling. "I guess I'm trying to understand my place in it all. I didn't understand that cryptogram, I didn't sense anything at the cemetery, but after hearing the ranger back at the Poe house, I feel like I'm supposed to be able to see something in all this."

"Maybe you're trying too hard."

"Or maybe I'm not trying hard enough," she said with a forlorn sigh. "I've always had trouble seeing things that are too close to me."

Mann looked at her curiously. "Why do you think that is?"

"Because it's easier to look at other people than it is to look inside. I think that's true for everybody."

"Yeah, but we're not talking about everybody right now."

Lenore knew he was right, but she didn't have an answer—at least, not one that she wanted to give.

Mann watched her for a few seconds. Then he looked off into the distance. "I would love to have a gift like yours," he said with more than a touch of envy in his voice. "To be able to look into people's lives and see the truth."

"It's more like a curse than a gift," Lenore said. "The truth is the ugliest thing in the world, and when you look in a person's face and see it, sometimes you just want to run and hide."

"Is that why you're hiding from yourself?" Mann asked.

Lenore looked at him and smirked. "I think you're the one who's the psychic."

"No, I'm just an observer. That's my job as a detective. I look at a set of facts and come up with a theory that fits."

"So what have you observed about me?"

"You want the truth?"

"I already told you the truth is ugly. Why would I want it?" Lenore asked with a grin. Her smile quickly faded when Mann began to speak.

"I've only got a few facts about you, but here they are," he said soberly. "Your father cheated on his wife with your mother, and because of that, you had a hard time in the town where you grew up. You can see things that other people can't, but you use that gift reluctantly, if at all. You're twenty-nine and you claim not to know who you are outside of your connections to other people. One of those people is a man who married you but doesn't seem to care for you. Another was your sister, who happened to be a serial killer. The fact that you came here to learn about a woman who didn't even like you is amazing to me. The fact that you stayed says even more."

Mann stopped and looked at Lenore as tears streamed down her cheeks. He felt no guilt for making her cry. At least the tears were honest.

"Then there's the biggest fact of all," he said, staring at her as he spoke. "Clarissa Bailey believed you could unlock the truth about Poe, and when she found you, someone killed her."

Lenore wiped her eyes and whispered the only question that mattered. "So based on the facts you have," she said in a raspy voice, "what's your theory?"

"I think you've always blamed yourself for the way Mary and her family treated you and your mother. You figured if you came here and found out some things about your sister, it might help you stop hating yourself. But when you got here and learned that you might actually have value, it scared you. Now you don't know what to do."

There was a long pause. Then she wiped her eyes again and looked at him. "So that's it, huh?"

"For the moment."

"And you're expecting more facts, I suppose?"

"Of course I am. Until we solve the crime, there's always more to learn."

"I guess I have more to learn, too," Lenore said. "Based on your facts, I live a pretty pitiful life."

"No, you live a life that a lot of women would kill to have. It's just that . . ." He let the sentence trail off.

"If you're trying to find a nice way to talk about John, don't bother. You've already said what you thought."

"So am I wrong to think that?"

Lenore rolled her eyes. "You can't judge him based on one phone call."

Mann laughed. "It's not just the phone call. He should be here right now."

"How could he be here when he doesn't know where I am?"

"He would find you if he really wanted to," Mann said, getting up and walking over to the window. "A man who really cares enough doesn't let his woman go if he can help it."

Sandy pulled up in her black Dodge Charger and stopped at the yellow barricades that stretched across the entrance to

Fairgrounds Cemetery. One of the cops who was posted there leaned into her open window with a flirty smile. His demeanor changed immediately when she flashed her badge.

"Go ahead, LT," he said in reference to her rank as he moved one of the barricades aside for her.

She smiled her thanks and drove up to the tarmac that had earlier been occupied by dozens of police cars. Now there were only two. Their dome lights flashed in the late-afternoon light. Sandy parked behind one of the cars and waved a greeting at the cop inside.

As she got out of the car and walked toward the spot where Clarissa's body had been found, she felt relieved to be in the place where it had all started. In a strange way, it helped her to deal with the fact that her friend Smitty was gone. If following orders meant helping to find the murderer who'd taken him far too soon, she was anxious to fall in line.

To that end, she'd called the Philadelphia Zoo as she drove to the cemetery from North Philly. She was trying to find out what she could about nesting locations for ravens. The zookeeper told her that the zoo hadn't kept ravens in 150 years. He did, however, tell her that ravens nest in cliff ledges, in cavities, or in trees, and he warned her that ravens are extremely territorial and secretive about their nests.

"Whatever you do, don't get too close," he'd said.

Sandy had thanked him and hung up before placing a call to the cemetery manager. He was all too anxious to be helpful after the debacle that morning. They had arranged to meet at Fairgrounds in twenty minutes. Sandy had made it there in ten. She took the opportunity to look around on her own.

She walked slowly along the grounds, watching as the afternoon sun glowed orange on the gray stone monuments. She looked up at the trees and down at the grass and watched as colorful leaves blew in circles. She watched the trees bend with a stiff breeze and felt goosebumps rise up on her skin.

She walked above the graves of the cemetery's long-dead residents and wondered if they knew their eternal home was now the center of attention. She looked at the hand-chiseled names on the mausoleums and the likenesses of the dead that had been carved into headstones. She tried to compare them to the makeshift memorials that lined too many Philadelphia streets, but it was more contrast than comparison. In a city where a quarter of the people lived in poverty, having one's life memorialized in anything more expensive than spray paint was unimaginable, and the opulence of a Fairgrounds burial was out of reach for most.

Sandy didn't want to resent the display of wealth, but she couldn't help thinking that some of those who were buried there had built their fortunes on war and slavery, pestilence and misery. But they were dead now. They deserved to rest in peace, and as Sandy strolled along, she kept that thought in mind.

But Sandy wasn't there for the dead. She was there for the living, and as she walked up the graveyard's incline while looking down on Kelly Drive below, she observed every detail of her surroundings. She watched as shadows crept over the headstones. She observed the trees growing from the rock face at the graveyard's west end, their exposed roots clinging to earth and stone while their trunks pointed across Kelly Drive.

She turned from the gate and walked up and over the hills that were dotted with every kind of grave marker imaginable. As she did so, she thought of the pigeons in North Philly and how they'd repeatedly come back to the same place for their daily bread. She hoped to learn if anyone had observed the raven doing the same.

"Lieutenant Jackson?" a voice called from behind her.

Sandy turned to find the cemetery manager walking across the graveyard. He looked frail, nervous, and small. She could tell he was anxious about something, but he tried to put on a happy face. It didn't work.

"I'm Mr. Vickers," he said, reaching out to shake her hand. "We spoke a few minutes ago. I understand you're working with Detective Coletti."

"Yes, that's right."

"Did he get the e-mail I forwarded to him earlier today?"

"Yes, that was very helpful," Sandy said pleasantly. "We were hoping you could help us with something else as well."

"Yes, I meant to ask you about that before you hung up. I wasn't sure if I'd heard you right. Just so I'm clear on what you were asking, you wanted to know about a raven?"

"Yes, we think there are ravens nesting nearby. Have you ever seen anything like that here?"

Vickers smiled nervously. "Are there ravens connected to the murder investigation now?"

"We don't know, Mr. Vickers. That's what we're trying to find out."

He looked away, and his face turned beet-red as he began to breathe faster. "Well, as you can imagine, we see a lot of strange things here. It's a cemetery, so nothing surprises us."

"Does that mean you've seen ravens here?" Sandy asked.

Vickers had an answer, but clearly he wasn't sure if he should say it. His nose started to twitch, and his eyes danced back and forth. He appeared to be weighing the benefits of answering honestly.

"It's a yes-or-no question, Mr. Vickers," Sandy said, her facial expression rapidly changing from cordial to menacing. "Before you decide how to answer, you need to know that this is a murder investigation. A police officer who was a friend of mine was killed today, and I'm upset about it. You can play with me if you want, but I wouldn't recommend it. Now, let's start again. Are there ravens nesting nearby or not?"

He licked his lips nervously and looked in her eyes. He could tell that she was serious. It was time for him to get serious, too. "There used to be two of them, right over there in that rock," he said, pointing to a cliff on the far end of the cemetery. "They lived in a crevice where they could look out, but it was very hard to see in. The female died about a year ago, and the male looked like he was on his way, too. But a young man who volunteered here stepped in and nursed the raven back to health. The raven still roosts in that rock."

"Do you remember that volunteer's name?"

"No. He was only with us for a few weeks—tending the grounds, helping with tours, that sort of thing."

"What did he look like?"

"Young white guy, kinda tall. He had blond hair, I think."

"How do we get in touch with him?"

Vickers began to look nervous again. "I'd really rather not get involved in this. The guy was referred to us by one of our major donors, and—"

"Would you rather get involved in obstruction of justice?"

The manager hesitated.

"Who's the donor, Mr. Vickers?" Sandy said forcefully.

He looked around like a trapped animal. When finally he looked Sandy in the eye, he had no choice but to answer the question. "His name is Irving Workman. He's a professor at Penn."

CHAPTER 10

The doorbell rang at the safe house. Mann looked out the blinds at the officers who were posted outside in the car. One of them nodded, and Mann opened the door.

Coletti, looking disheveled and worn, rushed inside. "Where is she?"

Mann pointed to the living room. "She's in there. What's wrong?"

"Nothing yet. I just need to talk to her."

Coletti hurried into the living room and stopped cold when he saw Lenore sitting in front of the television. Her eyes were red and puffy, and her facial expression was sad. Coletti looked back at Mann, who was walking into the living room behind him.

"I see you've broken our witness's heart already," Coletti deadpanned. "You work fast."

"She doesn't need me to break her heart," Mann said. "She's got a husband who's pretty good at it."

Coletti turned to her as the news droned on in the

background. "So you've talked to your husband? Is he on his way?"

"Not exactly. We had an argument earlier, and I hung up on him."

"Well, you might want to call him back," Coletti said, sitting down and looking at her with a grave expression. "He'll want to know what this is about, and there are things you'll want to tell him."

"If you're talking about the vision Poe supposedly wrote about in 'The Raven,' we heard about it when we went to the Poe house."

"Yes, but you're at the center of it: there are people who would kill for whatever the secret is, and we don't know who those people are," Coletti said. "If I were your husband, I'd want to know that."

"Then I guess I should've married you," Lenore said.

Coletti looked in her eyes and saw the heartbreak. For an awkward moment he considered asking about it. He didn't think it would help, though, so he asked her about something that might.

"We've been trying to reach your father," Coletti said. "We have reason to believe Clarissa Bailey might've been in touch with him."

Lenore looked confused, even worried, but it passed quickly. "Good luck finding my father," she said bitterly. "I haven't talked to him in years."

For a moment, neither said anything. Mann jumped in to fill the silence.

"So I'm assuming you found out what this is all about

when you went to Penn," he said, looking at Coletti expectantly.

"Yeah," Coletti said, tearing his eyes away from Lenore. "It all stems from Professor Irving Workman's theory that Poe's hidden message could unlock the power of the mind. Apparently there are others who believe the theory, too, but Workman says he doesn't know who they are."

"I can see a few crazy conspiracy theorists believing something like that," said a bewildered Mann. "But why would someone like Clarissa Bailey believe it?"

"That's the same question Clarissa's husband had. But it's not like they got this off the Internet. Workman is an established academic at an Ivy League institution. He's an authority on Poe, and for someone like Clarissa Bailey, who was a huge supporter of the arts and writing especially, Workman would be a voice worth listening to. And she wasn't alone. She was in a group called the Daughters of Independence. The rest of the group embraced Workman's theories, too."

"What kind of group is it?" Lenore asked as she glanced at the television.

Coletti checked his notes again. "They're involved in historic preservation. They were working on bringing the Gravedigger's Ball to an eighteenth-century mansion they maintain in the park. The two other ladies in the group were Violet Grant and Lily Thompkins. I've got calls into both of them, but I wanted to stop here first to tell you what I'd learned from Workman."

Mann looked at Coletti. "So did you think Workman was credible?"

Coletti's mind went through all the cases he'd seen over the course of his thirty-one-year career. The people he'd interviewed, the witnesses he'd talked to, the suspects he'd encountered. He settled on the one case he knew Mann would understand, and he started his answer there.

"We've both seen people commit murder because they believed in something or someone they shouldn't have. This is different. Workman didn't come off like a guy trying to get disciples. He just seemed like a harmless old nerd who was excited about his work. I will say this, though. Ellison Bailey didn't like the things Workman was telling his wife, and even though I wouldn't trust Ellison as far as I could throw him, I think Workman was holding something back."

"So what does your gut tell you?" Mann asked.

Coletti opened his mouth to answer, but it was Lenore whose gut spoke first.

"Whoever did this is looking for the kind of peace he couldn't find on his own," she said in a faraway voice. "He's lost something he can never get back, but he thinks he can replace it if he can find what Poe discovered at Fairgrounds."

She looked at Mann and then Coletti. "The man who killed Clarissa understands this whole thing in a way that not even Workman has figured out. The raven isn't just a poem for this guy. The raven is real and—"

Lenore wanted to go on, but she stopped when a familiar image popped up on the television screen. Surrounded by cameras and microphones, he was as dashing as always. His wavy brown hair was accented by a touch of gray at each temple. His eyes were an icy shade of blue, and his clean-shaven face was fixed in an intense expression. In his tailored suit and handmade shoes, John Wilkinson was a man who was accustomed to attention, and as he walked through New York's JFK International airport with his lawyer at his side, attention was what he received.

"Mr. Wilkinson, is it true that your wife witnessed the murder of Clarissa Bailey in Philadelphia this morning?" a reporter shouted.

"Do you know if she's cooperating with the police?" yelled another.

"Do you have any idea who the Gravedigger might be?" a third reporter asked.

The cameras flashed and the questions intensified, and John Wilkinson continued through the airport, his eyes straight ahead and his mouth set in a thin, determined line. When he'd had enough of the questions, he stopped in mid-stride, tightened the knot on his silk tie, and turned to his attorney.

Lenore watched along with millions as her husband allowed another man to state what he should have said for himself.

"Mr. Wilkinson is very concerned for his wife," the lawyer said, speaking quickly and with a distinct New York accent. "While he certainly offers his condolences to the families affected by this morning's events in Philadelphia, his wife's well-being is extremely important. For that reason, Mr. Wilkinson will have no further comment on the investigation. He's traveling to Philadelphia as a concerned husband, and he asks that his privacy be respected."

As cameras trailed John Wilkinson and his lawyer until they disappeared from sight, Mann looked at Lenore, who turned away from the TV looking troubled.

"You look like you don't want to see him," Coletti said.

"It's not that I don't want to see him," she said, looking back at the television screen. "It's just that he wants me to leave Philadelphia, and John can be rather convincing when he wants to be."

"If you don't want to leave, then don't," Mann said.

"It's not that simple," Lenore said.

She looked at the television screen as her husband's image was replaced by that of a host who promised ongoing coverage of the Gravedigger murders. Then the newscast went to a commercial.

As an actor blathered on about the latest miracle product, Lenore's mind ran through a series of images: her husband at the airport, the ranger at the Poe house, the raven at the cemetery, the poem in Clarissa Bailey's hand.

"I can't leave," she said, almost to herself. "Not until I find out why."

"Why what?" Mann asked as Coletti looked on.

"Out of all the Lenores in the world," she said, her face filled with wonder, "why would Clarissa Bailey choose me?"

Coletti's cell phone vibrated as he contemplated that question. He saw the number and connected the call immediately, then listened as Sandy Jackson gave him news that promised to get them closer to an answer.

"I was right about Workman holding something back," he told Mann and Lenore after hanging up. "He knew a man who worked with a raven at Fairgrounds. In fact, Workman was the one who brought the guy to the cemetery."

It was three thirty when Mann, Lenore, and Coletti left the safe house. Mann took two officers with him as he transported Lenore back to headquarters, and Coletti traveled alone as he raced to Penn in the hopes of finding the professor.

His engine hummed and his siren pulsed as he traversed the bumpy cobblestones of Germantown with his mind moving as quickly as the car. He thought of the theory the professor had espoused, the cryptogram they needed to solve, and the killer they had to catch. Workman was the key to all of it, and Coletti needed to get to him if he was to have any hope of piecing together the puzzle.

Coletti dove in and out of traffic, his dome lights splashing red and blue against the late afternoon as he turned onto the always-crowded expressway and sped along the shoulder. He fumbled with his cell phone, swerving once or twice while trying to dial Workman's office. The phone just rang, and by the third time Coletti pushed redial, it was clear that the professor wasn't in.

He dialed the main number and asked for the registrar's office, praying that they'd handled his request to pull the names and pictures of the students Workman had taught over the past year.

By the time the phone rang for the fifth time, Coletti was on the exit ramp at Grays Ferry Avenue, barreling through traffic as he headed for the university. He was about to disconnect the call when a young woman picked up.

"University of Pennsylvania registrar's office," she said, sounding annoyed.

"This is Detective Mike Coletti," he yelled over his blaring sirens. "I requested some records from Professor Workman's class a couple hours ago. I was told I'd have them by the end of the day."

"I'm sorry," the woman said, sounding rushed. "I don't see anything like that in the office, and—"

"Please check again," Coletti said as he pulled up at Thirty-fourth and Walnut. "I'm on my way in."

Coletti's car screeched to a halt, and he ran into the building where the registrar's office was located while dialing Professor Workman's office once again. There was no answer. Bounding up the steps to the second floor and through the glass doors of the registrar's office, Coletti stumbled to the desk and held up a single finger as he tried to catch his breath.

The young woman behind the counter watched with a look of concern as Coletti bent down, put his hands on his knees, and tried to pant his way through a formal introduction.

"I'm . . . Detective . . . Coletti," he said, huffing and puffing between each word.

"Do you need a glass of water or something?" she asked, coming out from behind the counter.

Coletti shook his head. Then he put one elbow on the

counter to balance himself as he tried to reach into his pocket to show her his badge.

"No need to show me that," she said, reaching over the counter and handing him an envelope. "We put together the information you asked for, so if you want to sit down for a moment and look through it, that's fine. You can stay as long as you'd like, sir."

Coletti hated it when young women called him sir. It made him feel a thousand years old. Of course, he looked about that age at the moment. Running was no longer his strength.

"I appreciate the offer," he said, standing up straight as the young woman gazed at him with a look of serious concern. "But I really can't stay. I need to find Professor Workman."

"Okay, well, let me call over to the English department for you, sir. I won't be a minute."

Coletti stood at the counter and opened the envelope, looking through the names and pictures inside. At first glance, none of them looked like a match. Not one of them had black hair, and though it was difficult to tell from headshots, only two of the men looked like they were big enough to be the Gravedigger.

He put the pictures back into the envelope and watched as the young woman filled a plastic cup at the water cooler. He grinned with appreciation as she bent slightly. Her tight sweater and snug skirt showed off curves and shapely legs that were accented by a pair of patent leather pumps.

She came back to the counter with a fluid walk and an

alluring smile. Coletti smiled back. Then she handed him the water and watched as he drank it.

"I hope you don't mind me saying this," she said in a velvety smooth voice. "But you are adorable."

He began to blush.

"You remind me so much of my grandfather."

Coletti nearly spit out the water as his fantasy moment shattered in a thousand pieces.

"Are you all right?" she asked.

"Yes," he said, grinning embarrassingly. "The water just went down the wrong pipe."

She grinned at him as if she wanted to reach out and pinch his grandfatherly cheek, her face fixed in the patronizing expression that the young reserve for the old.

Coletti decided to lay his pride aside and play the old-man card. "Can you do me a favor?" he asked.

"Of course."

"Can you e-mail a copy of these names and pictures to my partner? I'm not so good with the Internet."

"I'd be happy to," she said with a wide smile.

"One more thing. Did you have any luck getting in touch with Professor Workman?"

"I'm afraid not," she said, tilting her head in sympathy. "The department secretary said he went home early. He left about a half hour ago."

It was four o' clock, and the bird soared high above the streets, its wings stretched wide as the breeze carried it up toward the sun.

The killer looked up at the raven as he drove the stolen car. Then he glanced down at the cramped space between the glove compartment and the passenger seat. The car's dead owner looked back at him with vacant eyes. Her nose was a misshapen blob with shards of bone sticking out like macabre decorations. The killer smiled at his handiwork. Then he looked up at the road and panicked at the sight of a car that was stopped at a red light directly in front of him.

He slammed on the brakes, and the tires left foot-long skid marks before sliding to a halt. The driver of the other car turned around and yelled while giving him the finger. The killer stared passively, waiting for the light to change.

When it did, he drove on, crossing Cheltenham Avenue and leaving Philadelphia for a suburb called Elkins Park.

As the raven flew overhead, the killer drove down a winding street called Ashbourne Road, where grand estates were shaded by centuries-old trees that had witnessed the changes in the area. There were estates that had been divided into apartment complexes, and others that had been converted into museums, schools, and convents. In between were more modest homes in the three-hundred-thousand- to half-million-dollar range. The people who lived there were businessmen and doctors, lawyers and academics.

Irving Workman was among them, and as the raven alighted on the chimney of the professor's home, the killer pulled into the hundred-foot driveway behind Workman's twenty-year-old Volvo.

As he did every Wednesday, the professor had returned home early from the university. As he'd done the night before in preparation for this visit, the killer parked in front of Professor Workman's home.

Taking his time getting out of the car, the killer made no effort to hide the body that was slumped in front of the passenger seat. The professor's home was nestled among trees on nearly an acre of land. The killer had at least an hour before the professor's closest neighbors would return home, which would give him plenty of time to complete his deadly business.

Ambling up to the door, the killer rang the bell. He could hear Workman walking across the hardwood floor to answer. He could see the professor pull aside the curtain on the front window to see who'd come to visit. And when the professor opened the door, there was a glimmer of recognition in his eyes.

"What are you doing here?" Workman asked as he looked at him with a bemused expression on his face.

The killer grinned, revealing his black-toothed smile, and in two seconds, Workman's expression went from recognition to outright fear. By the time he tried to close the door, it was too late. The killer pushed open the door, and with a cool rush of air, the raven swept in and sunk his powerful bill into the professor's right eye.

There was a scream, and stumbling footsteps, and then the door slammed shut.

"It's been much too long since our last chat," the killer said as the professor stumbled to the floor with the raven stabbing at his face.

As Workman grunted and struggled with the bird, the

killer stood calmly over him, watching as the blood oozed from the professor's wounds and smeared the hardwood floor. After thirty seconds of listening to the raven's deep croak and Workman's pain-induced shrieks, the killer finally called off his accomplice.

"Prophet!" he shouted, his voice sharp and clear.

The raven flapped its wings and lifted itself a few feet in the air before roosting on a table on the other side of the vast living room.

As Workman lay on the floor, trying in vain to stanch the flow of blood with his hands, the killer bent down until his mouth was just inches from Workman's ear. "I named him Prophet," he said, his black-toothed smile spreading slowly across his face. "Do you like my choice, Professor?"

Workman struggled to prop himself up on his elbow, then dragged himself backward as the killer followed him across the floor, tormenting him with words the professor knew all to well.

"Prophet," he said with a chuckle. "Poe wrote that in his poem, didn't he? He said the raven was a prophet. But Poe wasn't sure if the prophet had been sent from heaven or hell. Which do you think it is, Professor? Do you think my prophet is a bird or a devil? Do you think he's from heaven or hell?"

With his one good eye, Workman turned and looked into the killer's face. What he saw confirmed what he'd initially believed. The man in his living room was a former student who'd excelled in Penn's master's of fine arts program two years ago. Workman had taken a liking to him and become a mentor. But halfway through the master's program the man disappeared. Now he was back, but something inside him had died.

"What happened to you?" Workman asked, his voice quaking with fear and exhaustion as the blood from his wounds ran down his face. "What turned you into this?"

The killer didn't answer. Instead, he walked over to the professor's coffee table and picked up the remote control. He turned on the TV and cranked up the sound. CNN was featuring yet another in a long line of so-called experts with opinions on the killings that had taken place that morning. An FBI psychiatrist was the latest talking head.

"All signs point to this so-called Gravedigger being a troubled individual," he said as the host nodded earnestly. "The mode of dress, the choice of an historic cemetery as the scene of the crime, all these things indicate that the killer is someone who's trying to recall a long-gone era. This killer might even be delusional enough to see himself as some figure from the distant past."

The killer smiled, turned to the professor, and began to laugh. "They've named me the Gravedigger. I think it suits me, Professor, don't you? I mean, it was you who introduced me to Fairgrounds. It was you who knew me best." The killer stopped, and his face clouded over with anger. "These people, they don't know me. If they knew me, they would know how much I've suffered. They'd know how many nights I lay awake, waiting for her to come back. They'd know how much it hurt to lose her the way I did."

"What are you talking about?" the professor asked, his voice weakening. "Who did you lose?"

"My wife, Professor. She was a nurse at Hahnemann Hospital who worked the late shift. One night she got into a cab and never made it home. Turns out the cabbie was wanted for two murders in Washington State. It wasn't hard to find him. The only thing that was hard was erasing the hate from my heart. Then I remembered you."

"What did it have to do with me?" the professor said, his tone desperate and his breathing heavy and labored. "I never even knew your wife died."

"What difference would it have made if you'd known? There was nothing you could've done about it."

"That's right," Workman said, his voice a near-whisper. "There was nothing you or I could do to bring her back then, and there's nothing we can do to bring her back now."

"That's what I thought, too. But when I went over your teachings, I discovered that my Helen was just like Lenore—young and beautiful and gone too soon. And I was just like the man in 'The Raven'—tortured by grief and looking for hope in things that weren't real. But if your theories are true, I can use my mind to bring her back, to make things like they were, to literally change everything."

"No, you can't," Workman said, his good eye fluttering as blood poured out the other. "My work is just a theory. There's no proof that it's true."

The killer smiled, again revealing teeth that were black and rotted. "Prophet!" he called sharply, and the bird flew over to him and roosted on his arm as the professor shrank back in fear.

"Did you know ravens are amongst the smartest birds, Professor? They can tell when you're afraid. They can tell when you're hurt. They can tell when you're defenseless." He looked at the bird, then back at the professor. "But the other amazing thing about ravens is that they sometimes eat sick and wounded animals while they're still alive."

"Please," the professor said as he slid away from the killer and his raven. "Just take what you want and let me go."

"I don't want things, Professor Workman. I want information. I want you to tell me exactly where Poe hid the secrets he found at Fairgrounds. There are people counting on me to get that information, Professor; people who've paid lots of money."

"I don't have the information you want."

The killer released the raven, and it gouged the professor's face with its powerful beak, tearing chunks of flesh from Workman's cheek and swallowing them whole as his victim screamed in pain.

"Prophet!" the killer shouted again, and the raven stopped its attack.

Workman was curled up in the fetal position, whimpering quietly as he trembled against the intense pain in his face.

"I don't want to kill you," his tormentor said. "That would mean I'd have to track down other people. Neither of us wants that, so please, just give me the information."

Workman looked up at the killer, and even with one

good eye, the professor could see that the man he'd once mentored had lost his grip on reality. There was no stopping the Gravedigger from killing Workman, and they both knew that. The only thing the professor could hope for was to prevent the killer from finding the truth that Workman and the Daughters of Independence had worked so hard to protect. There wasn't much time. His strength was leaving him in an endless flow of blood. There was only one option left.

"Okay," Workman said. "I'll give you what you want. It's right over here."

With a herculean effort, the professor dragged himself to his feet and stumbled across the living room floor to a glass cabinet filled with vodka, scotch, and rum. The killer was right behind him. Workman knew he only had a moment to act, and when the killer saw him reach for the cabinet, that moment grew even shorter.

The killer lunged for the professor, who managed to elude him. The raven attacked, and Workman reached for his lighter with one hand and pulled down the glass cabinet with the other. The structure fell on top of him, and the raven flew backward to avoid the spraying glass and alcohol. Then Workman lit the flame, and the alcohol-fueled fire spread across the wooden floor like a wave across the sea.

The raven flew up toward the ceiling, flapping helplessly as the room filled with smoke. The killer tried to douse the blaze, but as the flames licked the hardwood floors and climbed the drapes and wallpaper, it was clear that there was nothing he could do to stop their advance.

Workman's blood-soaked body was beneath the glass cabinet. His clothing was engulfed in flames. His one remaining eye was sizzling in his skull, but his dead face was fixed in the smile of the victor. He'd done what he could to protect what he knew, and nothing could get the secret from him now.

With the heat quickly building to unbearable temperatures and the smoke billowing up toward the ceiling, the killer dragged Workman's lifeless body to a sliding glass door on the side of the house. Then he opened the door and allowed the bird to fly out ahead of him. The killer then pulled the body fifty feet to an area just beyond the line of trees, and with a mighty heave, he pushed the professor's body into the hole he'd dug the night before.

A moment later, when he emerged from the woods and saw the balls of flame leaping out through the home's broken windows, the killer felt as if he'd seen the very maw of hell open up.

While the crackle of flames filled the air around him, the killer walked to the car, took a knife from his sock, and cut out the heart of the woman he'd killed earlier.

"Prophet!" he called to the raven, and tossed the heart onto the ground.

As the raven consumed it, the killer carried the woman's body to the grave where Workman lay. He threw her corpse on top of his. Then he looked back at the fire, got into the car, and drove away.

As he listened to the sound of sirens rising in the distance, a black-toothed grin spread across his face once more.

Workman had proven in no uncertain terms that the killer was chasing after truth, because the Gravedigger knew, just as his former mentor did, that truth was the only thing worth dying for.

CHAPTER 11

Mann pulled into the Police Administration Building's parking lot with Lenore, and John Wilkinson was standing there waiting. John's face, which had been impassive for most of the day, actually showed a glimmer of emotion when he saw her, and he smiled with something approaching gladness.

When Lenore started walking across the parking lot, however, John's smile quickly faded. His wife was surrounded by police officers, and instead of entering through the front door where he was waiting with his lawyer, she headed toward a side door and never even attempted to make eye contact with John.

"Lenore," John said as he walked in her direction. She didn't respond, so he called her again, louder this time. "Lenore!"

She glanced at him, her facial expression showing more hurt than anger, and continued to walk.

John caught up to them and tried to push past the cops to get to his wife. One of the uniformed officers nearly pushed him to the ground. John was about to push back when Lenore spoke up.

"Stop!" she said, as other officers in the parking lot watched.

She looked at her husband, who was red-faced and flustered. Then she looked at Mann, who appeared to be ready to take matters into his own hands. "I'd like to talk to John inside, if that's okay."

Mann glared at John. "He'll have to talk to me first," he muttered grudgingly. "He might want to bring his lawyer along, too."

They all walked in through the side entrance and took the long way around to homicide. Once they were there, Mann led Lenore into one of the interrogation rooms and had one of the uniformed cops stay with her. He led John and his lawyer into another room and sat them down at a table much like the one where he and Coletti had earlier questioned Lenore.

"Mr. Wilkinson, I need to know where you were today," Charlie said with a sigh.

John looked at his lawyer, who nodded.

"I've been in London for the past three days on business," he said. "I was on a long flight back today. Lenore knew that before she came here."

"Did the two of you also talk about her coming to Philadelphia?"

"Yes, right before I left for London she told me something about working on a ball for a historic cemetery."

"And you had no problem with her doing that, right?"

"Why would I have a problem with it? She works with charitable causes all the time."

"I was just wondering because I happened to be close by when the two of you talked earlier. I couldn't help overhearing you screaming at her on the phone."

The lawyer jumped in. "What does a personal disagreement between a husband and wife have to do with your case?" he said.

"I don't know . . . yet."

"So can we stick to things directly related to the case?" the lawyer asked.

"Sure," Mann said with a grin while turning back to John. "When did you find out that your wife was a murder witness?"

"When my flight from London landed, I got a text message from my lawyer. He met me at JFK airport, and we immediately got a flight to Philadelphia."

"So you never got the calls from Mrs. Wilkinson?"

"I was on a plane all day, so by necessity, my cell phone was off."

"Yes, but isn't your plane equipped with a phone?"

John laughed. "My plane? I fly commercial, Detective. I don't own a plane."

Mann looked at him quizzically. "I read last year that your company owned a 707. In fact, I specifically remember reading that in *Forbes*."

John's laughter turned to something else. He licked his lips nervously. "We sold it," he said. "We've been liquidating some of the company's assets over the past year.

In this economy, it's pretty important for any company to do that."

"Even your company, Mr. Wilkinson? That's kind of surprising."

"Why?" John said, sounding irritated. "I'm in real estate, Detective. In case you haven't heard, real estate's taken a beating over the past couple years."

"So how bad is it for you?" Mann asked.

The lawyer jumped in. "Detective, if you want my client's financial records, you'll have to get a warrant for them. And I don't see how that's relevant to your investigation anyway."

"It's relevant if they're having marital problems, or if he has any other motive to do her harm."

"Now wait a minute!" John said, his face turning red. "Let's get something straight. I love my wife, and I will not sit here and allow you or anyone else to imply that I would hurt her."

"I'm not implying anything, Mr. Wilkinson. I'm telling you in no uncertain terms that if you've got financial problems or anything else that might affect your relationship with your wife, we need to know that, because that would impact the way we're approaching this investigation."

"I don't know how many different ways I can say it," John said. "I love my wife, I'm here to see her, and unless you're going to charge me with something, I'd like to talk to her now."

Mann knew he had no choice but to allow Mr. Wilkinson to see Lenore. Neither John nor his wife had been charged with a crime.

Mann got up and led them to the room where Lenore was waiting. The uniformed cop stepped aside as Mann opened the door.

Mann looked at John's lawyer, then at Lenore. "Do you want this guy in here?" Mann asked.

"I really need a few minutes alone with my husband," Lenore said. "We've got a lot to talk about."

John considered saying something different, but Lenore gave him a warning glance, and he nodded in agreement with his wife.

"You can wait in the next room," Mann told the lawyer before closing the door so John and Lenore could be alone.

"Are you, um . . . are you all right?" John asked in a tone much gentler than the one he'd used when they'd spoken on the phone.

"Do you really care?" she asked, her eyes flashing angrily.

They were sitting across from each other in rickety chairs, speaking over one of the heavy tables where criminals cop pleas and make deals before cases ever make their way to a courtroom. They both knew the police might be listening, so they didn't say anything they didn't want them to hear.

"Before I say anything else, Lenore, I need you to know I'm sorry," John said, his tone sincere. "You know I just came in from London. It was a long flight, and I'm tired, so I might have been a little on edge."

Lenore looked at him in utter disbelief. When the words finally came, they weren't kind.

"You were a little on edge?" she asked. "Someone was murdered not fifty yards from where I stood, and if that wasn't bad enough, I found out that whoever killed her wants to come after me, too. So you'll excuse me if I'm a little more on edge than you are."

John sighed. "Look, Lenore, I know you must be tired and under a lot of stress. I am, too. So why don't we just go home, get some rest, and figure out what we're going to do tomorrow?"

"You haven't heard a thing I've said, have you? There's someone out there who wants to harm me, John. Even if I wanted to, which I don't, I couldn't just pick up and go home now. It's not that simple."

"Do you really think I would let someone harm you? I'd spend every dime I have to protect you, Lenore. You have to believe that."

"I believe what I see, and from all that you've said and done—or, rather, all you *haven't* said and done—I know I'm not your priority. You said it yourself. My involvement in a murder case might scare off your investors."

John stood up and closed his eyes tightly while squeezing the bridge of his nose. "Lenore, there's more to it than that."

"Like what? The fact that you want me at home doing charity work and playing bridge? Smiling and waving when I'm on your arm at black-tie functions? Never having a life or identity of my own?"

John knew that he had to get her to see things his way—a task that under normal circumstances would be easy. When she was upset, however, Lenore could be quite combative. The only way to gain the upper hand was to find and use a kernel of truth that she hadn't already discovered.

"I've never begrudged you your own life," he said. "In fact, I've always wanted you to have one. You just never seemed to want it for yourself."

"Until now," she said firmly.

John placed his hands on the table and bent down until they were nearly nose to nose. "So what does having your own life look like?" he asked. "Because I thought I'd provided you with a pretty great life as Mrs. Wilkinson."

"I'm not saying I don't want that life anymore, John. I love that life. But I want us to have that life together, not apart."

"Then come home with me now."

"I can't."

"Why?"

"Because for once I want to see something through. That's what having my own life looks like. And it doesn't mean I love you any less."

John looked in her eyes for a few minutes more. Then he walked across the small room and stood there with his back to his wife.

"If you love me at all, you'll do the right thing," he said. "Investors don't like controversy. That's why I need you to come home."

"I'm sorry," she said, "but the money and the deals aren't important to me."

"Then what is?"

"Happiness, John, and I'm staying here until I find it."

There was a knock on the door just then.

"Come in," Lenore said. "We're finished."

Charlie Mann walked into the interrogation room along with John's lawyer.

"Do you need anything more from my client?" the lawyer asked Mann as John stood up and prepared to leave.

"I need him to stay reachable," said Mann.

"That's fine," John said, turning to his wife with a hint of sadness in his eyes. "Lenore, are you absolutely sure you don't want to come with me? I can get you the best security money can buy, and when things are safer you can come back."

"I've made my decision, John," she said as her eyes grew moist with tears. "You've made yours, too, so please, get on with it."

He tried to hug her, but she pulled away. Duly chastised, John stood back and looked at her. Then he took out a business card, scribbled his personal numbers on the back, and handed it to Charlie Mann.

"I have to go back to New York to tie up some loose ends. These are all my phone numbers and e-mail addresses. You have my lawyer's numbers, too. I'll be back here as soon as I can."

He reached out to hold his wife once again. Her tears were flowing freely now, and John wanted to make them stop. He whispered the one thing they both knew for sure. "You're my biggest investment."

As Mann and the lawyer looked on, Lenore pulled gently away from her husband and touched him on his cheek. "One day soon, you'll act like it."

With a last glance at his wife, John left with his lawyer. Mann wanted to say something to make Lenore feel better, but he didn't have the words to do so. He was still trying to figure out what to do about his own relationship. Seconds later, opportunity knocked.

Sandy walked into the interrogation room, fresh off her interview with the cemetery manager, and Mann's eyes lingered on everything about her. Sandy liked that, but she wasn't about to be distracted by it.

"Hi, Lieutenant Jackson," Lenore said, her eyes filled with pain.

Sandy knew that pain all too well, and she couldn't help feeling sympathy for Lenore. "I assume that was your husband," she said.

Lenore nodded as a tear rolled down her cheek.

Sandy paused, unsure what to do. Then her humanity took over, and before she could stop herself, she was crossing the room to hug Lenore.

"It'll be okay, honey," she whispered as she held Lenore. "Men do what they do, and no matter what, we come out a little stronger in the end."

Their embrace lasted only a few seconds, but it was enough to let Sandy know they were more alike than they were different. When they released each other, Lenore smiled with gratitude. Then Sandy turned to Charlie Mann, who was still mesmerized by the sight of her in jeans and a tight leather jacket.

Sandy stood there for a moment, basking in the power of her raw sensuality. When she was satisfied that Charlie had seen all she needed him to see, she gave him the news she'd come to deliver.

"We just got word that Professor Workman's house burned down this afternoon. They found his body and a woman's body in a shallow grave on his property. Coletti's already there."

"What about the killer?" Mann asked.

"They think he's still in the area. They're searching for him now."

The Gravedigger drove the black Ford out of Elkins Park without incident, because from the outside, everything about the car appeared to be average. Its dull paint was speckled with water spots from the morning's rains. Its tires and rims were worn and dingy. Its engine was louder than most.

But on the inside, its charcoal gray-cloth seats and interior were soaked with the blood of its dead owner, and so were the Gravedigger's hands.

As he crossed back into Philadelphia, the killer knew, even as his sanity continued to crumble, that he'd need the help of his benefactor. When he received the text message saying a car would be waiting at Ogontz and Limekiln Pike in thirty minutes, he was grateful, but he was also afraid.

In the slow-moving after-work traffic, he risked being spotted, so he set out to get off the main streets.

He drove the labyrinth of one-way streets and twisting avenues on the Philadelphia side of the border, looking for a place to hide. Before long he was in a place where his heart had gone too many times over the last year, a place where he'd refused to go physically until now.

He drove along the stone wall that so often plagued his daydreams. He felt intensely lonely as he passed beneath the bare branches of the tree-lined street, and then he felt crippling sadness.

As he drew closer to the location where he knew his heart would take him, tears he hadn't cried for a year began streaming down his face. When finally he arrived there, with the raven circling above, he parked the car and told himself he desperately needed to leave. He sat there and chided himself for mourning all he'd lost. He looked at his hands and cursed himself for killing so many people. Then, as suddenly as they'd begun, the tears stopped, and he turned to look at the spot in Northwood Cemetery where he'd buried his wife a year before.

"I came back to see you, Helen," he said through trembling lips. "Did you miss me? Because I missed you more than you'll ever know."

He dried his eyes with his hands, streaking dirt and blood across his face. The red and brown smears looked almost like camouflage, which was fitting, because in the killer's mind, he was at war. He was fighting against himself, he was fighting against his grief, and he was fighting against the urge to simply kill everyone and everything in sight. Even as he continued to lose his tenuous grip on his sanity, though, he knew he couldn't totally lose control. There was a plan, after all, and that plan would allow him to get back the only thing that would make the pain go away. That plan would allow him to bring back his wife.

"I know you must be lonely, Helen," he said as the tears began anew. "I'm lonely, too. But it won't be that way for long. When I'm finished, we'll be together again."

The sobs began, softly at first. Then they rapidly grew into uncontrollable shrieks. He pounded his fists on the dashboard. He stomped his feet on the floor. He rocked back and forth in his seat. He gave in to his anger.

His tirade was visible from outside the car. It caught the attention of neighbors who watched him from their homes and called police. When a cruiser rolled slowly down the street and crept toward the car, the killer stopped and looked in the rearview mirror, and everything he'd worked for flashed before his eyes. He wasn't going to let it end this way, so he did what he had to do. He wiped the tears from his face once more, mouthed a silent good-bye to his wife, and put the car in gear. Then he gunned it.

The skidding of the tires was instantly followed by the sound of lights and sirens. As the black Ford and the cop car flew south on the residential street, the police officer reported the chase to radio, and every unit within five miles headed in that direction.

The Ford screamed down the road that ran along the

perimeter of the graveyard, then skidded onto a two-way street that ran between the graveyard and a school. By then, two more police cars had joined the chase, and all four vehicles were traveling at nearly a hundred miles per hour.

The Gravedigger looked nervously in the rearview mirror as the police cars closed in. Then he glanced at the blood on the seat. He knew he had to escape from them in order to have a chance to fulfill his promise to his wife. He would either succeed or die trying. He pressed the accelerator to the floor, pushing the black Ford around yet another corner and skidding on the blacktop as he barreled down a series of small, one-way streets with names like Bouvier and Gratz.

He sideswiped dozens of vehicles and barely missed a man and a woman who were returning home from work. As the chase intensified and police cars crisscrossed the tiny streets in an effort to cut him off, mothers herded their children inside. Teens dodged the speeding cars. The sound of wailing sirens filled the air.

The killer made a sudden right and hit the long block of Sixty-seventh Avenue that led toward Broad Street, barely missing an old woman as she disembarked from a bus. The policeman that was behind him wasn't so fortunate. He drove into the woman, knocking her twenty feet into the air, and skidded to a stop as other cars continued the pursuit.

As the killer approached a winding street called Old York Road, a police car came from the right and screeched to a halt, blocking the car's path. The killer skidded and swerved, clipping the front of the police car before heading south.

Police radios blared as commanders tried to give orders to break off the pursuit. But the calls for assistance drowned out the orders, and the police cars moved even faster.

The killer couldn't outrun them, but he knew he had to make it to Ogontz and Limekiln Pike, so he did the only thing he could to stop the chase. He began targeting pedestrians. He drove onto the sidewalk and hit a man. He swerved back into the street and hit another. And as the casualties began to pile up in his wake, the commanders' orders finally took hold.

The police broke off the pursuit. Five minutes later, they found the black Ford, but the Gravedigger was gone.

CHAPTER 12

Though Workman's home was still standing, the fire department wasn't sure if it was structurally sound. That was bad news for Coletti, because he wanted to see if there were things in the house that would indicate what else Workman had hidden when they talked.

As the fire marshall set about deciding when to let the police into the house, Coletti stood amidst spinning dome lights on the manicured lawn that encircled Workman's property. The stench of smoke still filled the air, and smoldering embers floated on the autumn breeze. Cheltenham Township police were on the scene, as were several fire companies from Philadelphia, Cheltenham, and La Mott.

The news media were there, too, including the woman who'd been hounding Coletti throughout the day. He tried to avoid Kirsten Douglas by standing far away from the gathered media, but it was hard for him to do so. She was yelling his name from beyond the perimeter, and her voice was louder than all the other reporters combined. For that reason alone, he was obliged to turn around and talk to her. He hadn't heard a woman yell his name in quite some time.

As crime scene officers busily took pictures and measurements, documenting every inch of the scene, Coletti walked to the edge of the crime scene tape that extended the length of Workman's property. He lifted the tape and made his way over to Kirsten. When the other reporters saw him, they flocked to the spot where Kirsten stood.

"I'll give you guys a statement in a few," Coletti said. "I need to talk to Ms. Douglas first."

Undaunted, the remaining members of the media followed Coletti, shouting questions as he calmly walked Kirsten to his car, which was parked at the end of the driveway. The reporters reversed course like camera-wielding lemmings when a township supervisor showed up to give a statement to a television station.

Kirsten and Coletti got into the car, and he turned to her with a weary grin. "Okay, the commissioner told me I should talk to you," he said. "What do you want to know?"

Kirsten knew he had no intention of helping her, and she understood from the numerous times she'd interviewed him over the years that he wouldn't tell her anything that wasn't in his own self-interest. Still, she had to ask him something, so rather than waste her time on questions he wouldn't answer, she asked him the one question she knew he would be officially free to address.

"Do the memories still haunt you?" she asked.

Coletti was taken aback. "I don't know what you mean."

"Mary Smithson. The Angel of Death. Do your memories from that case affect the way you're handling this one?"

"This is on background, right? No names?"

Kirsten nodded.

"Okay, then I'll answer it this way. Every case is different, including this one."

"So are you saying that what happened with Mary has no bearing on how you view Lenore?"

"I'm saying when someone's killed, we gather evidence, build a case, and take it to prosecutors. That's what we do. Anything that happens before or after that doesn't matter."

"All right," Kirsten said, her frustration mounting. "Let's go totally off the record."

"Okay."

"What I'm asking you is whether Mary's crimes affect how you view her sister. And if they do, should you really be working on this case?"

Coletti took a deep breath and looked out the car window at the crime scene. He considered his answer before he spoke.

"Look at all those people over there, Kirsten. They're all here for their own little piece of the pie. The politicians want to talk tough and make people think they're on top of things. The cops want to catch a killer. The firefighters want to put out fires. The reporters want to tell stories. All those people, no matter what their job, bring their own experiences with them. Some bring heartbreak, others bring loss, or grief, or fear. The one thing those people share is their humanity. Their experiences affect the way they see their jobs, so here's my question to you: Should *they* be working on this case?"

"You're trying to cloud the issue, Detective. Their connections to this aren't personal."

"How do we know that?" Coletti shot back. "And if we really want to be fair about it, the only person working on this case who has a definite personal connection is you, Kirsten. You even went on CNN and talked about how it affected you. Does that personal connection keep you from doing your job?"

"Of course not."

"Then what makes you think it would stop me from doing mine?"

Kirsten wanted to come back with a snappy answer, but she couldn't, so she turned and looked out over the crowd of cops and reporters who were milling about outside the house. She also looked inside herself.

"I guess I should consider myself corrected," she said with a wan smile.

"No, you should consider yourself lucky to be alive."

"I do," she said seriously. "I guess that's something we have in common."

Coletti looked at his watch. "Do you have any other questions for me?"

"Just one."

Coletti looked at her expectantly.

"Have you heard anything from Lenore's family?"

"You mean her husband?"

"No, I mean her family—her father especially."

"We've been trying to reach her father, but we haven't heard anything from him."

Kirsten smiled. "I have. He called the paper about an hour ago and asked to speak to me."

"Okay," Coletti said anxiously. "I need to speak to him, too. How do I reach him?"

"I'm sorry, but I can't reveal my sources," she said coyly.

"But you can get locked up for obstructing an investigation."

Kirsten's smile broadened. "Do you really want to go through the freedom-of-the-press thing and turn this into an even bigger media circus? There's an easier solution than that."

"What is it?"

"We can go up to Dunmore together."

Coletti stared at her, knowing that Clarissa Bailey had made several calls to Sean O'Hanlon in the days before her death. Coletti had to speak with him, and if Kirsten could make that happen, he'd gladly deal with the fallout later.

"All right," Coletti said. "You can do a ride-along to Dunmore, and if Sean O'Hanlon's okay with it, we both sit in on the interview. But after that we go our separate ways. Agreed?"

"Okay," said Kirsten.

Suddenly there was a tap on the car window. Coletti looked up and saw the lead detective from Cheltenham Township. Cheltenham had jurisdiction over the Workman scene, but the detective was an old friend who'd once worked with Coletti in Philadelphia's homicide unit. Coletti expected no contentious turf battles from him. But Coletti didn't know what to expect from his trip to Dunmore with Kirsten Douglas.

As the two of them got out of the car, Coletti was unsure what their unholy alliance would yield. But as Kirsten returned to her corner of the world and Coletti returned to his, he knew that they could learn more together than they could apart.

"You having a little one-on-one time with Kirsten?" Coletti's old friend asked while they watched the reporter walk away.

Coletti laughed it off. "I need that like I need a hole in my head," he said as they shook hands. "They finished with the scene yet?"

"Just about."

The two of them walked toward the line of trees where the bodies had been found, reminiscing about the days when they worked together in homicide.

"I still remember the time you had that foot pursuit down in South Philly," the detective said with a smile. "You were running so slow it looked like you were moving backwards."

"I was moving backwards," Coletti said. "I tricked the guy into thinking he was fast so you could catch him."

Their laughter faded as they walked between the trees, stood at the edge of more crime scene tape, and looked down into the shallow grave. The sight was grisly.

Workman's one remaining eye bugged out from his skull and stared up at them with a steadfastness that was sickening. There were third-degree burns over most of his body. The woman who lay on top of him had no such burns, but her smashed face and mutilated chest were covered with blood.

"We don't get much of this out here," said the Cheltenham detective.

"I wish we didn't either," Coletti said with a sigh. "If I was smart, I would've left for the suburbs, too."

As crime scene officers took pictures and blood samples, Coletti squinted and looked hard at Workman's dead body.

"I'm willing to bet that missing eye was gouged out with the same thing that made those gashes in his face," Coletti said.

"What do you think the killer used to do that?"

Coletti looked skyward, half expecting to see the bird circling overhead. When he didn't, he turned to his old friend and gave it to him straight.

"Those injuries came from a raven," he said. "My guess is the killer had the bird attack Workman to torture him into talking."

"What kind of information would Workman have had?"

Coletti explained while the two of them walked away from the ghoulish scene.

"Workman knew the Gravedigger," he said. "But for some reason he didn't tell me that when I spoke to him today. My guess is that whatever Workman was hiding from me is the same thing he tried to hide from the killer."

They walked to a spot in the grass where bits of bloody flesh were marked off with yellow markers. Officers in latex gloves and goggles collected samples.

"If I didn't know better, I'd think something had that for a meal," said the detective.

"Something did," Coletti said as he watched an officer pluck a black feather from the grass and deposit it in a plastic bag. "And I'm guessing it was the raven. It seems to show up wherever the killer does." He watched the crime scene cops for a few minutes more before turning to his friend. "So, in terms of sharing the evidence across jurisdictions—"

"Don't worry about it. We'll share whatever you need, whenever you need it. There won't be any delays or paperwork or red tape. Just let me know what you want, and you've got it."

"Thanks," said Coletti. "But the main thing I need is to find out what Workman really knew."

A woman's voice called out from beyond the perimeter. At first Coletti thought it was Kirsten again. The voice was too high, though. When they turned around to see who it was, there were two middle-aged women standing there. One of them had strawberry blond hair and a world-weary face. The other had short brown hair that was flecked with gray, and the low-cut blouse she wore beneath her coat showed pearls resting against a hint of cleavage. Both women had sadness in their eyes.

A uniformed officer walked over to the detectives to deliver the women's message.

"They say they need to talk to you, Detective Coletti."

"Who are they?" Coletti asked.

"Lily Thompkins and Violet Grant. They're with a group called the Daughters of Independence."

Coletti's eyes came to life. "Excuse me for a minute," he said to his friend. Then he hurried across the grass while taking his notepad from his pocket.

The press corps watched closely as he made his way over to the pair. Coletti pulled them inside the perimeter and walked along the edge of the scene until they reached a sprawling oak tree. The three of them stood beneath the tree as if it could hold the weight of all that had occurred that day.

"I'm Lily," said the one with the strawberry blond hair, "and this is Violet. We got here as soon as we heard."

"We've been trying to reach both of you," Coletti said. "How come I didn't hear from either of you before now?"

"We were afraid," Lily said.

"Afraid of what?"

"Afraid we were going to be next," said Violet.

Coletti took out a pen and began taking notes. "Why would you think that?"

"Because no one would kill Clarissa unless they wanted what she knew, and the only thing Irving Workman and Clarissa had in common was their belief in the professor's theories." Violet nervously played with her pearls. "For all we know, this killer could be tracking down everyone who believes. That would make us targets."

"That's right," said Lily.

"Had either of you ever met anyone other than the

members of your group who believed in Workman's theories?" Coletti asked.

Lily nodded. "There were a couple of young men from Penn, but they came and went."

"Wait here," Coletti said. He went to his car and retrieved the manila envelope containing the pictures he'd gotten from the university. He came back and showed them to both women. "You said there were a couple of young men who came and went. Do either of you see any of them here?"

They both looked through the pictures, their eyes lingering on one or two. "I can't say that I recognize any of them," Lily said.

"I don't recognize them, either," Violet said. "But you have to understand that people who weren't serious didn't stay around long enough for anyone to remember them. Professor Workman wouldn't let them. He only nurtured people who showed real fire."

"You make it sound like a cult," Coletti said, only half joking.

Lily smiled sadly. "It's not a cult. It's just a group of people who love the past even more than the present. Professor Workman gravitated toward people like us. That's why he trusted us with his theories."

"How'd you get to know Professor Workman?" Coletti asked.

"By getting to know each other," Lily said, as Violet nodded in agreement. "We were just three women who loved history. Not the tourist stuff they show you at the

Liberty Bell and Independence Hall. We loved the unusual—everything from Native American burial grounds to stops on the Underground Railroad."

"We wanted to see secret passages and hollow walls and long-lost documents and hundred-year-old secrets," Violet added. "But even when we saw those things, it was never enough for us. We wanted to be *in* the history, so when the Fairmount Park Commission came along and asked for a community group to maintain Tookesbury Mansion, we became one. We called ourselves the Daughters of Independence."

"Any significance to the name?" Coletti asked.

Violet and Lily exchanged a glance.

"We all lost our fathers pretty young," Lily said. "We used to joke that history was our dad, since we all loved it so much. It might sound corny, but we almost felt like history set us free to be ourselves. It gave us independence. That's where the name came from."

"So, how did you meet?"

"We met about two years ago," said Lily. "Violet and I already knew each other socially, and we'd occasionally visit historical sites around town. We started seeing Clarissa at some of the sites, and the more we ran into each other, the more we wanted to, so the three of us decided to start doing it together. We all have a role in getting into new sites. I'm an adjunct in Temple's history department, so I do the research."

"My background is as a business manager," Violet said, "so I'm the forceful one who persuades reluctant owners to let us into places that aren't open to the public. Clarissa? She's the sweet one. She's more caring than either of us, but also a lot richer. So if worse comes to worst, she buys our way in. Well . . . at least, she used to."

Violet stopped twirling her pearls around her fingers as a tear rolled down her cheek. She wiped it away quickly. "I'm sorry. It's just odd to think of her in the past tense."

"It's all right," Coletti said. "Please go on."

"The three of us were voracious learners," Lily said. "That's why we went to Fairgrounds Cemetery the first few times. It was right near the mansion, and the history was there to be studied. Eventually we met Irving Workman there, and he knew so much that we were immediately drawn to him."

"When did he bring up his theories about Poe being a seer?" Coletti asked.

"Fairgrounds gives tours of the more famous gravesites," said Violet. "We took one along with Irving. The tour guide mentioned the Gravedigger's Ball and started talking about the legend behind it. That's when Irving asked if the cemetery could substantiate the rumors of Poe working there as a gravedigger. The tour guide said no, but he invited Irving to share what he knew about it. By the time the professor finished speaking about Poe and the potential of the human mind being literally buried beneath our feet, it was almost like a whole new world opened up to us. The story was fascinating, his theories were riveting, but as entertaining as it was, we all had our doubts."

"Ellison Bailey did, too," Coletti said.

Lily rolled her eyes. "Ellison wouldn't know a historical fact from a hole in his head."

"Maybe you're right," Coletti said. "But he did say something I found interesting. He said he didn't trust Irving Workman. So my question is, why did you?"

Lily looked at the ground as she spoke. "Irving showed us things," she said softly. "He had handwritten drafts of 'The Raven,' with Poe's notations in the margins. He had the first draft of the 'Paean,' which Poe rewrote and later renamed 'Lenore.' He let Clarissa bring in an expert to authenticate the items. And when her expert proved they were real, we listened to the professor more closely. That's when he showed us how the poems went together to form a single message."

Violet jumped in, her eyes lighting up as she described the way the poems weaved together. "In 'Lenore,' Poe describes her as young, blond, beautiful, wealthy, and surrounded by people who don't really love her. By the end of the poem, there's a call for someone to sing to summon the gods. Irving believed Poe intended for that to be a call to Pallas Athena—the Greek goddess of wisdom and war.

"In 'The Raven,' Pallas arrives when the bird sits on a sculpture depicting her. Workman believed that finding Pallas was the key to unlocking the wisdom Poe hid at Fairgrounds."

"So if finding Pallas was the key to unlocking this mystery, why would Clarissa become so obsessed with finding Lenore?"

Violet looked at Lily, and they both turned to Coletti

with eyes that wanted to say more, but just as they were ready to speak, the detective from Cheltenham walked over to them.

"The firefighters found some stuff in the wall near the spot where the fire started."

"What kind of stuff?" Coletti asked.

The detective glanced at Lily and Violet before he spoke. "I can show you when you finish with your witnesses."

"It's all right," Coletti said. "I think they might need to see it, too."

The detective led the way as they crossed the lawn to the side of the house where the firefighters had piled items from what appeared to be an art collection. There were oils and sculptures, busts and reliefs. One bust in particular got Coletti's attention.

He bent down to look at it, and his face creased in a look of disbelief. He snatched a handkerchief out of his pocket. Then he picked it up and asked the question whose answer he already knew.

"Why would Workman have this?"

"Because that's a bust of Pallas," Lily said simply.

"Pallas?" Coletti repeated, sounding confused. "This is . . ."

The words trailed off as he looked at the bust. He couldn't believe what he was seeing, yet there it was, staring at them with hollow eyes and sculpted hair pinned up on a graceful neck. Even though it was chipped and charred, there was no mistaking the identity of the bust. It was Lenore Wilkinson, and it was haunting.

"That bust is why Clarissa was so obsessed with finding Lenore," Violet said. "It's the reason we all believed."

Coletti looked at the bust once more before calling over two cops from the crime scene unit. They bagged and tagged it. Then Coletti turned back to Lily and Violet before reaching into his pocket and extracting yet another piece of artwork.

"I almost forgot to show this to you," he said as he opened up the folded sheet of paper and held it in front of them. "It's a cryptogram that was tattooed on Clarissa Bailey's neck. Do either of you know what it means?"

Lily looked at the picture, and her face cycled through a number of emotions, not the least of which was fear.

"No," Lily said after staring at the picture for just a few seconds.

"I have no idea what it means," said Violet.

Both women looked sincere when they spoke, but Coletti had a nagging feeling that they knew more than they were saying.

The interrogation room was hot, and so was Sandy Jackson. She and a homicide detective had been questioning Vickers, the manager of Fairgrounds Cemetery, for the last forty-five minutes, and with each passing second, his answers grew more convoluted.

They still were uncertain about how much the manager

knew, but they were sure that he didn't want to be involved. That was apparent in the way he kept hedging on his answers.

First, he didn't know the man who'd volunteered at the cemetery. Then he wasn't sure. By the time the manager changed his mind again, Sandy was just about ready to employ a choke hold. She walked out into the hallway to get some air. That was when she spotted Charlie Mann.

"What are you doing out here?" she asked.

"Computer stuff," Mann said as he looked at two sheets of paper he was holding. "Penn sent over the names and pictures of Workman's students."

"Any hits?"

"Not yet, but I've got a couple other irons in the fire. I just left IT to check on the information from the Baileys' computers. Ellison's is filled with porn and not much else."

"What about his wife's?"

"Her C drive was corrupted, but they think they can repair it and save the information. It might take another half hour or so."

"Good, because I need your help."

Charlie smiled as he looked her up and down, his eyes drinking in the curves that were bursting at the seams of her clothing. "What'd you have in mind?"

Sandy liked his eyes on her, but she wasn't about to let him know it. She was all business now, and she needed Charlie to be that way, too.

"I'm questioning Vickers, the manager from the cemetery. I need you in on the interrogation."

"I thought he was cooperating."

"He was," Sandy said. "But I think he's scared."

"You think he knows something?"

"I think he knows everything," Sandy said. "He knew Workman and the guy who volunteered at the cemetery last year. He knew the volunteer was the one who found the raven and trained it, and he knows a lot more than that, but he's trying to hide it."

"Okay," Mann said. "Let's go."

Sandy opened the door to the interrogation room, and Mann walked in smiling. He nodded a greeting to his fellow detective. Then he made a beeline for Vickers.

"I'm Charlie Mann," he said, shaking Vickers's hand. "I saw you at the cemetery this morning, but I didn't get a chance to introduce myself."

"Nice to meet you," Vickers said nervously as Mann sat in the chair across from him.

"I'm not going to waste a lot of your time," Mann said. "Clarissa Bailey's dead, Irving Workman's dead, and the guy who trained the raven is out there somewhere. Whoever knows who he is and what he wants is in danger. I think that's you, Mr. Vickers, and the bottom line is this: if you don't help us find this guy, he's going to find you, and you'll be dead just like Clarissa Bailey and Irving Workman."

Mann stared at Vickers, and the nervous little man with the twitching nose and beady eyes looked back at him with eyes that seemed incapable of a steady gaze. It took Vickers a few minutes to absorb the truth in what Mann had said, but once he did, he shared some truth of his own.

"They always said that something was hidden at

Fairgrounds," Vickers began. "None of us believed it, really. It was just part of the mystique of the graveyard, and trust me, mystique is good for donations, so we don't discourage it. But beyond the mystique there were legends, and I knew all of them because that was my job: to know them and package them so our tour guides could thrill the tourists with ghost stories. I didn't really start believing that any of them were true until Professor Workman came along.

"I won't bore you with all the things you already know about Poe and the secrets and the message and Lenore. What I will tell you, though, is that the man Workman brought in to volunteer had problems that we couldn't solve."

"What kinds of problems?" Mann asked.

"He was just . . . strange. Eerily quiet. Angry. I was always nervous that he would explode one day and take some mourners or some tourists or even some of our employees with him."

"If he made you that uncomfortable, why didn't you try to get rid of him?" Sandy asked.

"It's like I told you earlier, Professor Workman was one of our biggest donors. I wasn't about to risk offending him. It was easier to just wait it out, but then . . ."

"Then what?" Mann said as Sandy and the other detective looked on.

"Then he found the raven," Vickers said. "At first, we were really happy because it gave him something to do other than standing around making everyone nervous. But when his time was up as a volunteer, he kept coming back, creeping around the back way, trying to avoid people on his way to see the raven. We pretended not to notice, but we saw him. For about ten months he spent a few hours each day with that raven. Then suddenly he just disappeared. It was the strangest thing. I hadn't seen him for weeks, but I never felt as if he were gone. His presence was still in the cemetery, still making everyone nervous."

"What can you tell us about his identity?" Sandy asked.

"I never knew his name," said Vickers. "He never told us, and we were afraid to ask. Workman never told us, either, so we kind of just stayed out of the guy's way and never spoke to him."

Mann placed the pictures of Workman's students on the table. "Do you recognize him in any of these pictures?"

He looked through the pictures several times to make sure he hadn't missed anything. "No, he's not there."

"Okay," Mann said as he removed the pictures from the table. "I need you to think hard, Mr. Vickers. Can you remember anything at all Workman might've told you about the man who volunteered at the cemetery?"

Vickers thought about it for a moment. "Yes, there was one thing. Workman told us that he was in the master's of fine arts program at Penn."

Mann wrote that down as he asked his next question. "And you're absolutely sure that you never had a name or address for him?"

"I'm sure," Vickers said. "But I wouldn't be surprised if he has an address for me. That's why I didn't want to be involved in this. I don't want to be his next victim."

"You won't be," Sandy said.

"You can't promise that."

Sandy paused, knowing he was right. When she answered him, she spoke quietly, in a tone that was reassuring in its compassion.

"Mr. Vickers, we understand your concerns," she said while staring at Charlie Mann. "We've dealt with murderers and suffered because of things they did. We don't want that for you or anyone else, so believe me, we'll protect you as best we can."

As she spoke, Mann thought back to Mary Smithson, and the way she'd driven a wedge between him and Sandy. Though Lenore had helped him deal with the pain, the rift remained, and despite his flirting eyes and teasing smiles, he still wasn't sure how to repair it.

He was barely listening when Sandy promised Vickers that there would be double patrols on his block and a detail at the cemetery. He was stuck in thought when the other detective escorted Vickers out. When Charlie got up to leave, however, he had no choice but to pay attention, because Sandy gently placed a hand against his chest to stop him.

"Where are you going?"

"To check with Penn," he said while avoiding her eyes. "Workman was an English professor, so the guy was probably getting an MFA in creative writing. It's a long shot, but I know a couple of professors in the creative writing program who might be able to give me some names."

"Are you all right?" she asked softly. "You seem distant."

Mann looked up at the ceiling. "I thought about the day I shot two people. That happens every once in a while. I'll be all right."

She watched his face go through a range of emotions that stemmed from that day. His eyes showed uncertainty, then apprehension, then guilt.

When she saw that his expression had moved from guilt to pain, she tried her best to wipe that pain away. "You did the right thing, you know. You had no choice."

"That's what they keep telling me," he said, squeezing the bridge of his nose between his thumb and forefinger. "But nobody told me that it's a lot different shooting a person than it is shooting a target."

Sandy went and locked the door to the interrogation room. Then she sat down on the table, looked Mann in the eye, and shared something she'd never told him before.

"The first time I shot a suspect, it was a foot pursuit down at Thirteenth and Walnut. It was around ten o'clock at night on a Thursday, so the traffic was relatively light.

"I came around the corner of Thirteenth Street and I saw this guy. He looked to be about seventeen or eighteen years old, and he was reaching inside the passenger door of this burgundy Buick—one of those long Roadmasters from the nineties. When I got a little closer, I saw that he wasn't reaching in, he was trying to get out, but the driver was holding his shirt. I hit my siren once, just to get their attention, and I guess I startled the driver just enough to make him let go. The boy popped out the window and fell hard on the sidewalk, and I finally saw what the two of them were struggling over. It was a gun."

Sandy's eyes grew vacant as she stared into a past that sometimes crept up on her in quiet moments.

"The boy was on that sidewalk with his torn shirt, and if he'd have stayed there a little longer I could've counted every one of his ribs. That's how skinny he was. But he didn't stay. He couldn't—not with that gun in his hand. He looked back at me, and he looked at the man in the car, and in that split second, he made a decision that changed everything. He ran.

"I got out of the car and chased him up Thirteenth toward Chestnut, past the theater and past the bars, past the bookstore and past a lot of people who were watching the whole thing like it was some kinda movie.

"I don't think the boy expected me to be as fast as I was, but when he turned on Chestnut Street and ran to Twelfth, I could see him getting tired. It's strange to say it now, but I could feel him getting scared, too. I tried to yell my location into my handset, but I was breathing heavy, and the dispatcher couldn't understand me. She was yelling for me to repeat my location, other cops were jumping on the air to say they were en route, and that's when it hit me: we were alone—just me and this scared boy with a gun— and it was this awful, frightening feeling.

"I watched him run past Twelfth Street. He turned on Eleventh, running toward Chestnut, and I was gaining on him. He turned down the back street behind the parking lot. There were Dumpsters on one side and a brick wall on the other, and in front of us, there was nothing but the dark. I saw him raising the gun and turning around, and right then, even before I saw the terrified look in his eyes, I was sorry for what I was about to do.

"The first bullet grazed his arm, and I could see him grimace in pain. Then he tried to raise the gun again, and the second bullet hit him dead center. The only thing I could hear was the echo of that shot, bouncing off the Dumpsters and brick walls. I couldn't hear the sirens. I couldn't hear the sound of the body hitting the ground. All I could hear was the gunshot.

"A few seconds later I heard something else. I didn't recognize it, at first, but the more I heard it, the louder it got. By the time my backup got to the scene I realized what I was hearing. It was the sound of my own breathing. Five years later, every time I remember that boy's face or hear a gunshot, it reminds me of that night . . . and the sound of my own breathing."

Charlie Mann looked at Sandy with a question in his eyes, and she answered before he could ask.

"As bad as I feel that I was on this side of those bullets," she said, taking his chin in her hand, "I'm glad I wasn't on the other side. I know you feel guilty about what happened on the train platform and in that warehouse, but think about the sound of your own breathing and how good it is to be alive, because if you would've hesitated a moment too long, maybe you wouldn't know that feeling anymore, and I wouldn't know how it feels to touch you."

He looked into her eyes. They were glistening in the

room's pale fluorescent light. The scent of her Angel perfume filled his nostrils. In that moment, she wasn't a woman who chased criminals and fired bullets. She was simply a woman, and she was beautiful.

He leaned over and brushed his lips against hers, softly at first, and then with a hunger that had been building with each passing second that their relationship had been in question. In that kiss there was tension, there was fear, there was anger, and there was relief.

They were each in need of someone who could relieve the emotions they'd been holding inside. They needed someone who could understand where they'd been and why. They needed to know they were safe from the world that existed outside that moment. They needed each other.

He wrapped his arms around her and pulled her close. She closed her eyes and allowed herself to experience what they felt for each other: love. It was stronger than life. It was stronger than death. It was stronger than any mistake they'd made in the past, and it was enough to carry them into the future.

Just then, Mann's iPhone began to vibrate. They ignored it at first, but it persisted. They both knew that the identity of the caller didn't matter. No matter what that person called themself, their name was duty, and Mann had an obligation to answer.

She sighed heavily and kissed him once more before he answered the call.

"Hello?"

He listened to the voice on the other end explain what

they'd found on Clarissa Bailey's hard drive. Then he disconnected the call and turned to Sandy.

"That was IT. They found the cryptogram on Clarissa's hard drive. It was decoded."

"So what does the cryptogram say?"

"It says, 'Start at the evergreen tree.'"

CHAPTER 13

As night settled upon what was left of Professor Workman's house, the billowing black smoke and leaping flames were a distant memory. A few crime scene cops remained, working by jury-rigged theater lighting, but the bodies of the victims were gone.

A security detail was posted around the perimeter of the house, and so were the media, though their frequent on-air reports had long ago become stale and repetitive.

Coletti looked around and knew that it was time to leave for Dunmore. There was nothing more for him to do in Elkins Park. He shook hands with his old friend who now worked for Cheltenham Township. Then he headed for his car. As he did so, Kirsten Douglas walked to hers.

She followed him until they'd left Ashbourne Road, but she got confused when he turned into a mall parking lot a few minutes later. He parked his car across from the bank. Then he got out and walked back to Kirsten's car while motioning for her to roll down the window.

"Why are you stopping here?" she asked.

He pointed to a brightly colored sign in the middle of the mall's parking lot. Kirsten saw it, but she couldn't believe it.

"Wendy's?" she asked incredulously. "You stopped in the middle of a murder investigation to go to Wendy's?"

Coletti looked down for a few seconds before staring off into the distance. "You're right—I shouldn't have done this," he said, shaking his head with fake regret. "I really should've gone to McDonald's."

Kirsten watched as Coletti walked toward the restaurant. He opened the glass door and turned around before he went inside. "You coming?" he asked.

She wanted to be professional, to stay on task, to do the right thing, but the smell of burgers and fries was wafting out the doors, and she hadn't eaten at all since early that morning. She put her car in park, turned off the engine, and walked in behind Coletti.

A few minutes later, after Kirsten parked her car and got in Coletti's, he took a triple cheeseburger out of his bag and mercilessly tore it apart. Kirsten wanted badly to do the same, but not in front of Coletti. He grinned with grease-stained lips when he saw her hesitation.

"Pretend it's fried raven," he said, stuffing fries into his mouth while starting the car.

She laughed. But a few seconds later, she was devouring a hamburger. Crumbs scattered across the seats, ketchup spilled on their clothes, and with each bite, their inhibitions faded just a little.

Within minutes, the hunger pangs were gone, and when they got on the road, their wariness began to give way to camaraderie. But even as they relaxed just a little, they both knew that the core problem remained. A killer was on the loose, and he needed to be caught before more lives were lost.

Kirsten placed a call to Sean O'Hanlon to tell him that she was bringing Coletti along. O'Hanlon responded with a long silence before he agreed to see the detective.

As Coletti drove north on Route 309 for the beginning of their two-hour trip, they were each lost in their own thoughts. Coletti wanted to know if it was possible for Lenore's father to know anything about a child he hadn't raised, and Kirsten wondered if traveling with Coletti would get her the story that she desired. Neither of them really wanted to be the first to speak. It was Kirsten who broke the ice.

"So, how close do you think you are to solving the case?" she asked while sipping her soda.

Coletti looked at her, and his mind took him back to the last time he'd traveled with a woman. The trip was to Graterford Prison to see Father Thomas O'Reilly, and the woman was Mary Smithson.

When he thought of that trip, he remembered seeing Mary in the very same seat where Kirsten sat now. He'd sat next to her and realized that he felt something far deeper than the collegial relationship he'd tried so hard to maintain. He remembered resisting the feelings he harbored for her, even as he let himself go in a haze of all the things he liked best: blond hair and blue eyes, Quarter Pounders and laughter, flirting and french fries.

Mary had sat where Kirsten was now, and from there she had asked about his dreams. Coletti surprised even himself by sharing them. He'd told her of his nightmares about the Confessional Murders. He'd told her of his doubts about the priest's guilt. He'd told her that he wanted to make it right. And when he made that admission, he knew that Mary had reached him in a place down deep. For that reason alone, he couldn't forget her. In truth, he didn't want to.

"Detective Coletti?" Kirsten said, shaking him from his thoughts. "Did you hear me? I asked if you thought we were close to solving the case."

He smiled nervously. "Yes, I heard you. I was just . . ."

"Just what?"

"I was thinking, that's all."

She observed him as he tightened his grip on the steering wheel and fixed his eyes on the road. He was rumpled and gruff, a cop's cop, and yet he was so comfortable with himself that he could eat burgers with a reporter. She wanted to know more about him, both for the story and for herself.

Coletti glanced at her, too. If nothing else, she was interesting to watch. With her intense brown eyes and curly hair to match, she looked like a woman who could juggle a million tasks while still holding herself together. She was dressed in clothes that were functional, but not alluring, and while her face was unremarkable, it was welcoming. In short, Kirsten Douglas was confident in who she was, and she could question herself openly without feeling stupid.

"I guess it was silly for me to ask if you were close to solving the case, huh?"

"Let me put it this way. If I was close, I wouldn't be riding to Dunmore with you."

"You sure know how to make a girl feel special."

"Anytime," he deadpanned. "I aim to please."

She looked out at the road flying by as Coletti drove way over the sixty-five-mile-per-hour speed limit. "How 'bout we start here," she said, kicking off her shoes and curling her feet underneath her. "What were you doing at the cemetery this morning?"

"Obviously, I was there to catch a murderer," he said as they turned onto I-476. "And obviously, I failed."

"No, I mean before all that happened. You were there visiting a grave, weren't you?"

Coletti shot a look in her direction. "You ask that question like you know the answer."

"You give that answer like you're avoiding the question."

He tensed up and hesitated a beat before he spoke. "I'd rather not talk about it, that's all."

"Well, is it all right if I talk about it?"

Coletti clenched his teeth and silently cursed himself for agreeing to travel with her. "It's a free country," he said tersely. "Talk about whatever you like."

"Okay," she said, turning in her seat to face him. "I know you went to Fairgrounds to visit Mary Smithson's grave."

She studied his face to gauge his reaction. He was

clearly hesitant to share his true feelings about Mary. When he spoke, he sounded uncomfortable.

"You must have really great sources," he said with a pasted-on grin. "The only people I saw there were Clarissa and Lenore. Clarissa's dead, and Lenore's under police protection. So who told you?"

"Does it matter?"

"Not really. No matter who you heard it from, it's still none of your business."

"Look, I'm not trying to pass judgment on you," she said softly. "I'm just trying to understand where you're coming from, because frankly, I don't see why you'd go to visit the grave of the woman who tried to kill you. It just doesn't make sense to me."

"So, why didn't you ask me about it earlier?"

"I didn't find out until after we'd talked."

They rode in silence for the next few seconds while Coletti considered whether to answer her. He thought he might, but first he had a question of his own.

"Have you ever wondered why somebody came into your life, and then wondered why they were gone?"

Kirsten thought of a loss that haunted her still. The memory of it was painful enough that she kept it locked away in a secret space in her heart.

"Yes, I've wondered about that," she said quietly.

"When did it happen?"

"Five years ago," she said, staring out the window as she spoke. "My mother had an aneurysm and died suddenly. It was awful, especially because we'd spent a lot of years angry at each other for basically no reason. Our relationship had been getting better, though, and then she was gone."

"That was five years ago, and I can tell it still hurts for you to talk about it," Coletti said. "I've only had two months, so whether I hated Mary Smithson or felt something else for her, don't you think it hurts me to talk about it, too?"

"Yes, but—"

"That's the one thing I've never understood about reporters. You get people at their most vulnerable moments, then you stick microphones in their faces and ask them to talk about the things that hurt them the most. And for what? To make your story juicy? To create some kinda scandal? To make people laugh at the poor old cop and the killer who pretended to . . ."

He stopped himself there, knowing he'd said too much, but it was too late to pull it back.

"If you don't want to answer my questions, it's okay," Kirsten said. "I can tell by the way you're acting that there was something more than hate between you and Mary, but that's all right. Keep it to yourself. Just remember that feelings are like acid. They can eat through the toughest surface if you give them enough time, even if that surface is a crusty old detective like you."

Coletti was in no mood to admit that she was right, so he drove the next two miles in silence. When he spoke again, she was surprised, not by what he said, but that he'd said anything at all.

"That's why I went there, you know."

She looked up, uncertain how to respond to what seemed like a random statement. "That's why you went where?"

"To the cemetery," he said. "I went so I could get out whatever it was I was feeling."

"And what exactly was that?"

"I don't want to call it love or hate," Coletti said. "To be honest with you, I really don't want to call it anything at all. I just don't want to be damaged by that acid you talked about. That's why I visited the cemetery. I was looking for closure."

"Did you find it?"

"No," Coletti said. "I didn't find closure. In fact, I opened a whole new can of worms. I just hope I can close it back up before more people get killed."

"Me, too," Kirsten said while looking out the window. "Me, too."

The gray, nondescript car had been left for him in front of the pizza place on Ogontz Avenue near Limekiln Pike. On a block where gunplay was lethal, where stickups were commonplace, and where death was ever-present, the sight of a man switching cars was not worth anyone's attention, and neither was the sound of sirens.

Under the fading light of day, the Gravedigger had maneuvered the car through traffic on the wide and winding street, slowly making his way onto the side roadways that extended like veins from Philadelphia's main arteries.

On those roads he'd made his way back to the art

museum area, and now that it was completely dark, he would make his way back underground.

He sat in the car on Fairmount Avenue, looking at the dried blood on his clothing and hands, silently cursing Workman for his refusal to tell what he knew. A simple act of submission would have saved countless lives, but now the Gravedigger would be forced to carry out the next phase of his plan, and even in his diminished mental state, he knew that the final phase wasn't something he wanted to do.

He told himself he would sit for a few minutes more, waiting for an opportune moment to walk away from the car. He was tired, though, and after his head bobbed for the third time he heard a loud pop at the entrance to Kelly Drive. His eyes snapped open to find that all the streetlights were out.

The Gravedigger looked calmly around him, waiting for the light to return. It didn't. Instead, the air began to move in a slow, whirling motion, causing sound and color and texture to spin like a top. He grabbed the car door in an effort to steady himself, but the spinning continued to whip everything in a circular motion. It continued for what seemed like an eternity. Then suddenly it stopped.

He was still for a few seconds before opening the car door and staggering out into the darkness, his equilibrium thrown off by the spinning. He couldn't see two feet in front of him, but he knew that he had to get to the underground, so he walked with his hands in front of him, groping for something to grab on to.

He listened for the croak of the raven, hoping it would circle overhead and guide him as it had done in the daytime. But in his heart the Gravedigger knew that Prophet couldn't guide him through this. No, this he had to face on his own, and if he survived it, perhaps he would be worthy of the treasure he so desperately sought.

He walked cautiously, hoping to find a wall, or a curb, or a sidewalk, or anything that would give substance to the darkness. He found nothing at all, and the more he pushed, the more he stumbled and flailed against the void.

As a sliver of light made its way through the dark, the Gravedigger could see that he had walked along Fairmount Avenue to Kelly Drive. He was now rounding the curve and approaching Boathouse Row. There were no lights on the iconic boathouses, however. Tonight there was only the blackness, and the statues that dotted the drive.

Behind him and to his right was Joan of Arc, riding on a golden horse while holding the banner of her armies. To his left was a crusader holding a cross, his helmeted face upturned. In the distance was a knight whose sword and shield were slung over his shoulder. Around the bend were a cavalry soldier and a Quaker with a massive bible.

The Gravedigger looked at the statues and wondered where the people were. As he tried to understand what he was seeing, there was a creaking sound. It stopped. There was a metallic squeal. It faded. For the next few seconds there was absolute silence. Then suddenly, there was the terrible grinding of metal.

The Gravedigger looked up and saw a horse and rider emerging from the darkness. He squinted, knowing that what he was witnessing was impossible, but when he heard the thunderous sound of hooves in the air, he knew that it was real. The statue of the cavalry soldier had come to life, and as it raced toward him through the blackness that surrounded him, the Gravedigger turned to run. The soldier fired a single shot. The killer dropped to his knees before rolling onto his back in agony.

A half minute later, as the Gravedigger's life's blood ran out from the bullet wound, the horse stopped, the rider dismounted, and the sound of heavy footsteps shook the ground.

The soldier stood over the Gravedigger with gun in hand, his upturned hat revealing a face whose scowl was permanent. The soldier pointed his rifle at the Gravedigger's face, and when the bullet exploded from the barrel in a flash of white-hot fire, the Gravedigger's eyes snapped open.

His face was covered with sweat and his breathing was rapid and shallow. He looked around quickly to get his bearings. He was sitting in the car. It was parked on Fairmount Avenue. The dream of the darkness was over.

The Gravedigger sat still, his heart beating wildly as the nightmare faded from his consciousness. As his mind returned him to the moment, he knew what he had to do. He would go underground and wait until he received word from his benefactor. Then he would move quickly to retrieve the treasure he'd been waiting for.

With that thought in mind, the Gravedigger slipped out of the gray car and into the darkness. Moments later, he was on his way back to the place where he felt safest.

He was on his way back to the grave.

* * *

Mann placed a call to one of his old professors at Penn, who promised to try to put together a list of students from the creative writing program.

Then he and Sandy walked over to the captain's office, where they sat with Commissioner Lynch and the captain, listening as a young computer technician walked them through the information that had been pulled from Clarissa Bailey's hard drive.

They understood some of it, like the bank records confirming that Clarissa had been tattooed at a South Philly shop, bought a gun at a Bucks County gun store, and stayed at a hotel in Scranton, all in the last week. They understood the e-mails indicating that she'd been in steady communication with Workman, Lily Thompkins, and Violet Grant about historical finds around the city. They understood that she kept records about the Gravedigger's Ball and Tookesbury Mansion in a file on her desktop. But there was much they didn't understand, because the computer technician spoke in the geeky jargon of a techie.

As he blathered on about the various bits and pieces they'd gleaned from the gigabytes of information on Clarissa's computer, even the tech-savvy Charlie Mann found himself lost. After a few minutes of listening to words like *code* and *algorithms* and *surrogate keys*, Mann had had enough.

"Do me a favor," he said. "Can you just tell us in plain language what we need to know?"

"I'm sorry," the young man said with a nervous laugh.

"Sometimes I get a little excited. Where do you want me to start?"

"Start with the cryptogram," Commissioner Lynch said.

"Sure, no problem. We found the cryptogram in Mrs. Bailey's 'My Documents' folder, along with some other things she'd stored in a subfolder called 'Poe.' It was a handwritten document that was scanned and saved as a PDF, and it contained a chart with two sets of symbols representing each letter in the cryptogram's code. The first set was the alphabet backward, so the letter *a* was represented by the letter *z* and so on. The second set was numbers, so the letter *a* was represented by the number 1 and so on. The cryptogram was pretty simple, really. It alternated between the letters and numbers. The method confused the computers, but anybody who was really into cryptograms should've been able to solve it pretty easily."

"And the solution to the cryptogram was written on that same document?" Mann asked.

"Yes. On the document, right under the cryptogram, was the answer. It said, 'Start at the evergreen tree.' Underneath that, someone had written three words, 'The Gold Bug.'"

Sandy glanced at Mann. "Isn't that the name of the story the ranger gave you back at the Poe house?"

"Yeah."

"Was there a map in the story?" the computer tech asked.

"Yeah," said Mann.

"Well, you might want to take a look at this. It was in the Poe folder on Clarissa's computer, too."

He handed them a picture of a map containing what appeared to be an overhead view of Fairgrounds Cemetery, complete with symbols for headstones, monuments, and mausoleums. In the upper-left-hand corner was a picture of a tree. A dotted line extended from the tree and wound around headstones and mausoleums in the graveyard. The line ended almost exactly at the point where Clarissa's body had been found that morning.

"Maybe this map leads to the secret Poe supposedly hid at the cemetery," Sandy said.

"But if Clarissa had a map, why would she need Lenore Wilkinson?" Mann asked. "Why would the whole thing about a seer even matter?"

"Maybe she tried to use the map and it didn't work," the captain said.

Mann turned to the computer technician. "When were these documents created?"

"The first one was created September fourth at nine A.M. The second was created about five minutes later. The properties in both documents list Clarissa Bailey as the author, which means she's the one who scanned them and saved them as PDFs."

"But that doesn't mean she created the documents, right?"

The technician nodded.

"So, in theory, she could've gotten these documents from anywhere and scanned them into her computer," Mann said.

"That's right."

"Then we need to figure out who created these documents for Clarissa."

"Not only that," Sandy said. "We need to figure out why she scanned them. If these documents were supposed to be the key to this secret and someone gave them to her on paper, she probably wouldn't have turned them into PDFs unless she intended to pass them on."

"Did she pass them on?" the commissioner asked the technician.

"Not by e-mail," the technician said.

"Maybe she got killed before she got the chance," said the commissioner.

They were quiet for a moment as they contemplated what it would mean if the commissioner was right.

"What else did you find on the computer?" the captain asked.

"E-mails. Lots of them."

The technician placed three sheets of paper on the captain's desk and began to explain. "Most of them were to and from Violet Grant and Lily Thompkins. She sent a couple to the cemetery manager, mostly about the Gravedigger's Ball. And then, of course, there was the e-mail address you asked us to try to trace—the fifth address Clarissa e-mailed with the information about Lenore Wilkinson coming to town."

"Were you able to find out anything about it?" Mann asked.

"Not based on the e-mail Mrs. Bailey sent, but when the person e-mailed Mrs. Bailey later that day, we were able to trace the IP address of the computer they used."

"What did the e-mail say?" Mann asked.

"It just said, 'Thanks.' "

"That's it? No signature?"

"Nope."

"So who sent it?" Sandy asked.

"We don't know. All we know is that the sender e-mailed Clarissa Bailey from a computer at the Free Library's central branch."

"So you don't have any other way of finding out who sent it?"

"Sure," the technician said. "We could send a warrant to the hosting company asking for the name of the person who registered the address, but it might take a while."

"Maybe we could see if they have surveillance video of the person who was sitting at the computer when the e-mail was sent," said Mann.

"They're both worth a shot," Commissioner Lynch said. "I'll get you the warrant. Mann, you get in touch with the Free Library and see if we can get that video."

"Did the Park Service ever send you the video from the Poe house?" Sandy asked.

"No," said Mann. "I circled back with them a couple hours ago and they still didn't have it, but I'll check with them again."

"So where does that leave us?" Sandy asked.

"Depends on what else we have," the commissioner said, as they all looked at the technician expectantly.

"We didn't really find anything else when we went

through her computer, and her husband's computer didn't contain much more than porn."

"What about her cell phone?" the captain asked.

"She got a text message yesterday that might have been significant," the technician said as he looked through the papers to see if he could find the cell phone records.

"Here it is," he said. "The bank sent her a text two days ago about check number 1766—a ten-thousand-dollar personal check that someone was trying to cash. Mrs. Bailey called the bank a few minutes later, apparently to okay the transaction."

"Do we know who the check was made out to?" the captain asked.

"We had to cross-check the bank records on her computer," the technician said while shuffling through the papers. "But it looks like the check was made out to someone named Sean O'Hanlon."

"That's Lenore Wilkinson's father," Mann said, sounding perplexed. "Did the check say what the payment was for?"

"In the memo line it just said 'research.'"

"Get the officers guarding Lenore Wilkinson on the phone," Commissioner Lynch said. "We need her back down here to answer some questions."

Mann made the call as the others watched. But as he listened to the response from the other end, his facial expression became apprehensive. Slowly he disconnected the call and looked up at the commissioner.

"They knocked on the bathroom door and she didn't

answer, so they went inside. They don't know how and they don't know why, but she's gone."

"What do you mean, 'she's gone'?" the commissioner asked.

"I mean, she walked away. They did say she left a note, though. It said, 'Don't try to find me.'"

Coletti got the call just as they pulled into Dunmore. Mann told him about Lenore, the documents, and the money Clarissa Bailey had paid Lenore's father.

The old detective turned ashen at the thought of Lenore gone missing, but when he saw the reporter looking at him, he tried to compose his face.

"Everything okay?" she asked.

"Yeah," he said, knowing he couldn't tell her everything. "Let's just go in."

Coletti parked the car in front of the house where Sean O'Hanlon was staying. As he did so, the pitch-black evening gave way to sleepy streetlights. It was hard to believe that this slice of small-town America was now infamous for being the Angel of Death's hometown.

Dunmore, after all, was a place where Catholicism flourished and violent crime was rare. Much like its better-known neighbor, Scranton, Dunmore was also a place where family mattered and where neighbors looked out for one another. By default, it was a place of law and order, since it housed the local state police barracks.

But like every small town, Dunmore was a place that held on to its secrets. While everyone within the tiny town's borders knew of the darkness that existed in his neighbor's house, nobody told outsiders. Dunmore's secrets were family business, and if you didn't live there, you weren't a part of the family.

That was what made it so odd that Sean O'Hanlon had not only agreed to speak with Kirsten Douglas, but had initiated the conversation. He had something he wanted to say, and he needed to say it in person, not over the phone, because here, speaking face-to-face was worth a two-hour drive.

Coletti and Kirsten got out of the car and walked toward the brick single home that was nestled among bushes and tall oaks. Kirsten looked at the house and then up at the stars that shone like crystals in the still and quiet sky.

The detective approached the front door with mixed emotions. Not just about the fact that Lenore was missing. He was also conflicted about Sean O'Hanlon, the man who'd fathered the two women who'd affected him the most. Coletti wanted to focus on the facts of the current case, but he couldn't help remembering the emotions from the last one.

They knocked. Sean O'Hanlon cracked the door open and glanced at Kirsten Douglas before turning his penetrating stare on the detective.

"Hi, Mr. O'Hanlon," Kirsten said with an easy smile. "This is Detective Coletti—the one I told you about."

O'Hanlon stared at him. "I know Detective Coletti," he said in a raspy voice. "I talked to him after my Mary died."

O'Hanlon shuffled backward to open the door. His unkempt blond hair was mostly gray, and his stubble-lined jaws were gaunt. His pale skin was punctuated by dark circles around his bloodshot eyes, and though his face showed hints of the looks he'd passed on to his daughters, he was clearly not the man he used to be.

"Come in," he said, walking with a pronounced limp as he escorted them into the living room. "Have a seat."

As they sat down on a couch across from him, Kirsten took note of the way O'Hanlon's flannel shirt hung limp from his shoulders, as if it were made for a much larger man. Coletti saw it, too, and he also saw the dozens of pill bottles on the end table next to his chair.

The walls were filled with photos of a family that had long since left Dunmore for greener pastures. A black and white wedding picture was there, fading badly after almost fifty years. The pictures of their six children were there, too. But even now, nearly thirty years after the divorce, there were no childhood pictures of Sean O'Hanlon's seventh child, Lenore. He still couldn't bring himself to put his illegitimate daughter's photo on the wall.

"I guess you're wondering why I called you," O'Hanlon said to Kirsten.

"Yes, I am," she said, taking out her notebook. "I'm especially curious about why you wanted me to come all the way out here to speak to you in person."

"Well, as you can see, I'm not in the best of health," he said with a cough. "The cancer's got me pretty good, so I don't get out much anymore, and with no one here to look after the old man, it's best that I do my talking face-to-face."

"I guess that's why you didn't answer the door when we sent the state police to knock," Coletti said.

"You sent them to the wrong door. This is my aunt's old house. I've been staying here for about a month because it's easier to get around with everything on one floor. All I had to move over here were my pills and my pictures."

"We called you, too, Mr. O'Hanlon," Coletti said. "In fact we called every number for every O'Hanlon in Dunmore, and you never answered the phone."

"Don't take it personal," O'Hanlon said. "I only wanted to talk to Kirsten. But when she told me you were coming, I thought it was for the best, since this Gravedigger thing seems to be centered on my daughter."

"Why would you think it was about her?" Coletti asked. "We never said that publicly."

"You didn't have to. Clarissa Bailey said it when she came to see me last week. She was asking all kinds of questions about Lenore, and I told her I couldn't answer them."

"Why couldn't you?" Kirsten asked.

"Because I didn't trust her," O'Hanlon said. "The things she was asking seemed odd. She wanted to know if Lenore had told me anything about Fairgrounds Cemetery, or if I'd ever heard Lenore mention some guy named Irving Workman. She wanted to know if Lenore had ever mentioned meeting her. All of it made me feel uneasy."

"But that's not what you called me to say," Kirsten said. "There's more to it than that, isn't there?"

"Yes," O'Hanlon said, taking a deep, ragged breath as he looked away from them and into the distance.

"So tell us why you called," Kirsten said gently.

He looked at them with a serious expression. "I called because Clarissa Bailey paid me ten thousand dollars to forget she'd ever been here. I was willing to keep my mouth shut until I turned on the news and saw Clarissa dead in the same cemetery she asked me about, and saw that my daughter was with her."

Coletti was getting fed up with O'Hanlon's self-righteous tone, so he did what he did best in interrogations. He went on the attack.

"So, let me guess," Coletti said cynically. "You're not speaking up because you want to come clean. You're speaking up because that ten thousand dollars connects you to a woman who was murdered."

"It has nothing to do with that," O'Hanlon said, his tone edgy but calm.

"Then why speak up?"

"Because I never spoke up about Mary."

"Sure you did," Coletti said with a cynical smile. "You trashed her after she was dead."

"And that was wrong," O'Hanlon said firmly. "I should've spoken about her when she was alive. Fact is, I knew the types of problems she had, and I never said anything to anyone. I kept my mouth shut, and all those people died because of it."

"Are you saying Lenore has the same types of problems?" Kirsten asked.

Coletti scoffed. "How could he say that? How could he say *anything*? He doesn't even know Lenore."

Kirsten looked confused. Coletti looked satisfied. He believed the emotion he'd conjured up might make O'Hanlon talk. When the old man's eyes filled up with pain and he opened his mouth to speak, Coletti knew his gamble was about to pay off.

"The detective's right," O'Hanlon said softly. "For a long time I didn't know anything about Lenore. She was born after I had an affair, and when the smoke cleared, my life was ruined. I had a wife who wanted to kill me. I had a daughter who didn't even know me. I had six other children who hated me because I'd hurt their mother so badly.

"I was a hypocrite, and I can see that, now that I'm seventy with only a few months to go before the cancer takes me. It's amazing that when you're old your eyesight gets bad, but your vision gets a whole lot clearer. When I look back, I see a life that was basically wasted. So I didn't just call you here to tell you about the ten thousand dollars. I called you here so I could make things right."

O'Hanlon grabbed a crumpled pack of cigarettes from amidst the pills on the end table.

"Do you think you should be doing that, Mr. O'Hanlon?" Kirsten asked worriedly.

"Doctor says I've got three months," he said while searching for a light. "I might as well die happy."

Coletti took a lighter from his pocket and leaned over to light the old man's cigarette for him. Kirsten gave the detective a dirty look, but Coletti didn't care. He understood where O'Hanlon was coming from. In a decade, that could be him.

"So, what is it that you need to make right?" Coletti asked.

The old man took a short drag on the cigarette. He exhaled the smoke and coughed a few times. Then he reached over to the end table for his glass. He took a swig of whiskey and savored it for a moment before leaning back in his chair and looking from the reporter to the detective.

"Lenore's mother was my wife's best friend," he said, his tone neither proud nor ashamed. "She lived a few blocks away, and she was at our house most days, talking to my wife or helping with the housework, or babysitting the kids. The affair happened over time, and when my wife found out about it she was hurt in ways I can't even explain. Even then, she was willing to forgive me, but when the town found out things got a lot harder."

"So, how did the town find out?" Coletti asked.

O'Hanlon puffed his cigarette and took another sip of his drink, grimacing as the alcohol burned in his chest.

"They found out because Lenore's birth was unusual," he said.

"You mean the veil?" Coletti asked.

O'Hanlon took another puff of his cigarette. "No, I never heard anything about a veil. Of course, it's possible that she was born with one—they didn't let fathers in the room back then, and even if they did I wouldn't have been there, since I was married."

"So what about her birth was unusual?" asked Kirsten.

He took another swig of his whiskey and swallowed hard as his eyes went vacant.

"Lenore came out bleeding. Turned out she was anemic, and she needed a blood transfusion. Her blood type was AB negative, which is very rare, so they did a big push for blood donors to save her—had it on the news and everything. When it turned out I was the only person in the entire Scranton-Dunmore area with that blood type, everyone started to suspect that I was the father. It didn't help that she looked just like me.

"My wife and I divorced right after that. She took our kids and moved in with her parents on the other side of town. Her friend took Lenore and made sure I never had a chance to be a father to her. When all my kids were old enough, they left town, and only two of them have ever come back."

He looked at Coletti as he spoke. "Mary came back to work at the state police barracks, probably just to torture me. She didn't just blame you for what happened to her in that cathedral when she was a child, Detective Coletti. She blamed me."

"Blamed you for what?" Kirsten asked.

"She was raped," said Coletti. "I caught the guy who did it. It was one of my first arrests, but they said his confession was coerced and they let him go."

"Mary blamed Detective Coletti for that," O'Hanlon explained. "But she blamed me even more. If I hadn't been distracted by the affair, if I would've watched her when she went in that bathroom in the cathedral, if I would've lived right, if I would've loved my wife . . . Mary gave me plenty of ifs over the years, and when she came back, she gave them to me again. She hated me for what happened to her, and I think that hate is the reason she turned out the way she did."

They were quiet for a few minutes, digesting what Sean O'Hanlon had shared.

"Who was the other kid who came back?" Kirsten asked.

O'Hanlon took a drag of his cigarette. "Lenore."

"Lenore?" Coletti said, sounding confused. "She told me she never knew you. She said she'd never talked to you before."

"That was true until about a year ago," O'Hanlon said. "But last fall she came back to Dunmore and showed up on my doorstep."

"And what did she say she wanted?" Coletti asked.

"She wanted to know who her father was," O'Hanlon said as tears sprung to his eyes. "I couldn't believe this person I'd only seen in passing a few times—this little girl I'd thought about every day for almost thirty years—had come back to Dunmore to find me."

O'Hanlon wiped his eyes and took another swig of his whiskey. "It seemed like we talked forever, catching up on everything about each other. She told me she had a master's degree and that she was married to John Wilkinson. She said she was interested in charities and history. She told me she'd met a group of women from Philadelphia who loved Poe, just like she did."

A chill went up Coletti's spine as he thought of everything Lenore had told him. She'd said that she wasn't interested in national historic landmarks. She'd feigned ignorance about the writings of Poe. She'd told him that she'd just met Clarissa Bailey for the first time. They were lies—all of them. But Coletti couldn't figure out why.

"Did the two of you stay in contact after that?" he asked.

"No, but she left something behind," O'Hanlon said, reaching into his pocket and unfolding two pieces of paper.

He laid them out on the coffee table for both Kirsten and Coletti to see. Kirsten was baffled. Coletti wasn't.

On one sheet of paper was the original of the map that Clarissa Bailey had scanned into her computer. On the other was the cryptogram and its answer.

"So I guess you're going to question Lenore now," O'Hanlon said sadly.

"Yes, we are," Coletti said with a sigh. "But first we have to find her."

"What do you mean?" O'Hanlon said as Kirsten looked at Coletti with shock etched on her face.

"Your daughter's missing, Mr. O'Hanlon. She disappeared from her hotel room about an hour ago."

CHAPTER 14

Police fanned out across the city to find Lenore. Bus stations, train stations, and the airport were checked. Calls were placed to Princeton and Manhattan. They called every number her husband had left, and neither John nor Lenore was anywhere to be found.

Commissioner Lynch could deal with many things, but incompetence wasn't one of them. As Mann, Sandy, and a team of homicide detectives pored over the material they'd collected over the course of the investigation, Lynch had the officers who'd been assigned to Lenore brought into an interrogation room in homicide. When they got there, he was waiting.

Lynch watched as cops from internal affairs brought the two patrolmen inside. One of the patrolmen was young and fresh-faced, with wide eyes and a nervous smile that he flashed to hide his fear. The other was older, more seasoned, and he wore the cynical expression of a man who'd been a cop too long.

"Have a seat, gentleman," Lynch said to the patrolmen.

Both of them sat in scarred metal chairs that were normally reserved for suspects. The cops from internal affairs stood silently at the door as the commissioner sat on the edge of the table and looked down at the patrolmen's faces.

"Officer Thomas," Lynch said, reading from the older patrolman's name tag. "When did you realize that Mrs. Wilkinson was missing?"

"Had to be about an hour ago," he said easily. "We were stationed outside her hotel room, and we were checking on her every ten minutes. The last time we went in to check, she was gone."

"Just like that?" Lynch asked. "She just disappeared into thin air while both of you were on your posts?"

The young one licked his lips nervously as Officer Thomas explained. "I'm sure she didn't disappear into thin air, sir, but I know we didn't leave our posts."

Lynch's eyes bored into Officer Thomas. "Her room was on the twentieth floor, correct?"

"Yes, sir."

"So she couldn't have jumped out the window, could she?"

"No, sir."

"And it wasn't a suite, so there was only one way in and one way out, right?"

"Yes, sir."

"So if she didn't jump out the window, and she didn't get out through an adjoining room, one or both of you must've left your posts. Otherwise, it would've been impossible for her to simply walk away."

Thomas shifted nervously in his chair. "I know it sounds crazy, Commissioner, and I've never seen anything like it in my twenty years on the force, but—"

"Put your badge and gun on the table, Officer Thomas," Lynch said.

"Commissioner, I—"

"Do it now!" Lynch shouted.

The old cop looked at the young one. Then he looked at Commissioner Lynch, and with a heavy sigh, he plucked his badge from his uniform, took his gun from its holster, and laid both on the table.

"Consider yourself fired," Lynch said. "And depending on what I find out, you might want to get ready to go to jail, too. The sergeant will escort you out."

Officer Thomas shot a look in the direction of the young officer, his eyes begging him to do anything but talk. The young cop refused to meet his gaze. He'd already seen enough.

When the door closed behind Officer Thomas, Lynch turned his withering stare on the young cop. Everything about the cop was new, from his uniform to his wedding band to the look in his bloodshot eyes.

"Officer Green," the commissioner said, reading from the young man's name tag, "I'm going to give you one chance to tell me the truth. If you do, I'll try to help you avoid jail time. If you don't, all bets are off."

Lynch paused and looked the young cop in the eye

before posing the question directly. "Where's Lenore Wilkinson?"

The cop twisted his wedding band around his finger. He wanted to weigh his options, but he knew he didn't have any. After a long moment he looked up at the commissioner with plaintive eyes.

"No jail time?" he asked.

"As long as nobody hurt her, no jail time."

Officer Green looked over his shoulder at the remaining cop from internal affairs. Then he allowed his gaze to rest on the commissioner. He sighed deeply before he began to speak.

"She came to the door and told us she wanted to go home," he said quietly. "I knew we couldn't hold her against her will, but I wanted to at least call it in to let someone know. She didn't want us to do that, though, so she offered us two thousand dollars each to look the other way. I wasn't going to take it at first, but Thomas, well, he said no one would ever know, and I believed him."

Lynch exchanged glances with the cop from internal affairs. Then he turned to the patrolman and asked the question they all wanted answered. "Where did she go when she left?"

"I don't know," Green said. "She just walked away."

The commissioner glared at the young cop, despising him as much for his stupidity as anything else. "Leave your gun and badge on the table," he said.

The cop did as he was told, and when he was escorted

out, there were tears in his eyes. Lynch hated watching a young cop's career end before it began, but what he hated even more was the fact that it was avoidable.

Mann knocked on the door and walked in with a laptop. Sandy and the captain were with him. Lynch tried to hide his troubled expression from them, but they all knew the case was getting to him. It was getting to all of them.

"They told us you were down here," the captain said. "Did you get what you needed?"

"I got what I didn't need," he said with a heavy sigh. "Lenore Wilkinson paid off the guys on the detail to let her walk away."

"I'm not surprised," Mann said. "Coletti just called on his way back from Dunmore. He talked to Lenore's father and apparently almost everything she told us was a lie. She knew Clarissa. She knew about Workman's theories. She knew everything."

"Did she know the killer?" the commissioner asked.

Mann opened the laptop and spoke as it booted up. "I'm not sure if she knew him or not," he said as he clicked on a pictures folder. "But my contacts down at Penn sent these over. These are the guys who were in the MFA program over the last two years."

They all looked at the pictures. There were two black men and three Asian men. Of the four white men, none of them had black hair.

"I don't see a match," the commissioner said.

"Neither did I," Mann said. "Not at first. But the

National Park Service came through with the surveillance video from the Poe house. They e-mailed it about fifteen minutes ago. Take a look."

He clicked on another folder, and the first of three surveillance videos popped up. In it, a young man with black hair and a mustache walked in behind Clarissa Bailey. In several shots, they walked through the house on the tour, seemingly unaware of one another. But in the final shot their proximity was so close as to be familiar. They appeared to know each other.

"That's interesting," Sandy said, "but we still don't know who he is."

Mann smiled. Then he took a still from the video and opened Adobe Photoshop. He superimposed the video still over the headshot of an unsmiling young man with blond hair and blue eyes from the master's program. It was a match.

"Dyed hair and contact lenses do wonders," Mann said. "This is our guy. According to my contacts at Penn, he never took a class with Workman, but the professor took him under his wing. His name is Lance Griggs, and he dropped out of the program after his wife was murdered. Nobody's seen Lance in months."

"Until today," the captain said.

The commissioner brightened. "Good work, Mann. What's his last known address?"

"With all due respect, Commissioner, I don't think his last known address is where we'll find him. This whole thing came down to the map of the cemetery, and that's where I think he is."

Lynch looked at the captain, who, along with Sandy, nodded in agreement. They all knew Mann was right. They simply needed Lynch's approval.

"Do it," Lynch said, and within a half hour, they were ready to hit the Gravedigger where he lived.

Four teams of homicide detectives walked in through Fairgrounds' various entrances, and did so with a single purpose. Follow the map to wherever it led them, and bring back whatever they found.

Mann and Sandy, joined by two M16-toting officers from the SWAT unit, made up team number 1. Teams 2 through 4 were also composed of detectives and SWAT officers. Between them, they had enough firepower to neutralize whatever they encountered, but as the teams got into position, the cemetery grew ever more still.

Pale yellow light filtered onto the cemetery grounds from the streetlamps along Kelly Drive. A sliver of moon and a smattering of stars shone dimly through the clouds.

The result was a graveyard that was darker than it should be. Occupied police cars sat at every entrance. Crime scene tape blocked off the empty grave where Clarissa's body had been found. Fallen leaves swirled in the night breeze.

Mann led Sandy and the others to the spot beneath the evergreen tree where Mary Smithson was buried. Sandy shone her flashlight on the tiny grave marker while shaking her head at the irony of the map's beginning there.

"Team 1 in position," Mann whispered into his handheld radio as Sandy unfolded the map.

The other three team leaders parroted those words, and flashlight beams stabbed through the darkness as Sandy and Mann began walking through the graveyard.

They followed the winding path laid out on the map, traversing mausoleums, headstones, and other monuments to the dead. When they reached the end point of the map, they looked down into the grave where they'd found Clarissa Bailey. There was nothing there.

For a full minute, they stood, staring into the hole as the darkness wrapped itself around them. Sandy bent down for a closer look, leaning in with her gun in one hand and her flashlight in the other. There was a swishing sound above their heads, almost like that of flapping wings. They all pointed their flashlights skyward in an effort to find out what the sound had come from.

When they didn't see anything, they returned their attention to the empty grave, and as Mann watched Sandy stare down into the hole, Poe's words came bubbling to the surface.

"Deep into that darkness peering . . ."

He tried to shake the phrase from his mind, but it was quickly followed by another.

"Long I stood there, wondering, fearing . . ."

Again, they heard the flapping of wings, this time punctuated by the deep croak of the raven. They looked up, all of them, with their weapons and flashlights aimed at the sky. When nothing appeared, Mann wasn't sure what he'd heard or seen. It was as if Poe's next line had come to life.

"Doubting, dreaming dreams no mortal ever dared to dream before . . ."

It was quiet now. The breeze was still, their guns were silent. Everything seemed to stop. Everything, that is, except for Mann's mind, which recalled the lines he'd looked up that morning while standing near that very spot.

"But the silence was unbroken, and the darkness gave no token,

"And the only word there spoken was the whispered word 'Lenore' . . ."

As soon as the thought of Lenore's name entered his mind, the raven dove from the sky with a deep, loud croak, and went for Sandy's face. She rolled left and the bird's sharp claws ripped through her soft leather jacket, scratching her upper arm. The raven tried to attack again, but Sandy rolled away once more.

A SWAT officer fired three shots in rapid succession, obliterating the bird and the ground beneath it. As blood and black feathers mingled with the dead grass and earth, a flurry of voices flooded their radios and the teams ran toward Mann and Sandy's position.

When Sandy rose to her feet, Mann took her by the hand. "Are you okay?" he asked.

She nodded. Then she looked at the dead raven and a chill went through her, because every time the raven had showed up that day, a body was not far behind.

By the time the three other teams reached them, Sandy was stepping away from the dead bird, and a quiet rumbling sound was bubbling up from the ground. Every cop in the cemetery listened as the sound grew steadily louder. In mere seconds it reached an ear-splitting volume, and the ground beneath Sandy's feet gave way. With Mann holding on to her, they both fell into the grave.

By the time the rumbling stopped, they were flat on their backs. They were startled, but neither of them was hurt. Sandy scrambled to her feet and pulled Mann upright. They both reached up so the other officers could grab their hands and pull them out. As they did so, the ground beneath them shook as if a heavy truck had driven by on the road. Suddenly the shaking became more violent. The officers who were standing over the grave fell backward. A chunk of earth came loose beneath Sandy and Mann, opening a hole that tunneled down into the earth.

By the time the ground stopped shaking and the other officers got to their feet, Mann and Sandy were no longer visible. They'd both been swallowed by the grave.

A homicide sergeant who commanded the second of the four teams jumped down into the grave with his back against the side, trying desperately to avoid the hole that had taken Mann and Sandy.

"Charlie!" he called into his handheld radio. "Lieutenant Jackson, come in!"

There was static on the other end. The sergeant leaned forward to look into the hole. He didn't see any signs of life, but approximately forty feet down he saw a faint blue light that brightened and dimmed, almost like the light from a gas-burning stove. As the ground started to shift again and the members of his team pulled him out of the grave, he felt like he'd just peered into hell.

"Call for an assist," he said as he caught his breath. "We've gotta get them outta there."

The harrowing slide through the deep, dark hole felt as if it would never end. They tumbled into and against one another for what seemed like forever, hurtling through a rock-strewn nightmare. When they came out the other end, some forty feet under the graveyard's surface, they slammed into the muddy wall of a much larger tunnel before landing in a bloody heap.

They both lay still for a few seconds, trying to reorient themselves. Once they both realized that they were still alive, they felt along the ground for their weapons. They retrieved them and struggled to their feet, thankful that the muddy wall had helped to break their fall, and anxious about their prospects for getting out.

Mann tried his radio, but it didn't work beneath the ground. Both of them tried yelling, but they couldn't hear anyone answer. The noise they made drew interest, however. The blue light from around the bend reflected in the eyes of gathering rats.

They each readied their weapons and checked their injuries. Mann's left arm was bloody and raw from the slide through the rocky tunnel. Sandy touched her left wrist and winced, realizing then that it might be broken.

"You gonna make it?" Mann asked.

"I'm breathing," Sandy said. "I'll be all right."

That was the optimistic view, because breathing had already become more difficult. The air in the tunnel was nothing like the air aboveground, and though neither of them said it aloud, they knew they couldn't survive in the tunnel for long.

"Come on," Mann said, walking cautiously toward the blue light that shone from around the bend.

Sandy followed him as rats scurried and squealed at their feet.

As they got closer to the curve in the tunnel where the blue light shone most brightly, they both held their guns out in front of them, and their breath came faster as adrenaline pumped through their veins.

They rounded the curve with a mixture of fear and excitement as the pulsing blue light shone brighter, and when they walked into the makeshift room that housed the source of the light, they were each shocked into silence by what they saw.

A small wooden chair held a laptop that had been left open. Its blue screen saver was pulsating, and Mann and Sandy both thought the same thing: the laptop's owner must be close by. They gripped their guns tightly and waited for someone to emerge from the shadows.

Aided by the light from the computer, they surveyed the small room that had been carved out of the dirt. They could see that it was a hub of some sort, with three other tunnels leading out.

"You hear something?" Sandy whispered.

At first he didn't, but when Mann listened more

closely, he could hear the rumbling sound returning. It was coming from somewhere behind them, and it was getting closer. They looked back into the tunnel they'd just come from and saw that its ceiling was giving way.

The collapse was moving quickly in their direction, so Mann grabbed the laptop from the chair and they ran to another tunnel, coughing and squinting from the dust that filled the air. When it settled, they could see that the room they'd just left had been obliterated.

That was when the voice spoke up. "Welcome," the killer said from somewhere in the darkness.

Both Mann and Sandy aimed their weapons in the direction that the sound had come from.

"Who are you?" Mann asked. "Lance?"

They could almost feel the Gravedigger's shock when Mann spoke his name. He didn't speak, but it felt as if he'd stopped breathing. This was no ordinary silence. It was a silence that was filled with grief.

"Lance, I know you're there," Mann said.

"Lance is dead!" the Gravedigger shouted from somewhere in the darkness, and then he was silent again.

His voice was still echoing through the tunnel when there was a sudden movement near the wall directly across from them. Both Mann and Sandy fired in that direction. Seconds later the rumbling began anew. Dust shook loose from the ceiling of the tunnel. It felt as if another collapse was imminent.

"What do you want?" Sandy asked.

"You know what I want," the killer said as his voice

moved closer. "I want the secret. That's why I agreed to do this."

"Agreed?" Mann said. "Agreed with who?"

"Come and see," the Gravedigger said, his voice so close they could almost feel him.

Mann raised his weapon to fire, but the Gravedigger knocked it out of his hand. Mann swung and caught him with a right that somehow found its mark in the darkness. Sandy heard the killer stumble, and she shot once in his direction. As the sound of the gunshot echoed through the passage, the rumbling in the tunnel began anew, and the Gravedigger ran away.

Mann and Sandy gave chase, but they were at a distinct disadvantage. The Gravedigger knew these mazelike passageways all too well. Mann and Sandy didn't know them at all. They banged into the dirt walls as they chased the sounds of footsteps and grunting, but as the killer rounded a curve and ran up a steep incline toward a room with dim yellow light, his silhouette emerged from the shadows. Sandy took aim. The Gravedigger dove toward the lighted room. Sandy fired once, and the killer dropped to his knees. Then he rolled onto his back in agony.

The Gravedigger remembered this scene from his dream. This was different, though. This time it wasn't the cavalry soldier standing over him and watching him die. This time it was two cops.

He winced as the wound began to throb, but he refused to let pain defeat him. Pushing himself along the tunnel's dirt floor with his forearms, he struggled to make it to the room. He told himself that if he believed in the secret the bleeding would stop; if he believed in the secret he'd see his wife again; if he believed in the secret his benefactor would fix it, just as he'd said he would.

But as the Gravedigger reached out for the man who'd promised him the world, he only saw a repeat of his dream. This time, when the white-hot light flashed in his face, it wasn't from the explosion of a bullet. It was the last gasp of a dying mind.

The Gravedigger was dead, and in his place was a man whose grief had given way to rage. Hints of his blond hair showed through the blackness. The contact over one of his eyes was gone. The stains on his blackened teeth were rubbed away, and all that remained was reality.

Lance Griggs smiled as his eyes went vacant. He'd soon be with his wife after all.

"You didn't have to kill him," said a robed man who'd appeared, as if from thin air, and was standing in the doorway of the dimly lit room. "He's not the one you wanted. I am."

Mann thought he recognized the voice. Sandy didn't.

"Don't move," she said, leveling her weapon as she and Mann walked up the incline.

The man stood there, calmly waiting for them to reach him. When they did, Mann and Sandy looked around and saw that they were in a crypt. Unlike the tunnels, it had walls of marble and concrete. There were metal drawers that looked as if they contained remains. And at the far end of the room, there appeared to be a door.

"Put your hands where I can see them," Sandy said as she pointed the gun at the man in the robe.

The robed figure complied. Then the light from the room washed over his face, and Charlie Mann and Sandy stared in disbelief.

John Wilkinson stared back at them without a hint of fear or apprehension. "Welcome," he said with an easy smile. "We were just finishing the ceremony."

"What ceremony?" Charlie asked. "I don't understand what you're talking about."

"Then maybe you should meet the other believers."

Lily Thompkins and Violet Grant emerged from the recesses of the room and stood near a candlelit altar with a yellowing parchment in the middle.

As Mann and Sandy watched, Lenore Wilkinson emerged from the shadows as well. John was about to walk back toward the altar when Sandy raised her gun.

"Stop right there!" she shouted. "Nobody moves unless I say so."

John's face creased in a relaxed smile. "I'm afraid you're not in charge, Lieutenant Jackson. Now that Lenore has deciphered Poe's secret, we answer to a higher authority. That's what the cryptogram was about. It's what the map was about. It was all for this time and this place. After a year of tunneling and searching for the truth, we finally found it here, and Lenore's gift was the key to it all."

Charlie looked at Lenore. "Is this true?"

"Of course it's true," she said with a patronizing smile.

"Out of everything I allowed you to see about me, it might be the only thing that's true. Well, that and the fact that I came here to find my purpose. And now that I've found it—now that I've deciphered Poe's secret—no one can take that power. Not even you."

"Is that why Clarissa and Workman died?" Charlie Mann asked while moving closer to John. "So you could have this power?"

"They died because they wanted to share it with the world," Violet said.

"And frankly, we don't share," Lily added.

"That's why when Lance Griggs came to us and asked if he could use the power to bring back his wife, we gave him conditions," said John. "We told him he'd have to kill Clarissa and Workman and anyone else who got in his way. Then he'd have to wait until we found the parchment and had Lenore decipher it. Of course, it was all a lie. We knew he couldn't bring his wife back, but we also knew Lance was a loose cannon who wouldn't make it to the end, and tonight he proved us right."

Charlie grabbed John's arms as Sandy pointed her weapon at his head. "You're all under arrest for murder," Mann said calmly.

He pulled John to the door at the other end of the room as Sandy followed with gun in hand. Charlie tried three times to open it, but the door was sealed shut.

"I'm afraid I can't let you leave," John said as he focused his mind on the walls of the crypt. "In fact, I can't let anyone leave. You see, now that Lenore has deciphered the parchment, I don't plan to share this power with anyone. Not Violet, not Lily, not even Lenore."

Just as he'd done before, John used his mind to make the ground rumble and the walls shake. Sandy's gun flew out of her hand and discharged into the ceiling. Charlie Mann was thrown against the altar, causing the candles to fall.

Violet and Lily dove for the parchment as it began to burn, but the flames leaped onto their robes and lit their bodies like oil-soaked rags. They tried to focus their minds as John had done, but their power was weak. John's mind was much stronger than theirs.

As the two women screamed in agony and Charlie and Sandy were pinned to the floor by John's powerful thoughts, Lenore lashed out against her husband's betrayal. She knew she was the only one who could stop him, so she closed her eyes and tapped into the power she'd always had inside.

Lenore's face turned a deep crimson as the veins in her forehead bulged. When she opened her eyes and looked at her husband, there appeared to be a fire within.

The crypt began crumbling and cracking as John was slammed into the wall. Rocks and dirt rained down from above them as the room fell quickly apart. Drawers flew open and bones were scattered and beams fell down from the ceiling.

The smell of burning flesh filled the room, along with smoke from the robes and the parchment. As John's power was overcome by Lenore's, his grip on Mann and Sandy was loosened. They scrambled to their feet while the room shook violently, causing the door to the crypt to swing open.

The distraction was enough to break Lenore's concentration, and when John's limp body fell down from the wall, a beam came down as well. It landed squarely on Lenore, knocking her to the floor, and as the flames began licking at the beam's dry wood, the room was filled with black smoke.

Mann scrambled across the floor, tripping over Violet's and Lily's dead bodies as the macabre scene grew more grisly.

"Sandy!" Mann yelled.

She didn't answer, but he heard a cough near the far wall, and he jumped the beam to get to her. He groped in the darkness until he found her and slung her over his shoulders. He stepped over bodies and rocks and beams to get to the door of the crypt. By the time he stumbled out into the graveyard, the smoke had seared his lungs to the point where he couldn't breathe.

He made it another twenty feet before he dropped to the ground with Sandy still draped around his shoulders. The faint sounds of firefighters and sirens filled his semiconscious mind, and as he looked up through bleary eyes, he saw the one cop whose presence mattered most.

"Charlie!" Coletti shouted as he jogged across the graveyard. "Charlie, I'm coming!"

Mann smiled faintly as the old man approached. But then he saw Coletti's facial expression change from gladness to fear. The old man's eyes grew wide, and the sounds of the sirens and voices seemed to fade. Coletti was shouting something. Mann couldn't hear it, but he could see the warning in Coletti's eyes.

He watched as his partner reached into his shoulder holster and grabbed his gun. Then everything seemed to slow down. The firefighters in the background looked faded and gray. The dome lights on the cars stopped flashing and were still. The look on Coletti's face seemed frozen in time.

Mann turned and saw John Wilkinson a few feet away. His body was in flames. He was holding Sandy's gun. He was aiming for Charlie's head.

He turned again and watched as Coletti stopped and fired. John Wilkinson hit the ground, the flames ignited the dry autumn grass, and in that moment, for Charlie Mann, everything in the world went black.

That was when the power of his mind took over. He saw Lance Griggs and Irving Workman, smiling as mentor and student. He saw Violet Grant and Lily Thompkins, their eyes filled with history's wonders. He glimpsed John and Lenore in the days when their love was new, and above it all, soaring high against the sky, he saw the raven. Its wings stretched wide as it was lifted toward the clouds, toward the sun, toward the heavens.

When the raven disappeared in the distance, Charlie Mann knew that the parchment and its secret were gone forever. Just as it had always been, the power of the mind could be used for good or for evil, and the secret Lenore had deciphered in the crypt would stay there to emerge nevermore.